I0678510

WHEN JUSTICE CALLS

Wilbur Brower

❦ ALSO BY DR. WILBUR L. BROWER ❦

Seven C's of Success—Developing the Attributes and Attitudes and Behaviors to Achieve All You Want Out of Life (2013)

Defining Your Success—You Decide What You Want Out of Life (2013)

Of Life, Love and Learning—Selected Poems and Educational Raps, Rhythms and Rhymes (2012)

English Grammar and Writing Made Easy—Learn to Communicate More Accurately, Clearly and Concisely (2012)

Personal Care Journal-The Adult Years (2000), co-authored with Lillery Fripp

A Little Book of Big Principles—Values and Virtues for a More Successful Life (1998 and 2012)

Traffic Signs on the Road of Life (2012), co-authored with Cynthia Brower

Me Teacher, Me...Please!---Observation about Parents, Students, Teachers and the Teaching-Learning Process (2001)

Visit the Author's Page:

http://tinyurl.com/ckw5ms8

This is a fictionalized account of some actual events. All of the names, characters, and places are products of the author's imagination or are used fictitiously. There are several historical facts cited, however.

Library of Congress Control Number: 2013910836

When Justice Calls / Wilbur L. Brower

ISBN: 978-0-9894838-3-4

THIS BOOK IS DEDICATED TO:

ALL THE PEOPLE WHO UNDERSTOOD THE POWER OF THEIR FUTURE BECAUSE THEY KNEW THE STRUGGLES OF THEIR PAST;

AND

THOSE WHO HAVE THE FUTURE IN THEIR HANDS BUT REFUSE TO SEE IT AND TO CLAIM IT.

ACKNOWLEDGEMENTS

In an attempt to create accurate fiction, I asked numerous, and often innocuous, questions of legal experts to gain a clearer understanding of some of the technical details of land ownership, and relied upon research librarians to provide me missing pieces of information that made the entire project come together. I relied upon many family members, colleagues and friends to read drafts of the manuscripts and to give me their most critical comments, which were invaluable. They allowed me to talk endlessly about some facets of my research and accidental findings, and endured my annoyances with their graciousness and generosity. I express my sincere gratitude to all of them. This was a labor of love that had to be shared, and a personal obligation that would have been infinitely more difficult to accomplish without their help.

Finally, I owe an enormous debt of gratitude to my wonderful wife Cynthia for her encouragement, patience and support, especially during times when she wanted to be pampered and I needed to write. Her superb computer applications and hardware skills helped to keep me out of technical trouble on numerous occasions. Thanks, Honey, for your understanding and belief in me as I've pursued those things that are important to me!

So they said, "Arise, let us go up against them. For we have seen the land, and indeed it is very good. Would you do nothing? Do not hesitate to go, and enter to possess the land. When you go, you will come to a secure people and a large land. For God has given it into your hands, a place where there is no lack of anything that is on the earth."

--Judges 18:9-10

1

Her heart pounded softly. Her hands trembled, ever so slightly. Yet, she felt composed, with a detached coolness that belied the churning of the thoughts swirling in her mind. What she was about to do was the right thing to do, she thought to herself. If she didn't do it, who would?

She meticulously and methodically removed the last letter from the printer, making sure again that the facial tissues she held in her hands to handle the paper did not let them collect any of her fingerprints. Again, she took great care inserting the letter into the envelope, just like she had done the other three. "I'd better read this one more time," she said to herself, as she thoughtfully opened the folder containing the only other copy besides the four resting snugly in plain white business envelopes and waiting to be sealed, stamped and mailed out. As she read, she smiled to herself and said inaudibly, "This should get somebody's attention." She mulled over in her mind what the reaction would be from the four individuals whose names and titles appeared at the bottom of the letter. They would be the only recipients of the letter; and they clearly had the power and resources to take some action, if they chose to. But, would they? Would they talk to each other as she had advised? Would they dismiss her anonymous letter as a hoax, an annoyance that interfered with their daily routines and their appointed and intended purposes? Or, would they spend all their time trying to figure out who sent it, and no time trying to investigate her allegations or validate her concerns?

She began thinking about sealing the envelopes, and replayed in her mind all the facts the missing county files revealed to her, stories that incomplete paper trails told her, the blank stares she got when she asked penetrating questions of clerical personnel in county offices; and the loud silence she could imagine swept across old, tired faces when the individuals realized they had been victimized once again by the very system that was supposed to help them and to protect them. "This is the only way I know to do it," she said to herself, as she focused on the content, tone and tenor of her message. However, her words were meant to convey a certain adeptness, intelligence, logic and a formality that suggested a special kind of knowledge that would give the savvy reader reasons to be attentive, but cautious. The tone conveyed a sense of urgency, yet a sense of a reasonable amount of time to act. She wanted to confuse and confound the recipients, while she was pointing them in the right direction at the same time. Her penchant for detail was unmistakable.

"Perfect!" she said out loud as she swiveled her chair around to a file cabinet next to her, pulled out the bottom drawer and carefully filed the unnamed folder in the very back of it for safekeeping. After turning back to her computer, she ran the letter through "Spell-check" once again. The one-page letter quickly showed that there were no misspelled words or other errors, and "Word count: 564 Press any key to continue" showed up at the bottom of the screen. She pressed her favorite key, "K", to continue, then logged off, logged back on, pulled up the File Directory and moved the cursor down to the file she had named "BIGTIME." She deleted the file with an assurance and a confidence she had not felt before, and sat quietly for a few moments at her computer gazing at the screen. She derived a lot of enjoyment from working with her older computer because it had served her well and served her purpose. Besides, she could find no logical reason to get rid of an excellent, "old workhorse," she often said jokingly, that was steady and reliable even though it was as "slow molasses in winter." She was often chided about it, but there was no time to dwell on that now. There was serious work to do.

Although the letter was no longer in her computer's memory, its precise wording, innuendoes and nuances were seared indelibly and permanently in hers. The copy she'd filed away would remain like a long-forgotten past—until she needed it again.

She carefully picked up the stack of envelopes with the bundles of tissues she had amassed and then bolted from her chair. Her small, 5'

2" frame glided quickly to another room in the apartment and abruptly stopped in front of a corner desk whose top was covered with several stacks of books, a caddy of pens and pencils, a newspaper, several sheets of paper, a stack of trays and a typewriter. Using her arms and elbows to clear away a spot to place the envelopes, she then laid them carefully in the spot she would use to perform another critical part of her operation. She carefully un-stacked the envelopes with the flaps up, so each could receive undisturbed, individual attention. Each envelope had been addressed, the words "<u>PERSONAL AND CONFIDENTIAL</u>" had been printed in bold type and underlined in the lower, left hand corner. Such marking should get the envelopes special attention, she reasoned, and may be opened and attended to only by the persons to whom they were addressed. At least, that was her desire.

She rummaged through the desk drawer a few moments and pulled out a small opaque bottle with a rubber-tipped lid, a large envelope and a book of postage stamps. Holding the bottle to the window in front of her and angling it toward the fading sun, she realized that it was empty. She placed the large envelope and book of stamps on top of a stack of books and left the room with the small opaque bottle. The large bathroom she entered was twice the normal size for units in that building. She carefully looked around it and thought for a moment how it all came to be. After she had purchased her unit, but before moving into it about two years earlier, she had the bathroom expanded to take up part of the bedroom. She reasoned that she only slept in the bedroom, but she always used the bathroom as a place to pamper herself. Shelves along one wall contained a large assortment of colognes, bath beads and body lotions and oils. As she hastily glanced at the full and nearly full bottles that gave her the assurance that she had been pampered, she filled the small, opaque bottle with warm water. She reasoned that warm water would make the envelopes seal better and faster. She could also see herself in the shell-shaped tub taking a long, soothing bath after completing the task at hand. Quickly returning to her operation and pressing the rubber tip of the opaque bottle repeatedly on one of the tissues she had laid nearby, she finally had an indication that the sponge tip would yield enough water to seal the envelopes. She used one hand protected by tissue to hold the envelope secure to the desk top, and used the other hand to moisten carefully and purposely the envelope flap.

Satisfied that the flap would hold securely, she quickly put down the water bottle, picked up a tissue, and used it to firmly press the flap against the envelope back. Feeling that this operation had been accomplished satisfactorily, she began to restack the envelopes. She proceeded to the second envelope, then the third and finally the fourth with the same meticulous care, completing each operation without leaving a trace of her presence. Putting the stamps on the letters would be the tricky part, but she had already figured out how to do it. She gingerly retrieved from the pen and pencil caddy an arts and crafts knife with a sharp, triangular blade. Unfolding the book of self-adhesive stamps she had specifically asked for at the post office earlier during the week, she used the tip of the knife blade to peel away artfully one stamp at a time and carefully place it on each envelope in turn, while holding each envelope in place with a hand full of tissues. She completed the postage stamp placement phase of the operation and carefully put the envelopes into the larger envelope and placed it in the desk drawer for mailing early the next morning.

2

k-be, Elizabeth Arden-5th Ave, Giorgio Red, Il Bacio, Nicole Miller, Ocean Dream, Opium, Pleasures, Spellbound and Volupte'. Bath Lotions, Body Splashes and Sprays, Colognes, Mineral Beads, Parfums, Satin Creams, Soaps and Toilettes. All containers stood stately against an elegant, pink background, waiting to be used lavishly and liberally by their owner to keep her dainty, dark-brown body smelling sweet and feeling supple. Like sentries waiting to be pressed into action, tall bottles and short jars, every conceivable shape and size and all sculpted to perfection, stood in great anticipation of the moment she would gently bang out the last few drops of the contents. Like Katherine Louise Webster, they, too, could hardly wait for this moment, and longed for the time they would become part of her bottle collection. Arrayed along a decorative rack were seaweed sponges, back brushes, back scrub labs, and emery boards. They, too, were ready. It was customary for Kaye Webster to indulge her body with the wonders they performed. In most cases, a shower would do. But she had made her tub baths a ritual for those special occasions. Sitting on the edge of the tub while letting the water run long and hot, she periodically would sprinkle in a mixture of bath crystals, hold a delicately manicured hand under the gold faucet, then close her eyes and sweep her tiny fingers through the rising suds and water below. This was one of her few passions. While deeply inhaling the fragrances and odors she had meticulously and ritualistically placed throughout the bathroom--inconspicuously scattered on shelves, secretly hidden in the toilet roll dispenser, delicately draped on the bathroom door and carefully tucked within the bathroom linen--Kaye reflected on their importance in her life and how they transformed her from within. How they were made was a marvel to her, and their recuperative powers were miraculous and mystical. That many of the fragrances' foundations are obtained from plants was difficult for her grasp; and many of the fixatives that are used to hold the fragrances together come from animals stretched her imagination. She could visualize and smell the bitter orange blossoms, citronella, geranium, jasmine, lavender and rose; the oil from the costus plant roots and leaves from the patchouli plant leaves. As she closed her eyes and waved her head back and forth, it seemed that a thousand varieties of citrus fruits wafted through the room, impregnating it with the indescribable power of their peels, leaves and shoots. Chasing close behind them were the aromas of cloves, gardenia, lily of the valley, mimosa, rosemary sandalwood, tuberose, vanilla and violet. Less appealing to her imagination was the idea that the items she bathe in, atomized over her delicate body and dabbed strategically in places to attract attention, all contained animal secretions from the civet cat, the male musk deer, the beaver, and a fatty substance from sperm whale known as ambergris. In their natural and undiluted state, they exude noxious and unpleasant odors; but when put in high alcohol dilution they lose their odor and act as mellowing and preserving agent. The balsams, coal tar, grains, molasses, resins and wood seemed to be more palatable, but they too gave her queasy feelings and a milder form of disgust. It all seemed so incongruous to her, and yet she knew it was so real. It didn't matter how many times she played this understanding in her mind and tested its validity, it was always new to her. She considered herself a closet connoisseur of perfumes, a "Sweet Maven" she often laughed to herself, and knew more about perfumery than she often wanted to know.

This ritual lasted for several minutes, allowing the tub to rise to the level that would consume all 110 pounds of her, while leaving her free to glide gently about the tub without pushing water over the edge. Kaye knew exactly when to turn off the gold faucet; she had done it so many times before. She would let no phone call, doorbell, or other outside disturbances intrude on these moments of intimacy. Kaye slipped the loosely fitted sweatshirt over her small head full of frizzy, black hair and proceeded to slip her arms through her delicate bra straps and turn the bra around in front of herself to unhook it. She had never developed the skill of reaching behind her back, unhooking the bra from behind and letting it slide down her arms. She then pushed and tugged at her tight jeans and skimpy panties simultaneously, while wiggling her round and tender buttocks, urging them to let go. Kaye slithered into the tub with deliberate care, leaned back, closed her eyes and relished in her accomplishment. She sighed and purred, then lay motionless for a while. She screamed "Boffo!" after a few minutes of silence, and began to wash her delicately strong body with a passionate purpose. Her unanticipated and, in many ways unwanted, meteoric graduation to this kind of luxury had taken her by surprise and made her blush when she took the time to bring it into her conscious mind. Her desire for it was probably always somewhere in her subconscious mind, but she never entertained thoughts of it until after it had happened. Only in her wildest dreams could she have imagined that she, a poor girl from Humphries, would relish the extravagance of such huge assortment of atomizers, perfume bottles and the sweet smells they held; and the exotic feelings their curious sizes and alluring shapes gave her. They contained many forms of freedom and liberation she never experienced growing up, and they filled her with a sense of awe and wonder she found hard to talk about and difficult to accept without talking herself through it. She was sure some people might consider her private and personal luxury a fetish, deserving of shame and scorn. Moreover, if she alluded to being a member of the International Perfume Bottle Association, because of her fascination with them, of all things, perfume bottles, they would know she was crazy. Therefore, she kept the fascination to herself and enjoyed it. Years away from her childhood hometown of Humphries, and away from her kinfolks there, had taught Kaye more about life than she sometimes wanted to know. After being back just a few months, she felt that Humphries, Sawyer Village, Perkins City and other surrounding towns, deep down, had changed very little since she had left nearly 20 years earlier. When she expressed her feelings, those who had not ventured far from Sawyer Village or understood how things really worked, cautioned her not to be too hasty. "Give it a chance, girl," and "Give yourself a chance," are directives and admonitions she had heard a thousand times if she had heard them once. In their minds, they had experienced monumental changes over the years, and they talked often about how things are now compared to the way they used to be. On the surface there was a small-town tranquility that lingered in the air, but Kaye Webster's basic instincts and big-city experiences told her something quite different. Although she could not readily identify what her senses were trying to tell her, early on she could sense that her mannerisms, presence and straight-talk caused people to look at her with curiosity. Therefore, she learned to be quiet, to listen and to observe. She worked at being inconspicuous. Socializing was low on her list of priorities, and working hard always gave her a sense of accomplishment. The less she socialized, the more she realized she didn't miss it. The harder she worked, the more she realized that long, hot showers or long, soapy baths gave her more determination and energy to do all the things that were important to her. After a restful night, Katherine Louise Webster was up and stirring about just before the sun began to peep over the horizon, getting ready to complete her mission. The cold January morning was filled with gray skies, and the little patches of frost or thin layers of ice on the roads caused panic. It seemed that drivers either inched along as if they were carrying dynamite, or they drove as if they were in pursuit of dangerous speed records. Driving the additional thirty miles to go to Perkins City and back this morning required that she leave much earlier to avoid the panic, make her drop, stop to get breakfast, and get to work before it was time for her to be there, as was customary for her. It was also customary for her to wear non-descript, casual office clothing, but today she felt more daring. Therefore, she searched through her small, walk-in closet and came out with a dressy blue suit and blue shoes, a cream-colored blouse and a blue and cream scarf she had learned to fashion around her neck with a certain elegance. She walked blithely to the spare bedroom, where she always kept ready the iron and ironing board, and steamed out the few wrinkles she saw. As she dressed herself in front of the full-length mirror symmetrically positioned on the spare bedroom door, she admired herself and marveled at her contentment. Hints of her curvaceous body were showing through her attire; and this was a rarity for her because she normally wore clothing that allowed none of her enticing feminine qualities and physical stature to be noticeable. Her attire today was the antithesis of how colleagues and friends often implied about her, if not to her face, then stated explicitly among themselves behind her back. She had the intuition to know that, but not to let it define how she elected to dress. She reasoned that her clothes didn't make her the person she was, unlike many people she knew who used them in an attempt to mask and cover many of their deep-seated imperfections that could only be cured by laying them bare and methodically excising them from their inner being.

She bundled herself up snugly in a dressy gray coat with a matching hat, turned her coat collar up slightly, and pirouetted in front of the mirror several times, admiring what she saw and feeling good about how she felt. Kaye put on her gloves, went to the corner-desk drawer and pulled out the large envelope. She then gracefully left her second-floor condominium unit, bounced down the steps, and strutted directly to her 10-year old sedan. As she gingerly unlocked the door, she surveyed the landscape around her as if she were expecting to see somebody spying on her. She let her car warm up a few minutes and slowly backed out of her assigned parking space, then moved forward slowly as she rotated from looking into the rearview mirror and at the road ahead of her. Rather than driving the most direct route to Perkins, she took a very circuitous route that had her crisscrossing patches of road she had traveled only minutes earlier. The normal thirty miles to Perkins City had taken her more than an hour and covered nearly forty five miles. Kaye confidently drove the thirty miles to Perkins City, eagerly approached the isolated mail box she had scouted out weeks earlier, and shook the four small envelopes from the larger one, making sure that they all fell out and being careful that her fingers or any part of her hand had not touched them. "Mission accomplished," she told herself when she realized the large envelope was empty. She had accomplished another phase of a project she started three months earlier. "This should shake them up," Kaye said as she drove off smiling at herself. "All these facts coming to them at the State Capitol, and being mailed to them from a different county, 30 miles away from the scene of the crimes."

3

As Kaye walked into *Mamma's Dining Room*, the place she usually had breakfast and occasionally would have dinner, her cousin John's dejected demeanor flashed before her eyes and his resigned voice rang clearly in her ears. Somewhere out of sight, before she could sit, a familiar voice yelled out to Kaye. "Hi, honey…. You're a little early this morning…..The usual?" The voice said and asked in one continuous sentence, as if it had been said numerous times before. It was the voice of the woman everybody called Mamma Sylvia, owner of *Mamma's Dining Room*. Sitting in the corner in the rear of the restaurant was a lone man sipping long and hard from a cup--or maybe he was just holding the cup to his lips, with both hands, as if he was praying or worshipping whatever he was drinking--and watching Kaye with intent interest. She ignored his presence and yelled back, "You got it!," as she positioned herself at her favorite table. Her mind slipped immediately to the conversation she had with John three months earlier at the very same table. It was just like he was still sitting there. Her attention focused intensely on that discussion:

"Explain that to me one more time," Kaye demanded. "I want to make sure I understand what happened." Her mind re-played every detail of that meeting.

The mousy-looking little man lowered his head and began recounting what undoubtedly was a painful experience. "I received a call from this fellow named Anders Zorn telling me Dad borrowed $1000.00 from him 'bout 30 years earlier, but never paid him back. He wanted me to come see him and arrange to pay back the loan, or he was going to take the land for the loan."

"Again, how much land are you talking about?" Kaye asked as she feverishly scrawled notes on the pad in front of her while looking at him with empathy.

"It's about 25 acres." The man nervously rolled out a plat. "This is it here," he said, pointing to an area familiar to Kaye because she had grown up near it. Then he handed her several documents.

"The guy who got you to sign these, where does he live?"

"Oh, he's dead, now."

"Well, who are you paying the money to?" The more Kaye asked questions, the more intense she became. She would close her eyes as John Wilkinson, Jr., began to talk, and then she would attack her note pad when John dragged a relevant answer out of himself.

"His son Bennett inherited everything the old man left; so, I'm paying his son now."

"But, this guy gave you no proof that Uncle John had ever borrowed the money from him, is that right?" Kaye asked with an air of disbelief.

"Yeah, that's right," the little fellow said nervously, and with a growing sense that he had done something horribly wrong.

"And, he gave you no proof that Uncle John put the land up for any money?" Kaye asked again to be sure she fully understood what had happened.

"Yeah, that's right. I just saw a blue copy of something with my Pop's name on it, and I got real scared of what could happen. It said 'deed.' Pops told me that whatever I did, to never let the land get away from me and Sister." A look of dread slowly came over his face and tears began to form in the corners of his eyes and creep down his face.

"And, all of this happened about 20 years after Uncle John died. Is that right?" Kaye asked as agitation and fury crept into her voice.

"Yeah, that's right. I know I should'a got a lawyer, but they told me I didn't need one," he said with obvious pain and profound embarrassment at his lack of business sense.

"So, you signed this *Deed of Trust* and Promissory Note without any legal advice?" she asked in disbelief, but she already knew the answer.

The more questions Kaye asked, the more the little man realized what mistakes he had made. They all made him feel so inadequate and completely unaware of the magnitude of the problem that he earlier had created for himself.

"Yeah. I gave the old man $2,000 when I signed them and agreed to pay him $22,000 more." "Do you have any idea how much you've paid them?" she asked in a tone of continuing disbelief? She knew that peppering John with additional questions would probably yield no useful information, but she was optimistic.

"I'm not sure; but I was out of work for 'bout two years and couldn't pay anything. I have a rough idea," John said as he lowered his eyes, showing signs of additional embarrassment. "What's a rough idea?" Kaye demanded to know.

"Probably 'bout $15,000."

"How long have you been paying these people?"

"It's been 'bout twelve years."

"Do you know how much you owe? Do you have any idea?" she asked again, still disbelieving what she was hearing.

"I'm not sure about that either."

"Do they give you a statement or something every time you pay some money or at the end of each year?" Kaye asked as she examined the documents closely and periodically shook her head.

"No," he replied sadly. "Have these people ever given you a 1099-Interest form, showing how much money you've paid in interest?" Kaye knew the answer to the question before she asked it, but she had to hear the answer from John.

"I'm not sure; what's that?"

"That's not important for now. But, it probably means that they're not reporting a penny of the money to the IRS. Here's how I'm understanding this: You, your wife Clara and your sons signed these documents saying you'll pay $22,000; and if you and Clara don't pay it, your sons will; and if they don't pay it, their kids will," Kaye pointed out to him matter-of-factly. "It also says that you're to pay $150 per month at 12% interest. Do you realize that at that rate, you can never pay it back? You're further in the hole every time you make a payment. Did you know that?" Kaye did not expect an answer, and wasn't sure why she had asked.

"Nope, I didn't know it, but that's what I'm scared of."

"It also says that if the money is not paid, they can have the land instead. That's what the *Deed of Trust* is for."

John Wilkinson, Jr., just shook his head.

Kaye poured over her notes and began to draw lines connecting pieces of information she had written on the note pad. After some reflection, she looked at John empathetically and said, "Those bastards think they are slick."

"What do you think we can do?" John wanted to know.

"We can't lay down on this one; we got to do something," Kaye said as she rhythmically tapped the ballpoint pen on her forehead.

"When is the last time you made a payment, and when is the last time you've seen the son...What's his name?"

"Bennett Zorn. I haven't made a payment in 'bout three months, but I plan to get some money to him next week," he said with some anxiety. They sat and said nothing to each other for several minutes. "I know this is messed up," John finally said sadly.

"Yeah, but we'll get it straight. Tell you what: Why don't you go to see this guy Bennett Zorn to find out exactly how much you owe him. Maybe you can negotiate a reasonable payoff amount. If you need me to go with you I will," Kaye offered. "If he's adding penalties for late payments and adding to the principal the amount you are short each time you make a payment, he'll probably say you owe him a fortune."

Kaye's words were not reassuring to John, and she could detect it.

"I need to do a little research on this, and then talk with an attorney friend of mine. I got a hunch about something," Kaye said mysteriously. She looked at John seriously and said, "I don't think they have a legal claim against the land, and I'll be willing to bet you Uncle John never borrowed the money. Or, if he did, knowing Uncle John, he paid it back, with interest and on time. What I'm concerned about though is the statute of limitations on this thing."

John looked as if he wanted to ask what was meant by "statute of limitations." Instead, he asked, "What do you think this will cost? I'm low on funds, right now."

"Don't worry about it now. I'll pay for it. Let's get this straight first and we can work out something about the land later," Kaye assured him. John Wilkinson, Jr., gave Kaye a big hug and a smile and vanished as quietly and quickly as he had appeared. "Keep me on board," she yelled after him, knowing that he probably would not unless there was an emergency.

Kaye Webster's discussion with John caused her to have pity and sympathy for him, and simultaneously blamed him for being so gullible and naïve.

John Jr. was John and Clara Wilkinson's only son; and John had twin boys whom he had not seen in several years. Kaye Webster was John Jr.'s younger cousin, but they had not spent a lot of time with each other while they were growing up. The woman John referred to as "Sister" was his only sibling, whose given name was Doreena. Although she was older than John, she had no interest in her mother's estate or the land and, therefore, signed over her interest to her brother John after their mother's death. Therefore, it was up to John to keep the land and to protect it, but he sees it slipping away from him despite his efforts to hold on to it.

Mamma's Dining Room was clean, quiet and quaint, the antithesis of what its location and ownership might have suggested. It was the ideal place for the unhurried diner, the diner who wanted a meal with anonymity, or for the diner who wanted a healthy, home-cooked meal for a price that was reasonable. In fact, it was the place for the discriminating diner who wanted all three. Located somewhat off the beaten path, out of the easy reach of annoying traffic and away from the goggling and unwelcome eyes, it was a place that one undoubtedly had intentions of going to, rather than stumbling upon it serendipitously. Nestled among a row of houses off one of the lesser traveled streets leading into Humphries, the non-descript place had the usual façade of the neighborhood buildings, but the ornately decorated front entrance was seldom used. Those unaware of its purpose mistook the building as just another house in desperate need of urgent repair, on a street that received little attention and even less care. Its shabby exterior belied the comfort and modernity of its interior. The narrow driveway beside the building emptied precipitously, even carelessly, into an unusually large parking lot in the rear that appeared to belong to another place and from another time. *Mamma's Dining Room* was a place where any real news or useless speculation worthy of comment or commentary would probably be discussed by someone there. The news or speculation was seldom a matter of public comment at *Mamma's Dining Room*, however, but it was sure to be a matter of serious private conversation; and real talk could take place without pretense, varnish or veneer. People came and went unconcerned at *Mamma's Dining Room* because of the anonymity the place assured them and the unspoken code of confidentiality confirmed by its patrons.

Sylvia Hamilton was a short, buxom woman, given to the genteel art of easiness and familiarity that engendered trust, both with those who met her for the first time and those who had known her and been loyal customers since she opened the doors of *Mamma's Dining Room* for business more than twenty years earlier. Her ever-ready smile, inviting facial features and youthful stride masked her true age; and her propensity for the dramatic concealed her true feelings about things on which she had very strong, but unvoiced opinions. She had learned how to hear everything, but pretend not to, and to say nothing, even when she wanted to; and she learned to do that very well and expected the same from the few people who worked for her. Hers was a place whose atmosphere exuded warmth and whose employees were the epitome of honesty and sincerity.

When anything big was about to happen in Humphries or Thompson

County, the goings and comings at *Mamma's Dining Room* foretold it; and when something significant had happened, the patrons Mama Sylvia discreetly called "irregulars" stopped in to whisper about it among themselves. Whether it was some official County business or the usual questionable dealings and skullduggery, it was probably discussed at some point in time in *Mamma's Dining Room*.

4

"Attorney Freeman, this is Kaye Webster," she said hesitantly and in a manner to suggest he knew who she was.

"Yes?" the voice on the other end said with a question. "You probably don't know me, but I know you through my younger brothers and sisters. I think you went to school with some of them. Clayton Webster, we call him Clay, Doretha Webster, Ken Webster,..."

"Oh, yeah, yeah! Sure I know them," the voice interjected without giving her a chance to finish. "What can I do for you?" he asked, anxious to get to the purpose of her call.

"I have a minor problem in Thompson County I may need some help with." Kaye stated with some doubt about his ability to help.

"I'll do what I can. What do you have?"

Kaye painstakingly told him the story, as she had understood it from John Wilkinson, Jr.

"You'll be amazed at how often this happens," Attorney Freeman informed her, "especially to people who are afraid to ask questions or to use a little common sense."

Every time she told the story or thought about it for long, she experienced an inexplicable fatigue, an unexplained weariness that seemed to bore deeper into her bones; and an unquenchable longing for any type of resolution. "Your cousin John never consulted an attorney?" he asked, feeling quite confident that he probably hadn't.

"No, he didn't."

"*Deed of Trust*! That's a shame! I don't normally do work in Thompson County; but why don't you come in to see me and let me see what I can do. What kinds of documents do you have?" Atty. Jarvis Freeman wanted to know. Kaye flipped through the documents in the folder spread across her desk and identified them by names: "A Purchase Money, a Promissory Note, and a General Warranty Deed," as she carefully examined the front of each document as she called out the names.

"You need to bring those with you, and anything else that you think might be helpful. Hold on and my assistant will give you an appointment and tell you about my fees."

A high-pitched male voice came on the line after a few minutes. "Hi, this is Antonio. Attorney said he'll probably just have to write a letter for you, and he might have to have a title search done. That will be $300. He'll need half of it up front. Is that okay? You still want to come in to see him?" he asked in a way that said she probably didn't.

"Yeah, I guess so," Kaye said reluctantly. "If I get an appointment in some reasonable time. When can I get one?"

"Jus' hold on, Sugah, I'll get to that in a minute." After a short delay, Antonio asked, "How's one week from today, at 2 o'clock?"

"You got it" Kaye snapped. "1210 Jasper, right?"

"You got it," Antonio snapped back.

"I'll be there."

Antonio held the phone handset out from himself, looked at it and said, "Huh!" as he dropped it onto the cradle, as if he were dropping something hot.

Kaye knew that one-week would give her enough time to do her own research to see what she could determine. She didn't know everything she was looking for; but she knew that if there was a legitimate claim against her Uncle John's property more than forty years earlier, there should be a record of it somewhere in the Thompson County Courthouse, in the Register of Deeds' Office. There was an Information

Desk positioned at the entrance of the Thompson County Courthouse. Humphries was the county seat for Thompson County, and it had a long history of discrimination against Blacks. The often-repeated history of the Information Desk is that it was a checkpoint specifically for Blacks until the early '70s. Blacks had to stop, identify themselves and explain their reason for being in the building. If the attendant was suspicious of them or was not satisfied with the explanation, they were turned away. Now, the Information Desk, usually staffed by retirees, was there more as a courtesy than it was as a checkpoint. Blacks were now actually serving as voluntary Information Desk Attendants. Kaye walked quietly up to the Desk and explained to the attendant what she was looking for. The man looked skeptically at her, pointed one hand toward the ceiling and jabbed it back and forth. To the casual observer, the interpretation of his directions was: Go up to the next level of the two-story building, then go toward the other end of the building. He never said anything.

Kaye followed his directions and ended up at an office with the word "Records" boldly etched in the wood over the entryway. She walked hesitantly into the room and immediately noticed several older women sitting at cluttered desks arrayed behind a chest-high service counter. Many of them were laughing and talking. A few were fidgeting with stacks of papers on their desks, giving the impression that they were busy. The woman who was sitting at the front of the space enclosed by the counter was engaged in a humorous conversation with an older man. She and the old man ignored Kaye Webster's presence for several minutes while they laughed, talked, and slapped their hands together.

Kaye stood patiently and silently, observing as much of the scene as she could take in. The woman suddenly stopped laughing, turned to Kaye and asked curtly, "May I help you?"

"No, I'll wait until you're finished with him," Kaye said.

"Oh, that's okay. He's just visiting. He used to work here; he's retired now," the woman explained.

"Oh, I'll just wait 'til you've finished. I have some personal questions to ask and I need to keep them private," Kaye shot back. They looked at her disapprovingly, and she immediately realized that she needed to smile at the woman and man to smooth away the unintended sharp edges of her comments. She reasoned that her drab, frumpy clothing belied her air of certainty and confidence.

The old man slyly walked away, and occasionally turned to look at Kaye. The woman walked sheepishly up to the counter and grudgingly asked "What can I help you with?"

"I'm looking for a copy of a lien that may have been filed about forty years ago."

"Wow! That was a long time ago," the woman exclaimed. "If it was filed, it will be back there in the *Books of Liens and Judgments*," the woman said as she pointed toward an inner room toward the back. She stared blankly at Kaye then walked away without offering an explanation about how to use them or suggesting any additional information that might be helpful to her.

"Thank you so much, Ma'am. You've been very helpful," Kaye said cordially as she headed toward the room the woman had pointed out to her. Most of the women in the room turned in her direction and looked at her intently as she negotiated the maze of desks in the larger room to make her way to the inner room in the rear. She began to walk without purpose, hoping and wishing that the older women would continue their talking and laughing. She anxiously stepped through the narrow doorway and entered the small room filled with many volumes of large, official-looking books stacked neatly on rows of shelves extending from the floor to the ceiling. Stationed strategically about the room were several computer terminals and printers. Kaye wondered why the woman assisting her did not mention them to her. "Maybe judgments and liens from forty years ago had not been put in a computerized system," Kaye thought to herself. "Or, maybe the woman assumed I have no familiarity with computers," was another thought that entered her mind. Kaye decided to still herself to determine what she should do first. She noticed that there were some numbers printed neatly on labels and attached to the shelves. Other numbers were printed directly on the spine of each book. She randomly picked out a shelf, eased her way toward it and studied the numbers on the shelf and the numbers on one of the books, trying to decipher how they were related. After studying the numbers carefully for only a few minutes, Kaye figured out the filing system and determined that she was in a section that was too current. She studied the numbers on a book to her right and determined that it was more current and ended only ten years earlier. Kaye concluded that it was from that point that the information was put in a central data-base, accessible by way of the computers in the room. She had to move in the opposite direction. She walked slowly to her left, tracing her small hands up and down the book spines and along the numbered shelves, up one row of shelves and down another. High above her head at the end of one shelf she came upon the book containing information for the year she was looking for. She quickly reached up, pulled it down and, with it resting securely on her right hip, walked briskly toward a small table in the corner of the room. Upon reaching the table, she let her shoulder bag slide down her arm and drop onto it with a thump. She then wrestled the large book onto the table and began searching carefully through the shoulder bag. She delicately pulled out a pair of eyeglasses, a note pad and pen. She placed the eyeglasses neatly upon her dark, round face, and positioned the note pad and pen next to the large volume.

Kaye opened the book, studied the pages a few seconds and began to flip pages, one at a time, from right to left, quickly looking at each one in turn. After studying the last page in the volume, she closed the book, stood it on its edge and studied it's spine for a few seconds. She then laid the volume flat on the table again and began thumbing through it page by page again. With a quizzical look on her face, she hoisted the large volume up from the table, struggled to get it across the room and back up on the shelf from where she had gotten it. She then moved between the shelves toward the volumes of books that were more current. Again, tracing her small hands up and down the book spines and along the numbered shelves. She suddenly stopped at a volume directly in front of her, struggled to pull it out and, again, placed it on her hip and headed toward the table in the corner. After flipping and studying several pages, she stopped at one page and studied it in great detail. She smiled to herself, picked up the pen and began to write hurriedly on the note pad. Satisfied that she had found what she was looking for in that volume, Kaye struggled to put it back on the shelf in its assigned spot, and struggled again to pull down several more volumes that she had randomly identified. She carefully leafed through volume after volume, now looking for nothing specific, but was finding a treasure trove of information that was helping to clarify her understanding of what had happened in Thompson County in the past, and no doubt was still happening, but in a way that was more difficult to detect. After randomly perusing several pages of entries from several other books she had pulled from the shelves, Kaye was intrigued with the answers and information that they were revealing. She read some of the entries aloud and reflected on what they meant and their legal significance. When she thought they revealed a new insight, she made notes to herself on the note pad, and underlined those that she wanted to explore further. She suddenly moved from the mount of books she had surrounded herself with and went to the computer terminal. She punched in a few keys and several columns of information popped up on the screen in front of her. She sent a command to the computer to print some of the information, then raced to the printer before the pages began to appear in the paper tray. Then she went back to the table of books with the printed pages and thumbed through a book, as if the paper was telling her exactly where to look. Kaye Webster was also getting a clearer picture of what was stilling going on in Thompson County. She became so engrossed in the task that more than an hour passed without her noticing it. Suddenly sensing an immediate urge to escape the confines of the small inner room, she hurriedly gathered up her note pad and pen and stuffed them into her shoulder bag, leaving the mount of volumes stacked on the table on which she had been working, and securely stuck the shoulder bag under her left arm and quietly walked from the inner room into the larger room and back through the door that had "Records" etched above it. She wasn't sure any of the old women in the room had seen her leave. Nor did she care.

Kaye walked quickly, but quietly down the hallway and approached the staircase with a sigh of relief. She bounced gracefully down the stair steps and headed in the direction of the Information Desk. She had moved only a few steps down the corridor when she looked to her right and saw a door with the words "Property Taxes" painted on it. It was like some supernatural force had directed her attention to the door. Kaye stopped suddenly, and a pressing feeling entered her chest and constrained her breathing. She put her hand over her heart and left breast for a few seconds, gently patting and rubbing and trying to compose herself. After calming down and feeling that she could conduct herself with poise and a sense of purpose, Kaye opened the glass door carefully and stepped up to the counter with a quiet confidence. "May I help you?" a voice asked, as a young man seemed to materialize from nowhere and approached the counter.

"Yes, sir," she said with a disarming smile and a playful tone of voice, as she hoisted the shoulder bag onto the counter and searched for the notes she had taken while looking through the *Books of Liens and Judgments* and retrieving information from the computer files. After a few moments, she produced a list of numbers and said gleefully, "Oh, here it is!" She placed the list on the counter and pointed to several notes she had made. "Could you give me the tax histories on these properties with these Property Identification Numbers?" she asked the young man.

"I don't see why not," he said with a broad smile and look of admiration. "They are matters of public record," he said with confidence as he wrote down the numbers.

"Can you also let me know who owns the properties?" she asked.

"Sure, I can do that," he said with greater assurance.

The young man walked briskly to a computer behind him and punched at a few keys. A few seconds later, a printer nearby began to churn and print out several sheets of paper. He pulled the sheets from the printer tray and scanned them as he walked back toward the counter where Kaye was waiting patiently.

"That's strange," he said as he approached the counter. "The complete tax history is missing from some of these printouts; and it looks like there's information missing about the ownership of some." The young man looked bewildered and at a loss for an explanation.

"I don't know what to tell you, Miss," he said apologetically as he pushed the sheet in Kaye's direction.

"Oh, that's okay. I'll be able to figure it out," she said as she slowly took the sheets from the young man and put them into her shoulder bag that was still placed on the counter. "You've been so helpful," she assured him and reached out to shake his hand. The young man beamed with delight and gingerly grasped her delicate hand and shook it.

Indeed, Kaye had already figured it out. She had found another piece of the puzzle that somebody in Thompson County had attempted to hide. She went out the door as quietly as she had entered it, and again walked in the direction of the Information Desk. Upon approaching it, she extended her hand to the same attendant who had given here directions and said, "Thanks, you've really been a big help." The man looked at her then looked at her extended hand and said, "That's what I'm here for." She withdrew her hand, smiled cordially and said, "Take care, sir." She shook her head as she gracefully moved from the Information Desk and headed toward the door through which she had entered.

Kaye was beginning to understand the context of all the land issues in Thompson County. She believed it was a context in which simple wrongdoings, undoubtedly, first were allowed to evolve to major malfeasance by violating the public trust. Then the malfeasance became a conspiracy of silence, germinating additional opportunities for wrong-doings and later unwittingly ensnaring individuals who, under less enticing circumstances, never would have become involved. That they had become involved saddened her; but she reasoned that it was either their choice to participate, or to tell on those who did.

5

1210 Jasper Street was in a section of the quaint town of Humphries, a section with which Kaye Webster was unfamiliar. Most of the buildings were large houses that were owned by the town's ruling class at one time. But, now most of them housed lawyers' offices and small service businesses. It was hard to say who owned the buildings now, but it was safe to assume that they did not belong to anybody who did not have money or did not have an inextricable connection to it. The tree-lined street and driveways still portrayed an aura of money, nobility and power. It was a section of town she was cautioned to stay out of when she was growing up there. She wasn't exactly sure why.

The office of Atty. Jarvis L. Freeman was listed as "Suite 2" on the sign out front of the large antebellum structure. Posted in front of the parking area was a sign with an arrow pointing to the right. Printed under the arrow was "Suite 2." Kaye gathered a map and a folder from the back seat of her sedan and headed in that direction. Nestled among the tall trees to the side and slightly behind the larger building was a smaller one. She quickly reasoned that the building she was approaching probably was the maid's quarters at some point in time, but now had been converted to prime office space for an exorbitant monthly fee. Looking at her watch as she opened the door, Kaye realized that she was fifteen minutes early for her appointment, which had long been her practice. After carefully closing the door, she stopped momentarily to determine what she should do, stepped up to the glass enclosure with a sliding window and announced her arrival. "I'm Kaye Webster," she said. "I have a 2 o'clock appointment with Atty. Freeman, but I'm a little early."

"Ooohh," the young man said as he looked her up and down

with a smirk forming on his boyish face. "What have we here?" was the question that quickly leapt into his mind, but he didn't have the audacity to articulate it because of Kaye's demeanor. He then handed her a clipboard and coldly said, "You need to fill this out on both sides, Honey. Let me have it back as soon as you finish. Attorney will see you in a few minutes." Kaye looked directly and sternly at Antonio for a few seconds, then slowly turned around and walked defiantly toward an armchair she spotted beside a lamp on a table, next to a light blue door. "Why does he always say, 'Attorney' as if Jarvis L. Freeman does not have a name?" she said to herself as she studied the information requested.

Name. Address. Social Security Number. Home Telephone Number. *Driver's License Number. Employer. How long employed. Income. Work Telephone Number. The nature of your legal problem.* Kaye thought that the information requested would never end. "They want your whole life's history," she said to herself as she flipped the sheet over to complete the reverse side. However, she completed the form, signed it and immediately took it up to Antonio. As Kaye stood patiently before Antonio, he studied the form, looked up and studied Kaye a few seconds, then mumbled something inaudible.

"Is there a problem?" Kaye asked with a serious tone of concern. Antonio ignored her question and appeared to become more absorbed with and consumed by the information she had provided. He studied the form some more, looked at Kaye again, then asked her, "Where do you hang out?" with a slight inflection in his voice.

"I don't!" she replied as she turned curtly and went back to her seat, thinking that he was presumptuous, trying to become too familiar with her and was too impertinent for his position. She gracefully sat down and looked sternly at him for several minutes without blinking.

After a few minutes past, a medium-sized, muscular man opened the light blue door and asked, "Ms. Webster?"

"Yes," she said while getting up, walking toward him and extending her hand.

"Hi, I'm Jarvis Freeman. Come on back," while leading her to an inner office.

"Thanks for agreeing to take a look at this for me," she said as he directed her toward a chair in front of his desk.

"That's what we're here for. Why don't you tell me that story again," he directed her and began writing notes on a legal pad.

Kaye Webster retold Atty. Freeman the story as her cousin John Wilkinson, Jr., had told it to her. After asking a few questions for clarity, Freeman wanted to know information about John's educational background. "The arrogance of those people," he said. "They knew he didn't know what he was signing."

"Here's something else you might find interesting. I did a search and found no official record of any kind pertaining to the $1000 loan," Kaye said.

"Oh, that doesn't surprise me. It happened thousands of times in the past and it still happens today. People just don't know any better. But, you found the documents your cousin signed thirty years after the fact, right?" Jarvis asked in a way that said he already knew the answer.

"Right. That has to be criminal," Kaye offered.

"Yeah. It's criminal and it's unconscionable. But, if people can get away with it, they'll do it." "How do you fight these kinds of cases?" Kaye wanted to know.

"In cases like this when you catch them with their hands in the cookie jar, sometimes they'll just go away, forget about it and you'll never hear from them again. In others, they'll bluff you, try to call in the loan and hope you won't contest it in court," Freeman explained. "They obviously have done this to many more people. They must have it down to a science by now. They're good at it, but they can be stopped. Somebody's just got to go after them."

"That has to be an expensive proposition," Kaye speculated.

"Yeah, it can be expensive and it's time consuming, too," Freeman replied.

Freeman asked for any documents that Kaye had brought with her, and she produced a carefully prepared folder. He shook his head as he poured over them. "Any decent attorney would've never let your cousin sign these," he said with a look of exasperation. "And your cousin never even consulted an attorney. Wow! I can't believe it."

Kaye thought she had seen and heard enough, and began directing Atty. Freeman to take some specific action for her. "I need to know if you'll write this guy Bennett Zorn a letter and ask for proof that Uncle John borrowed $1000 from his father more than forty years ago that resulted in a lien against the 25 acres of land. Also, ask him to provide the payoff balance. You're actually representing my cousin John, but I'll take care of all the legal expenses. I don't want my name associated with this at all. But, I need to be kept informed of all the details. Is that alright?" Kaye wanted to know.

"That's no problem with me," said Freeman as he looked at her curiously.

"You might want to do another title search. I'm not an expert at this, but I do have a little bit of common sense."

"No, it sounds to me like you know exactly what you're doing," he said with a chuckle. "But, I have a woman in Thompson County that I use to do work like this for me. She's good. I'll have her take a look. If there was an original lien, she'll find it. I'll get back to you in a couple of weeks," Freeman assured her as he scribbled on a notepad. After exchanging a few departing pleasantries with Freeman, Kaye left his office and went to the glass enclosure. Antonio was standing as if he was expecting her departure. "That will be $300, Ms. Webster. How would you like to pay it?" he asked with obvious joy spreading across his smiling face.

Without saying anything, Kaye reached into her shoulder bag, pulled out four crisp $100 bills and handed them to Antonio. The look of joy faded from his boyish face as he searched through a moneybag in his desk drawer trying to find change for her. He counted the change several times before handing it to her. He said nothing. "Thank you, Sweetheart," Kaye said as she winked at him. She dropped the change into her large shoulder bag, slung it over her shoulder and strolled gracefully out the door. Antonio looked at her with disdain, smirked and rolled his eyes toward the ceiling.

6

Kaye Webster left Suite 2 at 1210 Jasper Street and drove aimlessly through that section of town. In an effort to become more familiar with it, she drove up one street and down another, seeing things as she had never seen them before. She drove with a purpose on the main drags and lurched along the side streets speculating on who lived there, based on the conditions of the general surroundings. She marveled at how much it had changed and how much it had remained the same. After more than an hour of a destination to nowhere in particular, this section of town was etched in her memory. She drove down Jasper Street again and then headed directly to *Mamma's Dining Room* to meet John Wilkinson, Jr. This late September afternoon, John was already at *Mamma's Dining Room* when Kaye arrived, sitting in the same place he did the first time they met there to discuss the issues with the land. He jumped when she walked up and said, "Hi, Cuz," and hugged her as he customarily did.

"Been waiting long?" Kaye asked.

"Jus' a few minutes," John said with a sound of sorrow in his voice.

"What's new?" she asked, not really expecting anything beyond the customary replay of his ordinary existence.

"Well, I went to see Bennett Zorn," he said sadly. Kaye looked at him with surprise and a tip of her head that asked what he had learned.

Before John could explain, a young server rushed up with glasses of water, silverware and menus. As she began to place the items neatly on the table, Kaye said, "Let me have the usual, Sweetheart."

"I'll have the same thing," John said without knowing exactly what he was ordering.

"Thank you," the server said as she briskly walked away. "That was painless. Two Thursday Specials with sweet tea coming up."

"Where were we? Oh, yeah. You said you went to see Bennett Zorn. What did you find out?" Kaye asked as she looked carefully at him to get a feeling of how he responded, rather than what he said.

"He didn't want to talk about any kind of paperwork Pops signed for the loan more than forty years ago," he said with disbelief. "He kept saying, 'Your dad's dead and my dad's dead. What went on between them, we'll never know. We can't bring them back. All I can go on is what I have here. So, this is between us.' He had everything laid out on his desk," John said with obvious anguish and growing disappointment. "You mean everything you, Clara and the boys signed?" she asked.

"Yeah, and he had something showing how much I've paid and how much I'm supposed to still owe him," he said while casting his eyes downward.

"How much did he say you owe?" "You were right. He's telling me that I really owe him about $42,000 now. But, if I pay him $30,000 before the end of the year, he'll forget about the rest of it," John said with a tone of confusion.

"And, all of this for a $1000 loan. That's very kind of him," Kaye said with obvious cynicism and sarcasm.

"He said something else very interesting. He told me that I shouldn't go to the court house checking on the loan. He also said everything was legal because Dent Madden, the county land attorney, approved it; and I could trust them. Why do you think he said that?" he asked in a way that said he knew he had made a mistake.

"You don't know why he told you that?" Kaye asked incredulously.

"No, I'm not sure," John responded with a quizzical look on his face. "I never heard of Dent Madden. I remember hearing about an Estelle Madden. I believe she was the Register of Deeds at one time," he added. Kaye quickly wrote down their names.

"He knew you wouldn't find any proof that Uncle John borrowed any money from his old man," she said with assurance. "This Dent Madden guy was probably involved with what happened later and made it appear to be legal," Kaye explained. "That should've been a red flag to you. Besides, they knew you trusted them," she said with a feeling of pity for him. Kaye had seen the name Estelle Madden listed at the Register of Deeds on several documents she had seen in the *Books of Liens and Judgments*, but she could not recall seeing the name Dent Madden on any of them.

"You mean there is no proof?" John asked with a quizzical look and dejected demeanor.

"No, there is no proof. I've already checked records for liens and judgments during that period. There were no claims filed against Uncle John. The only thing that's on file are the Promissory Note and *Deed of Trust* you guys signed thirty years after the fact and nearly twenty years after Uncle John died," Kaye announced, knowing that John Jr. probably did not understand the importance of what she was telling him.

"What do we do now?" John wanted to know, showing signs of frustration.

"Let me tell you what I've done," Kaye said, and started to tell John about her meeting with Jarvis Freeman and her agreement with him.

Shortly after she started explaining, the waitress arrived with two servings of broiled, sautéed chicken breasts, buttered corn, green beans, applesauce and toast, and, with a sassy attitude, placed them in front of Kaye and John. With a similar flair, she set down two large glasses of tea with numerous pieces of lemon hugging the brims. "Anything else, folks?" she wanted to know.

"Not now. Maybe dessert later," Kaye said.

Kaye continued to explain to John what she had done. He was amazed at how smart she was, and he was delighted that she was taking on his problem as her own. He latched onto every word she uttered, and smiled broadly at her simplistic manner. Her air of confidence was something John had seldom seen. He began to experience a sense of hope, as well as a feeling of relief. The more she explained, the more confident he became that she was the answer to his many prayers.

Their dessert was a slice of pound cake with a scoop of vanilla ice cream. John launched into how his father used to make hand-made ice cream and how his mother would bake. Kaye delighted in his joy, but was sadden by his circumstances. She only hinted to John her strategy as they departed. "I've got to come at them from different directions," Kaye said as she looked off in the distance, and talking as though she was speaking to no one in particular. John was curious about what she was saying, but he did not ask any questions and she did not bother to explain it to him.

"See you later, Cuz," he said and hugged her.

"Take care," she responded. They freed themselves and went their separate ways.

Kaye Webster felt a special obligation to assist John Wilkinson with the untenable position he managed to get himself in. She had a lot of empathy for him. He, like his father, was a trusting kind of guy, believing in the unearned goodness of others. She knew that was part of his upbringing, having grown up in a very strict and religious family and learning that all people would elect to deal with him the way he had internalized to deal with them. He could only see the goodness in people, even when their evil actions were apparent and their less-than-honorable intentions were obvious and unmistakable. It was almost inconceivable to him that people would elect to deal with him in a manner to take advantage of his kindness and generosity. Too trusting was probably too generous a description for him. John grew up in a place and during a time when the words of a man like Anders Zorn, for all practical reasons, were sacrosanct and infallible. If they said something, it was to be taken at-face-value, even when commonsense and logic dictated otherwise. Zorn was a pillar of the community, and his name carried significant currency in Thompson County and the surrounding areas, opening doors and removing obstacles, advancing his agenda and impeding others' rights when they interfered with his goals and objectives. He was a man whom people like John had learned to respect, even to the point of not looking him in the eye during face-to-face conversations, a respect that came with his name and influence, rather than from merit or from his acts of true altruism. Zorn, like many people with whom he associated, was motivated by greed and self-interest; and John Wilkinson, Sr.'s property was just one more means for him to accomplish his financial goals. John would automatically believe a man like Anders Zorn before he could find the inner capacity to believe himself. And, he could not find it within himself to believe that anybody he knew personally could possibly refute anything Anders Zorn had told him. He was at the mercy of men like Zorn in more ways than he ever realized, and they realized it more than he.

John Wilkinson was a perfect dope for a man like Zorn, gullible to his gift of gab and in awe of his apparent knowledge of the intricacies of real estate transactions. To be sure, John Wilkinson, Jr. reasoned to himself, Bennett Zorn had learned from his father and was simply carrying out what all of the parties, past and present, had agreed to. He was oblivious to the reality that it is because of people like the Wilkinsons that men like the Zorns become parasites, living well off their hosts and fooling themselves into believing they're living on their own. These parasitic creatures have developed the fine art of hoodwinking their hosts into believing that their relationships are mutually beneficial, and even to the point of being symbiotic. As long as people like John Wilkinson continue to labor under such illusions, men like Bennett Zorn will continue to exploit the ideal situation they've created for themselves.

7

Kaye Webster's presence in Humphries and Thompson County had not escaped the attention of Judge Frank Wilcox. Several custodians of the records had gotten word to him that she had been examining records in the County Courthouse and asking questions of several people in the County. After inquiring about who was examining records and asking questions, his initial response was that there was nothing to worry about. But, he told himself that he had to call "The Enforcer" to be certain. As was customary, Wilcox immediately called Sheriff Johnny "Big Boy" Dawson and asked him to find out whatever he could about her. Sheriff understood that these were the kinds of assignments that he could not entrust to any of his deputies and would have to perform himself, and he also knew that Judge Wilcox wanted this little assignment to be confidential. In fact, he could not even mention to his deputies that he was performing these kinds of services for any county officials because they would know they were personal and could not be interpreted as part of their official duties. Known for his size, standing more than 6' 8" and weighing more than 300 pounds, and overly aggressive nature, Sheriff Dawson was feared by most of Thompson County's residents or any non-resident who encountered him under the wrong set of circumstances. He made great efforts to exude congeniality and passivity, but the slightest provocation brought out his wrath. He was famous for pulling out his service revolver and putting it against a suspect's head if he felt that he was not getting the cooperation he was seeking. "Hey, Big Boy," Judge Wilcox said cheerfully as Sheriff Dawson answered his personal cell phone. "Got a minute?"

"Of course, Judge," Dawson said in a way that was meant to please. "I got a little something I need you to checkout for me."

Wilcox told Sheriff Dawson what he had heard and from whom he had heard it, and instructed him to find out all he could about her and to report back to him within a week. "You know you can count on me, Judge," Dawson said in a manner that was clearly ingratiating and servile, attitudes and behaviors to which Judge Wilcox had become accustomed.

Sheriff Dawson immediately called the Chief Deputy and told her that he had a special assignment that he had to complete on short notice and would be incommunicado for several days, but that she had to keep that information to herself. He instructed her to let the other deputies know that she was their point of contact for any atypical emergency that might arise during his absence. He also instructed her to call him on his work cell phone if she needed to. Sheriff Dawson then went to the County Courthouse to inquire of Judge Wilcox's source about his suspicions. These inquiries led him to the surveillance video cameras that record all entrances to, activities within and exits from the Courthouse. The courthouse informant identified Kaye as the person who had been examining records and asking questions, and Sheriff Dawson began his sleuthing, something that gave him a heightened sense of importance and indispensability.

After determining her name, where she worked and her general patterns of movement, Sheriff Dawson examined her paper trails and, to his disappointment, found nothing unusual. No criminal record. No traffic violations. No behaviors considered outside the norms of civility and decorum. "No Life! Boring!" Sheriff thought to himself. He, nevertheless, staked out her apartment building several consecutive nights and followed her to work the next day. Then he would go home, sleep, return to her place of employment before she got off work then follow her back home. He, stuffed into his small pickup truck, remained as inconspicuous as he could, as he watched her stop for gasoline, stop to eat or to shop for household items. He was struck by her beauty, simplicity and unassuming presence and was beguiled by these characteristics and traits that fed his ego and self-assurance. What Sheriff Dawson didn't know was that she accomplished much of what she wanted to do during the time that he was following her. She had done it while he was sleeping, and she did it via the Internet and in the confines of her home. He concluded that she was not someone Judge Wilcox had to fear. He could detect no apparent personal or professional ambitions that he should be concerned about.

At the end of the one-week period, Sheriff Dawson called Judge Wilcox as he promised.

"What'cha got for me?" Wilcox asked after recognizing Sheriff Dawson's number on the caller ID and answering the phone.

Sheriff Dawson was a little miffed that Judge Wilcox did not even answer his phone with a simple "Hello," but he was not surprised. Over the years he had learned that the judge was not one for a lot of small talk; he was one for getting right to the point.

"Found out that her name is Kaye Webster. She's a Claims Adjuster and works for that big insurance company over on Popular. Gotta be something related to her job that she's been checking into," Dawson said with great confidence. "Nothing in her background that I think you have to be concerned about, Judge. Typical stuff—grew up here, moved away for awhile, came back, knows her place."

"You can't be too careful nowadays. You know how they are. You let'em get a little education, give them a decent job and they think they're as good as you," Wilcox said with an air of confidence and superiority.

"Yeah, you got the right," Dawson said in full support of the judge's sentiments.

Judge Wilcox was amply satisfied with the report Sheriff Dawson gave him and completely dismissed the courthouse informant's suspicions from his mind. Besides, he told himself, there was no way she was smart enough to uncover any legal or more offenses that he may have committed.

8

ohn Wilkinson, Jr. was a man to be pitied in some respects, and to be envied in many others. "I am a God-fearing man," he often said of himself, "and I believe God will look after his own." Like his father, he was a hardworking man, accustomed to asking nobody for anything he could find the energy to acquire or do on his own. He suffered from the illusion that hard work was all that was necessary for him to succeed in life, but he had not always seen life that way. He was to be envied for his diligence and self-reliance. He was to be pitied because he did not always know what was in his best interest, or when others claimed his interest as theirs. His lack of education and limited exposure was a great disadvantage he was able to recognize on some levels and unable to accept on others. In some ways, he was pathetic, and even tragic.

John Wilkinson, Jr. left school after only six years, but he had virtually left the earnest pursuit of an education long before that. All of his years of schooling were interrupted by chores he had to help his father to perform on the family farm; and it was rare that he completed a week of school without missing a day or two. Many days he would stop the mule in the fields and momentarily daydream about school and what he was probably missing. Those moments were soon ended when his father would seem to appear from nowhere and yell at him. "Stop daydreaming and get back to work," John Wilkinson, Sr. would scold. "That mule needs to be worked, boy, not allowed to stand around and do nothing all day." "I was just thinking about school," he would say in defense of his actions, and with the hope that his father would be sympathetic to his yearnings.

"School ain't never made nobody rich; hard work has," his father would admonish him with contempt and ridicule. It was difficult for John Jr. to determine if his dad was just mean and crotchety or was succumbing to the ravages of high-blood pressure and heart disease that had plagued him for many years. John Sr. was fond of saying he had worked hard all his life; and it was obvious that he expected his only son to do the same. When John Sr. talked about working hard, John Jr. always wanted to reply, "We're working hard but we ain't rich," but he knew better than to let those words form in his mouth or attempt to issue from his lips. And, he was even careful how he allowed them to form in his mind. Somehow, he could not see how working hard and school were incompatible, although he was unable to articulate that view. It was not long before he gave up on the idea of school altogether. He could not be there as often as he wished, and he was not allowed to show an outward appearance of thinking about it when he wasn't. On several occasions when John Jr. was working in the fields, and off in the distance when he could hear the rumbling and whining sounds of the school bus coming in his direction, he would stop the mule as quickly as he could and streak toward the nearest hiding place, in a nearby patch of trees, within a stand of taller crop, or flat on his stomach in the middle of the field, anywhere he thought he could not be seen. The taunting and teasing by the students who did not have to endure his fate were more than he could endure. He reveled in a great sense of accomplishment when he was able to elude them, and to peer from behind and through those obstructions that had saved him. When the bus had rumbled from his sight, he would dance and frolic about, clapping and laughing, rejoicing that he had done it again. "I won again! I won again!" he would shout with delight and shake his clenched fists in the direction of the school bus. At times, it appeared that the school bus driver, who was only a few years older than John Jr., would stealthily approach the field where it was expected that he would be working, then bear down on the horn when he was spotted languidly walking behind the mule or methodically tending a crop by hand. And, the students rejoiced when they caught him. It had become a game and he had won more times than they.

When he was not fast enough to avoid detection, or they caught him by surprise, they'd yell, "Gee! Haw!", "Getup!" and "Whoa!", as the bus passed by; and they'd laugh with obvious delight when the mule wanted to follow their directions, or was completely confused by them.

The embarrassment, humiliation and shame were more than he could take. Each one caused his shoulders to droop a little more and his head to bow unwillingly. Having felt that he had suffered enough, and did not want to face the students again each time after they had caught him, John Jr. came to the painful decision to distance himself from school and the process of academic learning, and to immerse himself in spiritual learning, a world beyond his rational understanding. He was relieved because he would not have to endure their ridicule and torture again.

The transition was an easy one for John Jr., since he had always been enamored with the religious life, and felt a kindred connection with it. Early on, he had learned the books of the Bible, and could name them sequentially on demand, backward and forward. He could recite passages from the Bible, chapter and verse, and give what he thought were accurate interpretations of them. He was always fascinated by the various parables and stories embedded in them, and had learned them before he learned to read. He could find in them justifications for circumstances and situations in his personal life, even when the justifications clearly weren't there. He developed a way of thinking to make the parables and stories relevant by contouring and stretching their meanings until they gave him the lessons he wanted to learn. John Wilkinson, Jr.'s life after school was a difficult one, but one which he learned to accept and to accommodate himself to. When he was not working on the family farm, which was getting more difficulty every year to produce a livelihood, he worked at odd jobs wherever he could find them in and around Thompson County and at whatever wage anybody was willing to pay him. What he lacked in skills and abilities, he worked hard to make up for with determination, faith and perseverance. In spite of his best efforts, there were many opportunities that escaped him because he did not have the requisite skills and abilities to overcome the distinct disadvantages he faced; and he had come to terms with that reality. Nonetheless, he remained optimistic that, in the end, his undying faithfulness and obedience to God's word would overcome any worldly disadvantages he faced. Moreover, he was willing to stake his life on that proposition, and was committed to and held fast to that belief. It was reinforced two to three times each week when he attended church services, praising and worshipping, and several times each day when he prayed. These were times that sustained him and gave him the strength to continue the struggles he faced. They were a kind of reality that gave him an inner peace and a sense of hope that he could find in no other place and at no other time.

John later came to terms with a different reality. His father died suddenly from a massive heart attack, and his only sibling Doreena, who long had been estranged from the family for many years, could not be located and informed of his death. Within months of his Dad's death, John Jr. soon married his childhood sweetheart, the first girl he had dated. Although he was only sixteen years old at the time he made a lifetime commitment, he gave the appearance and demonstrated the behaviors of being much older. In less than a year after his marriage, John Jr. was the proud, yet apprehensive father of twin boys. With a fifteen-year old wife and newborn babies to provide for, it was difficult for him to make a life for them and for himself in and around Thompson County. He soon came to the realization that providing food, shelter and clothing for his family out- weighed the test of his faith and obedience. It was a reality that said attending church services two to three times each week and praying several times each day did not guarantee him and his family the basic necessities of life. It was a reality that also said he probably needed to leave Thompson County and to expose himself to opportunities he undoubtedly never would receive if he chose to stay there.

Armed with his sixth-grade education and his wife and children in tow, John Jr. struck out for the big city, just two hundred miles from Thompson County. His vow never to return was soon nullified by the cold, hard reality of big-city life. He began to have second thoughts about his vow after being there only one month. Insensitive and uncaring hearts seemed to await him at every turn he attempted to make. And, his ability to navigate the complexities of city life was compromised by his inability to read and comprehend the economic and social milieus that were foreign to Thompson County and the surrounding areas. Although he was determined to seek out a living there, his mother called frequently asking him to return to Thompson County. Her comments about not being able to live without his father, and beliefs that she didn't have much longer to live, soon convinced him that he should return. When John Jr. told his wife of his decision, she was adamant that she and the twins were not going to return because there was no place she could conceive of that was as bad as Thompson County. She was prepared to do whatever was necessary to fend for herself and the boys. Her strong defense for not returning to Thompson County was puzzling, since she was living in the only place she had ever lived after leaving. If he wanted to return, she told him, it was his choice. While it was a difficult choice for him, he returned and picked up his life there were he had left it; and only saw his wife and sons briefly and sporadically after returning to Thompson County. It was on one of those rare occasions when they visited him in Thompson County many years later that John Jr. convinced them to sign the documents that had become his financial and legal nightmare. He vowed that if he ever got it straight, he would never find himself in such a predicament again. However, when he could bring himself to reflect on his life, depression tended to consume his waking moments and to frustrate those moments that he attempted to sleep.

9

Weeks passed, and there had been no word from Freeman. Every time Kaye called, Antonio was there to answer with his high-pitched, proper greeting. Kaye could not determine if his voice was real or effected. However, he was always polite but never very helpful. When she inquired about the status of the work they were supposed to be doing for her, Antonio knew nothing. However, her intuition told her that Antonio was somehow involved with her case, but she dared not ask him, and she dared not express her concern--at least not to him. Leaving a message with him requesting that Freeman return her call was the same as leaving no message at all. Freeman never returned her calls, and there was no way that she could be sure he had ever received them. Although she could not be sure that Freeman was doing anything, Kaye made sure she was still busy stringing together bits and pieces of information, like stringing together a large variety of ugly beads, forming a pattern that was becoming more pleasant to look at. Asking a few simple questions in the right places produced important tidbits that became treasure troves when she began putting them together later. Kaye used informal discussion periods before and after Sunday morning worship service to find out all she could. Some of the same people who had asked her to "Give it a chance," and "Give yourself a chance," were eager to talk what seemed like forever if she asked them a simple question. She often jokingly said, "Them brothers and sisters know everything." She knew that many of them had difficulty reading and writing; but she marveled at their ability to remember. Asking them to recall an incident or to explain a particular event was an open invitation for them to help add a few missing pieces to a complex puzzle she was putting together. They did not know it and she could not tell them. Eventually they would find out about it; and they may eventually benefit from it.

More than two months had past, and still no word from Freeman. Kaye called and left a message with Antonio to give Atty. Freeman. The message was: "I want my work done now, or I want my money back. If you can't do the work, let me know. I will be in you office today at 3 o'clock; I'll talk with you then." Within five minutes, Antonio called to confirm the 3 o'clock appointment. Kaye was there on time and was not asked to wait. Antonio was cordial and polite, and Freeman was profusely apologetic. Kaye sat quietly and let Freeman explain why the work had not been done. He stated that he would understand if she took the case from him and gave it to another attorney. "No, I don't want anyone else involved with this, since you're already involved," she said emphatically. "I just want you to handle the case if you're serious about doing it. If you can't, let me know," Kaye continued emotionless and without blinking an eye.

Freeman tried to interject a few comments to soften Kaye's anger. "We've had a few unexpected cases we were assigned by the courts," he offered as an explanation. "You know how that goes."

Showing a desire to hold her frustration, she said, "Yeah, I understand all of that, but I need these things taken care of." Kaye said. "Now," she tagged on a few seconds later.

"We've done some work, Ms. Webster. As I said, the person who does work for me in Thompson County was stranded on vacation. So, my office assistant and secretary, Antonio, went down there and did a preliminary title search. He had a few problems at first, but didn't come up with anything either." While looking at a calendar on his desk, he said, "My person down in Thompson County should be back Monday of next week. I promise to get that letter out to Zorn no later than Friday of next week," he said with assurance.

Feeling assured that she had his attention and that he knew she was not joking, Kaye shared with Freeman some of the information she had gathered since they last met. He shook his head and chuckled as she spoke.

"This sounds like a class-action to me," Freeman said after she finished.

"Could be," replied Kaye. "Let's try to make some headway on this one first," she continued in the form of a demand, rather than in the form of a request. Freeman assured her that he would follow through as he had promised and would keep her informed about what he was doing and finding out about the issues. Kaye was relieved that she had finally gotten his attention and secured his commitment to work on her case. "Attorney Freeman," Kaye said as she looked him squarely in eyes, "I'm counting on you." She reached out to shake his hand as she stood up. As Freeman attempted to stand, she told him he didn't have to get up and that she could see herself out. She stepped out of his office and into the reception area where she expected to see Antonio, because she was very anxious to see him before she left; but he was nowhere to be found. She suspected that Antonio also knew she was anxious to see him, and made sure he was nowhere near when she finished her meeting with Atty. Freeman.

🐚 10 🐚

rue to his word, this time, Freeman sent Bennett Zorn a letter the following Friday asking that Zorn furnish proof that John Wilkinson, Sr., in fact, had borrowed $1000 from Bennett's father. He also stated that it was his initial conclusion that John Wilkinson, Jr. had been intimidated into signing the Promissory Note and *Deed of Trust* thirty years later, since Freeman was unable to find any official record of the initial transaction. If the transaction with his father more than thirty years earlier was legitimate and Bennett Zorn had inherited the instruments from his father at the time of his death, then there must be a paper trail for the entire transaction, Freeman stated to him.

Kaye was impressed with Freeman's grasp of the facts and how he had stated them. But, she felt that his use of the phrase, "Have a nice day," at the end of the letter diminished the seriousness of what had occurred and minimized the resolve she had about correcting it. Nevertheless, she passed a copy of the letter on to John Jr. and continued to plan and plot her own strategy. She could not share it with Freeman or with John. In fact, she could not share it with anyone.

By continuing to ask questions, to listen and to observe, more pieces of the puzzle came to Kaye and she methodically placed them into the vacant spaces in the puzzle. Many of the pieces fell into place with a loud thump. Others had to be massaged and nudged a bit before they found their rightful place. Information came not only from Thompson County, but it also came from surrounding counties and neighboring states. For example:

- Several hundred acres of land were "sold" for a few thousand dollars, and it was "discovered" that the land contained a large reserve of oil and leased to a major oil company.

- An illiterate woman lost more than 195 acres of land because she allowed her son to use it as collateral for a loan to buy two used automobiles. The loan was never fully repaid, according to the "official" records.

- Three hundred acres of land were forfeited because of missing one car payment. The land was used as collateral for the car loan, and the fine print stated that missing one payment could result in loss of the land.

- Laws had been enacted stating that acreage of land could not be parceled and sold in order to pay back taxes on the land.

- Unsuspecting landowners signed documents to lease their land for a specific period of time. But, at the end of the lease period they discovered that they in fact had signed the land over to the lessee at the end of the lease period, never to get it back.

These examples and others that Kaye Webster uncovered enraged her. On the face of it, they all appeared to be fair, legitimate business transactions. Not only did they occur in the past, they were still occurring and Kaye knew it. But, how could she prove it, she wondered. Behind the thin veneer of legitimacy lurked an ugly truth that she was determined to expose. Several weeks had past since Freeman had sent the letter to Zorn. Kaye had not heard from Freeman and assumed that Zorn had not responded to the letter. Therefore, she made a surprise visit to Suite 2 at 1210 Jasper Street to push Freeman gently to turn up the heat on Zorn. Antonio was unusually polite toward Kaye and got her in to see Freeman as soon as she arrived.

After exchanging the normal salutations with Winfield, Kaye moved quickly to the purpose of her visit. "I hadn't heard anything from you about the letter you sent Zorn, so, I decided to come by to see what's going on," she said.

"Oh, I got a call from Zorn a couple of days after we sent out the letter," Freeman quickly explained. "Said he had proof that his old man had a legitimate claim against that property. In fact, he was supposed to send a copy of it right out to me. But, I haven't gotten anything from him, yet. I know it's been at least a couple of weeks."

"Yeah, I know," Kaye replied.

"My guess is he doesn't have anything."

"Whatever he has, it doesn't go back forty years," Kaye said confidently.

"Here's what I need you to do," she directed. "Send Zorn another letter asking him to provide some proof within a week. If he doesn't provide it, let him know that we will file a lawsuit asking to have all of John's money refunded to him and to have the judgment against the property set aside. Also, ask for a 1099-Interest form showing how much money John has paid in interest to Zorn and his old man over the years."

Freeman finished scribbling down exactly what Kaye wanted him to say in the letter to Zorn. He then stated again that the case probably should be a class action, but that he would not be able to provide any additional legal help on it because of his current case load and lack of legal resources. Besides, Thompson County was not a county he normally considered in his practice, he informed her. Kaye knew she could demand nothing else of Winfield, and Winfield knew it, too. "If you can get this letter out this week, I would really appreciate it," she stated with sincerity as she left him.

"That should be no problem," he responded skeptically. As Kaye left Winfield's inner office and entered the reception area, Antonio smiled and waved at her. She did not smile or wave at him; but she gracefully sauntered across the room and carried her trade-mark walk out the door. Her fertile mind was churning many thoughts and she could sense that more of the puzzle pieces were within her grasp; she just hadn't yet been able to discern them in order to put them all together, confirming in her rationale mind the complete picture of what her gut sense already knew.

11

Kaye approached her car with deep thoughts of what she had learned about the land issues. A sense of dread crept over her as she methodically and slowly opened the car door and slumped heavily into the seat. She slung her purse into the passenger seat and sat immobile for a few minutes, running many uneasy thoughts through her mind, biting nervously at her lower lip and staring in the distance. As was her custom, she gradually surveyed the landscape all around her to ensure, the best she could, that nobody was watching her. She eventually started her car and slowly backed out of the parking space and headed toward Jasper Street. When she reached the street, indecision overcame her; she didn't know which way to turn. She stopped the car and just gripped the steering wheel as though she wanted to rip it away from the shaft. Her dread and indecision had turned to a quiet rage she had never experienced before. She could only see a blur of images as they streaked before her eyes. A gentle beep from the car behind Kaye's awakened her from a momentary state of possessed anger and brought her back to rational thought. She pulled the car onto Jasper Street, and it seemed as though it turned right against her will and headed toward a section of Humphries that was called and known as "the worst section of town."

She wandered around aimlessly, and saw and understood Humphries like never before. She saw a section of town that was the polar opposite of others she had seen before. There were abandoned buildings as plentiful as abandoned cars, battered and smashed, precariously parked among the trash, strewn and piled along the streets. It appeared to be a God-forsaken place, a veritable wasteland teeming with desolation and neglect. Meandering and milling all around her were very familiar faces, some etched with the pain of despair and neglect, and others beaming with hope, promise and possibilities. They were imbued with a flair and style that was uniquely original, yet comfortably familiar. It was like she was seeing with a new set of eyes, calibrated to 20/10 vision. She saw the contrasting conditions and understood that some were derived from undeserved necessity and that the others were created for unearned convenience. She asked herself, "How did this happen?" Her mind drifted back to the issues involving the land. "It all makes more sense now," she said audibly, time and time again. "It's about information and knowledge," she said as she chuckled and shook her head. "It's all so simple. You don't have to know a lot; you just have to make sure that others don't know as much as you." Those words reverberated through her mind. "My people perish from lack of knowledge. Hosea 5:4," she said in a conversational tone.

Kaye knew that she was approaching a sad reality of something she should have known a long time ago. She had a new awareness, a personal renaissance, about herself and all those she often jokingly called, "My folk!" She was upset with herself about what she was thinking, but at the same time glad she was thinking it. It was an epiphany that she had been searching for, but never realized it until it was upon her. A series of questions coursed through her nimble mind as she continued to drive and really see and experience things like never before. How many people really want to be here? How many lost their land because they or their forbearers didn't know what they were doing? How many of them were too trusting, believing somebody else had their interest at heart? How would their lives be different if they had the opportunity to acquire the knowledge and understanding that others took for granted? How many would believe me if I tried to tell them all they need to know? When will we learn that people are motivated by self-interest? These questions generated many more; and she felt herself slowly becoming consumed by anger and fear; anger at what she was seeing, and fear that she may not be able to do anything about it. She had discovered her calling, her true purpose, the profound sense of what she must do with the rest of her life. She knew that her inner-self would accept nothing less.

As Kaye Webster crisscrossed Humphries, meandering in and out of the Sawyer Village section, and finally headed toward her office, she knew that her work, which she once said was her life-blood, was no longer important to her. The place was just somewhere to go as a ritualistic practice, and the activity itself was something that was expected of her. While she was good at both, lately neither had any significant value for her. She reasoned that she had probably found her real purpose in life, her real work, and she pondered where it might lead or take her. The work she had been doing all of her professional life was inconsequential, but work she had done with pride and precision.

When Kaye returned to her office, there were piles of folders on her desk that required her attention and notes that requested phone calls to be returned. Armed with the lackluster desire to be the consummate professional, she tackled the tasks with a half-hearted effort, giving them the best she had at the moment. While she finished them to perfection, her heart for the work was nowhere to be found. Her preoccupation with the land issues had saturated her entire existence, and had begun to gnaw at the core of her being. There had been a growing awareness that the land issues had begun to consume all of her thoughts during her waking hours, and troubled her peace during the times she should have been sleeping. True to his word, again, Winfield sent Zorn a letter the next day stating exactly what Kaye wanted it to say. John received a copy of it from Kaye and read it several times before calling her to discuss it. "You mean I might actually get my $15,000 back?" he urgently wanted to know. "It's possible. Let's just wait and see what happens," she cautioned him. Kaye was amazed at her cousin John's naiveté and his willingness to trust people who did not have his best interest at heart. She did not have the heart to tell him that, at one time, he did not actually own the land Bennett Zorn was now trying to take from him. Kaye had discovered in the Liens and Judgments and Property Tax Offices that John had always paid taxes on the land he had inherited from his dad, assuming that they owned it continuously from the time of his death. He got a tax bill each year, and paid it, not knowing that during some of that time, Anders Zorn, Bennett's father, was actually the owner of record. When John signed the deed and promissory note many years after his mother's death, it was to transfer the property back into his name. Kaye also reasoned that, even if she were to explain to John exactly how Zorn and others pulled off the trick, he probably would not grasp it. Kaye had determined that the only reason Zorn probably had transferred the property back to John was to clean up some title transfer problems that undoubtedly would surface later if he did not. He knew that John wasn't knowledgeable to ask questions or to consult an attorney on the matter. Once John signed the documentation he had prepared, Zorn's paper trail on the questionable transaction would be covered and John was the perfect patsy to help him do it.

12

"J.P.?"

"Yeah?"

"This is Mac. What the hell's going on down there?"

"What're you talking about, Mac?"

"I got a letter today. We need to talk. Call me at home tonight."

"Who...?" There was no response. The caller had hung up before J. P. could ask the question.

James Preston Sellers placed the handset on the cradle, and sat staring at the phone. "It's gotta be summin real hot if Mac can't talk 'bout it on his office phone," he told himself. He arduously pulled himself from his chair, walked haltingly over to the window across the room, and looked nervously up and down Main Street.

J. P. Sellers and Heywood Bradford "Mac" Mc Lauren had watched out for each other as boyhood friends. Nearly thirty-five years later, they're still looking out for each other. Mac Mc Lauren had the good fortune of living up in Sawyer Village, an exclusive section of Humphries, and J. P. Sellers had the misfortune of growing up in Humphries. Although they lived just walking distance from each other, it was like they were from different worlds because of the contrasts in their physical surroundings and the resulting perceptions created by them. It didn't matter; they would always be friends.

After high school, J. P. joined the Army and Mac went off to college, but their friendship remained intact during their six-year physical absence from each other. The occasional letter kept them as close as ever. J. P. re-enlisted after his first hitch, and Mac went to law school immediately after college. They both ended up back in Thompson County about the same time. Mac went to work in his father's small law practice, and J. P. took a job in a local feed and hardware store full-time and dabbled in real estate on the side. Sawyer Village and Thompson County had been good to both of them, J. P. thought to himself. Besides, he was lucky and had befriended the right people in the right places. Mac was now in a position to open greater opportunities for him, and he would do anything he could to continue helping Mac in Thompson County. Mac's called spooked J. P., but he knew that Mac, with his vast resources and network, would take care of the problem, no matter what it was. He decided not to worry about it. J. P. finished up some paperwork, or "grunt work" as he called it, and left his office an hour earlier than he normally did. After all, he was now his own boss and could make his own hours. His side job in real estate thrived, and he was able to leave the hardware store much sooner than he realized. In fact, after working in real estate for only two years, J. P. was able to establish his own real estate business, selling very little but getting involved with deals that others put together and invited him to participate in, and managing a few properties that others owned.

He cruised around Humphries and Sawyer Village for an hour or so with no particular destination in mind. He was really at home in Humphries, and easily learned to be at home after he moved to Sawyer Village. On the off chance that he would see some of the people he often referred to as "The Big Mucks," but never to their faces, he decided to swing by The Belmont Club for a cocktail or two before heading home. He stopped his new sports utility vehicle (suv), which he referred to as his truck, at the valet parking area, as was required of all members, boldly rolled his stumpy body out and threw the keys to the young attendant holding his door. "I'll take care of it for you, Mr. Sellers," she said with great familiarity as she jumped into the vehicle and quickly moved it from in front of the entryway toward the back of The Club. J. P. watched the vehicle admiringly as the attendant drove it out of view. He smiled broadly and walked with confidence toward the opened door that awaited him. The Belmont Club was the place for anybody of any significant economic and social standing in and around

Humphries and Thompson County. From the time of its inception to its subsequent completion, The Belmont Club was meant to be the private domain for men only; more specifically for white men who could afford to pay the initial $25,000.00 membership fee, and a $5,000.00 annual participation fee. Without a sponsor, however, no amount of money could secure a membership in The Belmont Club. Initially, women were only allowed in the main clubhouse three times a year: Mother's Day, Christmas Day and New Year's Eve, and they had to be accompanied by a club member in good standing. While there had been recent attempts to change the Club's membership policy, its history probably would make it difficult to change the practice. Members frequented the place when special occasions dictated it and when other occasions allowed for easy conversation and frivolity among men of like minds and common purposes. It was also a place where questionable business transactions conducted there could more easily take on an aura of legitimacy and respectability, and all with the assurance that even the walls would maintain their silence about them. The grand and imposing structure demanded that; and those who were welcomed into its culture of secrecy had an implicit understanding of the dos and don'ts regarding the sanctity of their common bond.

The Belmont Club was nowhere near the main thoroughfares of Humphries, but nestled in a grove of tall, red oak trees bordering the Sawyer Village section of town. It could not be seen from the road winding lazily in front of the driveway leading into the property. It was a place that was difficult to find without specific directions to get there, and could be a little intimidating to the person who happened to stumble upon it by accident. The tall, red oak trees lined each side of the long driveway to the main clubhouse, and had been trained to form an archway of shade and tranquility, darkening the stately main clubhouse standing at the very end. Carefully and strategically erected behind the main clubhouse were several buildings, angled in such a way that they could not be seen from the driveway. It was club policy for all club members to drive their vehicles directly to the valet stand, which could accommodate six cars abreast, under the ornately decorated archway at the main entrance to the clubhouse. The valets were diligent in moving the cars and parking them out of sight as quickly as possible. Unless two members arrived at The Belmont Club about the same time, they would not know who else was there. The words that best describe the interior of The Belmont Club are impressive and palatial. Some would even say that it was lavish and ostentatious. The grandeur of the cavernous vestibule foretold what the remainder of the main clubhouse probably looked like. Large leather chairs, accompanied by Tiffany lamps on marble topped tables, rested quietly and comfortably along each side of the plush, burgundy, carpeted corridor leading to the member reception area. It appeared that the chairs and tables were seldom, if ever, used, and were placed there as much for their grandiosity as they were placed there for their practical use. Paintings neatly hanging along the corridor walls gave away potential secrets about the attitudes, lives and times of those whom the club represented. There were stern-faced men, loftily perched on horses; paintings of battle scenes, portraits, apparently of families, intently following all who walked by; and pictures of workers in fields, engaged in various kinds of manual labor. These images were integrated with an assortment of religious symbols that ornately adorned the walls. The collection of images and symbols portrayed a common theme from the alcove up to the stand where members announced their presence, and highlighted by a row of chandeliers that rivaled many European palaces.

The Belmont Club was very accommodating to all its members, providing them an opportunity to entertain themselves and their guests in private elegance, and sending them a bill at the end of each month for almost any kind of service they had requested. Drinks and meals were standard fare. Occasionally, however, other requests were "accommodated," or "procured," without hesitation or question, no matter how unusual or difficult they were to fulfill. The more unusual and difficult the request, the more it would cost. There were also a few private suites to accommodate members who preferred staying overnight, and meeting rooms for private discussions for those who wanted to conduct business or hold court out of the sight of other members. The members' parlor was appointed with the finest oak and leather furniture, and served by a wait staff dressed in black and burgundy uniforms. The staff attended to the needs and whims of those they served, getting cocktails, emptying ashtrays, finding a newspaper, shining a pair of shoes, or arranging to secure a table in the dining room. The staff had been known to procure conveniences, items and services that bordered on the illegal and immoral. No request was left unexplored and, usually, unfulfilled. The Belmont Club was a place that was conceived, built and operated to make the average man feel like a king and the uncommon man to feel untouchable. J. P. Sellers was no exception. J. P. walked up to the member host's desk with a big smile. His strut, bordering on a swagger, was the epitome of self-confidence and his stance exuded a self-assurance that stated that he had earned the divine right to be there; a right that was reserved for a select few, and J. P. knew it and was forever grateful to his wife for helping him to understand it. "Good evening, Mr. Sellers," the host said with an easy familiarity and a business-like sincerity. "Doing great," J. P. said with a smile and a wink. "Probably couldn't stand it if it got any better," he added while thinking about the conversation he'd had with Mac Mc Lauren. He was laboring over the desperate tone in Mac's voice and words that Mc Lauren was unable to share with him earlier. But, now was no time for such concerns to interfere with his sense of the importance of himself. "What will it be for you this evening?" the host asked as he motioned for one of the wait staff to come to the host stand, and reached in the host stand for a statement ticket to keep track of J. P.s charges.

"Just a couple of cocktails in the parlor," J. P. replied as he looked in the direction of a huge leather chair in one corner of the parlor.

"Mr. Sellers will just be having cocktails this evening," the host informed the wait staff as he approached. He handed him the charge statement and said, "Take good care of Mr. Sellers." "Of course," the young man said. He then turned to J. P. and asked, "Will there be anyone joining you, sir?"

"No, not this evening," J. P. responded with a worried look on his face.

"Any particular place you want to sit? Or, are you going to the bar?"

"Back there," J. P. said while pointing with authority to the chair in a dimly-lit area in the rear corner of the parlor, declining to go to a conspicuous area in the parlor where he usually went.

J. P. plopped down in the big chair and ordered himself an extra dry martini barely before his backside touched the cushion. In a matter of minutes, the wait staff had returned with the cocktail. As soon as he placed it on a decorative coaster on the table in front of him and set the cocktail on it, J. P. grabbed the drink and started gulping it. "Let me have another," J. P. demanded before the wait staff could finish the setup on his table.

The wait staff then placed the basket of snacks on the table and left as J. P. was turning up the glass to coax out the olive and remaining cocktail. The Wait Staff returned a few minutes later, moved the empty glass from the coaster and replaced it with another extra dry martini. J. P. finished it in a few minutes and was ready to leave. He motioned for the wait staff to bring his check by holding up his left hand and pretending that he was writing in it with his right hand. J. P. was ready to go.

The valet saw J. P. purposefully walking down the long corridor leading toward the main entrance in less than twenty minutes after he had arrived. She quickly grabbed his key from the key board, ran toward the back of the building and moments later drove his sports utility vehicle back to the entryway before he arrived there. He winked and gave her a small wad of money as she smiled and held his door opened for him. "Thank you, Mr. Seller," she said.

"Anything for you, honey," he said in a flirtatious manner as she closed the door.

J. P. sped away thinking how fortunate he was to have the adoration and respect he had deserved. After all, he had grown up poor, had worked hard, and had gotten a few lucky breaks. If everybody followed his formula and worked the way he did, he thought to himself, they, too, can make it big. Even make it big in Thompson County and Sawyer Village. Then he suddenly thought about the phone call he had received from Mac Mc Lauren earlier during the day. It gave him a cold and clammy feeling. He figured that Mac would be home by then, so he decided to go back to his office to call him from there. Besides, he didn't want to get home too early. Waiting for him was his wife Maureen who always asked him numerous questions about what he had done for the day, and how he was planning to make *her* life better. It didn't seem that his life really mattered. He would do anything he could to avoid that. And, he would do anything he could to please her. He told himself many times that she loved him in her own way. She had stopped saying it to him within the first few years of their marriage, but he knew she did.

She was demanding, even to the point of encouraging him to do things that initially pricked his conscious and caused him many restless nights. Like J. P., she too had grown up poor, and now saw an opportunity to gain positive community standing and social recognition. She was not going to pass it up. She considered herself the brain of their marriage, and instructed J. P. on what he should do, and how he was to do it.. He resented her pushiness at first, then resigned himself to accept it. Any time that it appeared he was not following her directions, the Damocles Sword she held over him were the words, "If you really love me, you'll find a way to do it." They were enough to make him forget his upbringing and violate his basic principles.

It was because of Maureen that he got involved with his first real estate transaction that was highly questionable and, he thought, even bordered on being illegal. Her assurance that it would work out okay began to assuage his conscious after she told him she just happened to mention it to a Judge Frank Wilcox's wife during one of their social gatherings. The woman called Maureen back later and said that the transaction would, "withstand legal muster; we'll make sure of that." That was all Maureen needed to prod him in the direction she wanted him to go. J. P. thought it sounded too good to be true, but he was not going to question it. Words from the judge's wife were just as good as, or maybe better than, words from the judge himself, J. P. reasoned. Women had a way of inducing men to do things they didn't want to do, or simply thought were impossible. The apparent success of that transaction absolved him of any residue of guilty feelings, or feelings of questionable ethics. Within months, James Preston Sellers was getting the lesson of a lifetime, and he had Maureen to thank. After many years of success with his business and giving her the life style she wanted and demanded, he still feared her wrath. Regardless of what J. P. was able to provide, she always wanted more, and expected J. P. to provide it. Caught between being his own man and anticipating and pleasing her wishes, avoiding her as much as he could was his only saving grace, and he did it as much as he could.

13

"This is Mac Mc Lauren," the authoritative but cautious voice said.

"Mac, this is J. P. What was that call 'bout today?" Sellers asked without engaging in the customary and irrelevant greetings.

"You alone?" Mac Mc Lauren asked, sounding more informal, but no less apprehensive.

"You betcha. What's up?" J. P. asked without any pretense of being cautious.

"I got a letter today, naming some names in connection with some of those land deals in Thompson County," he attempted to say quietly and emotionlessly. But, every word he uttered dripped with the intensity of his worse fears.

"Holy Crappoly! Who's it naming?"

"Can't say right now. It's not us," Mc Lauren said with an artificial sigh of relief. "The letter also went to some pretty big folks up here." "Who else did it go to?"

"Can't say that right now... either," Mc Lauren said haltingly.

"Why did you call me and want me to call you for then, Mac? What the hell *can* you say?" J. P. asked in an irritated fashion.

"Just wanted to give you a 'heads up,' buddy." That was one of J. P. Sellers' favorite expressions, and he used it freely and reverently. Mc Lauren thought J. P. would appreciate his using it. "I'm afraid this whole damn thing might blow up, if we're not careful." His voice noted a tinge of caution and a sense of urgency.

"What the hell you talking 'bout Mac?" J. P. asked anxiously.

"It's a hot letter, J. P. Somebody apparently got hold of some of the facts on some of the land deals that weren't exactly kosher, and they're spreadin 'em around like free government cheese, powdered milk and peanut butter." The comparison was humorous to J. P. but he wouldn't dare say it to Mac Mc Lauren. "Gotta be somebody inside," he said instead, forcing himself not to laugh.

"That's what I figure, or they got hold of somebody inside and been pumpin 'em for info." "You talk to the other,..uh… fellows, yet?" J. P. asked with a note of caution in his voice.

"No, not yet. Don't know if I'm gonna." Mc Lauren said with reservation.

"What you want me to do?" J. P. asked quietly, hoping that Mc Lauren didn't want him to do anything.

"Check your sources to see who's been asking questions. Get back to me as soon as you can, but only if you come up with something." Mc Lauren hung up without giving J.P. an opportunity to say if he would or if he wouldn't.

It was clear that J. P. had been given an order, and the expectation was that he would carry it out, whether he wanted to or not. He also knew not to call Mac unless he had something significant to report, anything that demonstrated to him that an effort was made to carry our his order. They both understood that.

J. P. Sellers softly placed the handset on the cradle and looked around his office as if he were expecting to see someone. He picked up the handset again, tugged at the mouthpiece cover until it was unscrewed, then suspiciously peered into the opening without knowing exactly what he was looking at or looking for. After replacing the mouthpiece cover, he gently put the handset back on the cradle, grabbed his briefcase from his desk, looked suspiciously around his office and hurriedly headed toward the door. Before opening it, he stood there momentarily trying to compose himself. Mac's comments and assignment startled J. P.; and what Mac chose not to tell him about the letter concerned him even more. If J. P. were not somehow implicated in the letter, why would Mac have called him? What if he could not find out who had been asking questions? Would Mac and the others protect his interest? Would they stick together and leave him hanging, fending for himself? These questions and related ones flung themselves at J. P. as he tried unsuccessfully to dodge them mentally or fling them away from him and out of his mind.

As if nothing had happened, he nonchalantly opened the office door and sauntered toward his Ford Expedition. He proudly pressed the remote keyless entry system to deactivate the alarm and to unlock the doors and tailgate long before he reached the vehicle. The quick beeps, signaling the disengagement of the security system, stopped J. P. Sellers in his tracks. Although he had heard these beeps many times before, they startled him. He could hear himself breathing heavily and feel his heart pounding in his burly chest. He eased up to the vehicle, slowly opened the door, bounced his stubby, 350-pound frame up on the sleek leather seat, and slung his briefcase, which he usually left in his office, into the passenger seat. He rested his head on the steering wheel while he tried to compose himself. He could now hear his heartbeat echoing in his square, bald head. It was throbbing rhythmically with the pounding he was experiencing in his chest and radiating into his arms. After several minutes, J. P. struggled to hold his head up, looked stealthily around him, started the engine and just sat gripping the steering wheel and thinking. He played back what Mac Mc Lauren had said, and wondered what it all meant for him, James Preston Sellers, a local boy who had done well, a self-made man who started out with nothing, but now was living a good life--nice home, cars, a boat, vacations, invitations to important social gatherings. Real estate had been good to him. He had friends among those at the centers of power in Thompson County and Humphries , and he was known as a person to be trusted. Somewhere in the back of his mind, he had anticipated a day like this. A day when one small piece of information in the wrong hands could or would spell trouble for him and many of those who ran in the same circle. Information just like that which Mac Mc Lauren had just told him, but without really telling him much of anything at all that was useful. J. P. thought how quickly things could change. Just a few minutes earlier, he felt that Humphries and Thompson County would be his perennial playground. Now, he wasn't sure. But he would do his homework, starting the next day, and not stop until he got to the bottom of what Mac Mc Lauren was not telling him.

For days J. P. skulked and snooped around asking questions and huddling with those who were supposed to know, but was coming up with nothing that was useful. The days quickly turned into weeks, and the weeks, just as quickly, turned into months. Still, this intense, surreptitious effort yielded him nothing. He began to think that maybe the whole thing was a joke intended to spook Mac, and Mac panicked, potentially exposing them all for no apparent reason. Or, maybe there was no letter at all and Mac was just up to one of his legal tricks. He knew that Mac had many of them, and was known for his histrionics and practical jokes. But, this was no joking matter, and J. P. could detect no reason for laughter in anything that Mac had said. The more he thought about all that Mac had said and implied, the more concerned and worried he became. J. P. raised his eyebrows without being aware of it, and feelings of fear imperceptibly crept upon him. Before he realized it, J. P. was struggling to abate his desire to flee the uneasiness and desperation that were absorbing his weary consciousness and saturating his troubled mind.

14

S awyer Village had an unusual history that was whispered about by some people in Thompson County and not thought about at all by others. Still, there were others who were completely oblivious to how Sawyer Villagers, as they identified and referred to themselves, were able to do what they had done for many generations and were still doing. Anybody who was somebody either lived in Sawyer Village or was trying to move there. How it was established had been a subject of debate among those who were brave enough to think it. Early in its history as a section of Humphries, Sawyer Village was known as a place where the poor could come to work, but not a place to tarry too long or to go to without a specific destination and purpose in mind. Many stories circulated about its history of having people arrested who didn't live there and had no clear and convincing purpose for being there. There were many stories told of people literally being run or escorted out of that section of Humphries, and encouraged not to return. While that was in the past, the history was whispered still among those who remembered it or were victims of it. There was no question that it was a segregated community in the past, but, for all intense and purpose, it was a gated community now without the gates, but segregated just the same.

At one time, Sawyer Village was actually the eastern section of Humphries, an area that was reserved for those who had the economic means, the legal know-how and the political connections to keep it that way. In an attempt to isolate themselves from the remainder of Thompson County and to solidify their status and stature, Sawyer Village residents set about building a transparent wall of protection around them, using the economic base and the legal mechanisms of the County to do it. It was a wall that could not be seen, but one that easily could be felt.

When Sawyer Village cut itself off from the west, it expanded eastward and identified less and less with the remainder of Humphries. Many of the residents in Sawyer Village were actually Thompson County employees, but they did not identify with the rest of the County and, in many ways, did not see themselves as residents of the County. However, they held most of the key positions in the County and were instrumental in using resources allocated to all Thompson County to build, enhance and expand Sawyer Village. They convoluted and tortured County and state statutes, and federal laws to accomplish their economic and social objectives. For example, monies that the County received to construct water and sewage facilities for rural areas went toward the construction of a small airport that was used almost exclusively by owners of small aircraft. Monies obtained under the guise of economic development for the County were used to build a County golf course in Sawyer Village. The County Golf Club just happened to be directly behind The Belmont Club, and the only easy access to it was via The Belmont Club. If there was anything left after the Sawyer Villagers got what they wanted, which wasn't often, Humphries and the rest of Thompson County got it. In more ways than can be imagined, the level of affluence in Sawyer Village was a direct result of the poverty and economic deprivation and social isolation in the remainder of Thompson County, conditions that did not occur as a natural phenomenon. They were conditions that were created either by design or by benign neglect. As a result, there were still houses without in-door plumbing, houses that still had dirt floors, houses that still relied upon pump-wells that yielded water at their convenience, and houses that were considered uninhabitable by any standard of measure. In spite of these conditions, those who controlled the county resources did not consider the conditions intolerable enough for Thompson County Government to do anything about them. The disparity became an unquestioned economic condition and social custom that was the normal basis of differential treatment. The people who were economically and socially disadvantaged by how Thompson County operated were blamed for the economic and social conditions they were in. The prevailing attitude was that if the people in Sawyer Village had achieved such successes, so could the remainder of Thompson County if they wanted to. They just had to try a little harder. It seemed that for many years, three of the five Thompson County Commissioners lived in Sawyer Village. County rules were changed to allow commissioners to live anywhere in the county, but they could represent specific voting districts. In other words, they did not have to live in the district they purported to represent, and usually made no obvious attempt to. The net result was that the County Commissioners, as a governing body, favored Sawyer Villagers over the other citizens in Thompson County.

Kaye Webster had heard whispers of the situation as she grew up in Humphries and Thompson County. She had not fully grasped the long-term implications of it until now. She also understood that, while the disparity had been minimized, the entrenched pervasive nature of its history would not allow any semblance of equity to come about for some time. That weighed heavily on her mind, to the point of sadness and almost to the point of intense anger. She now realized that these circumstances conditioned her to live with a certain caution, a keen, but unspoken awareness that her life had prescribed limits, limits that were not of her choosing. They were limits that denied her full humanity; and did not allow for the fullness of her being. They, in deed, were meant to circumscribe her possibilities and to interfere with her personal sense of her true potential, and did not come about as happenstance or random chance. Kaye realized that the physical and symbolic barriers could no longer stand in her way, no matter how they were presented or portrayed. Her newfound awareness and personal integrity would not allow it. Coming to that realization was liberating for her; and with every new insight came a clearer understanding of her mission. She became more circumspect each day, and scrupulously looked at herself and those around her in a very different way. She was moving ever closer to making life-changing decisions that those who thought they knew her would find improbable. And, she was certain that some would find insane.

15

Mac Mc Lauren was Chairman of the State Board of Ethics, and had been since being appointed by the governor to that position three years earlier. He knew that if he received a call from any of the others who received the letter, they would probably want him to launch an investigation. If he started to investigate and asked too many questions, how would it be perceived by J. P. and the others? If there was someone who had been asking questions, he needed to know who it was, and what kind of information they had been provided. Mac Mc Lauren was sure that the ""State Boys"" would conduct their investigations, but he could deal with them. He knew what they would find out before they would, but he didn't want them to get to the person who had written the letter before he and J. P. did. Mac Mc Lauren was unsure what the judge could do, or what he would do.

For several days after receiving his letter, he anticipated telephone calls from somebody; but there were none. He became more anxious and nervous the longer he waited and nobody called him. Therefore, he decided to drop by the office of one of the ""State Boys"" who was supposed to get a copy also, the one he was most friendly with. Mac stepped in with his usual jaunty walk and fixed, phony smile. "Just stopped by to find out what's new," Mac said as he studied Robert Stanton's face very carefully to see if he could detect any change in his demeanor, or any hint of unusual concern. There was nothing there for Mac Mc Lauren to hold on to.

"Not much. SOS," Stanton said with a chuckle. "What's new with you?" he asked.

"The ethics business is always a hot area," he said jokingly. He was trying to give Stanton a wide opening to mention the letter, an opportunity to tell him all that he wanted to know. He would take it anyway he could get it, directly or indirectly, explicitly or implicitly. He just needed to know something. But, Stanton did not honor Mc Lauren's wishes, and didn't show any particular warmth or pleasure with his presence.

"Yeah, I bet it is," Stanton said nonchalantly and with an air of disgust. "I'm sure it's going to get hotter," he added almost as an afterthought intended to inflict a little pain.

Mac Mc Lauren was caught completely off guard by that offhanded comment from Stanton. He wasn't sure what Stanton meant by it and he was afraid to ask him. He wanted to know if Stanton had talked recently with the other State boy who was supposed to get a copy of the letter, but he knew better than to ask, directly or indirectly. Instead, he rambled a few minutes about current happenings around the State, the weather, sports, and vacation. Stanton looked at Mc Lauren without any obvious emotions as he struggled to make light conversation. Mc Lauren became unnerved by Stanton's cold look. He excused himself abruptly and rushed out of Stanton's office more anxious and nervous than he did when he walked in. His jaunty walk had been reduced to a labored shuffle and his fixed, phony smile had become one of genuine concern.

Mac Mc Lauren went back to his office, buzzed his administrative assistant and asked her to hold all calls. He frantically paced about his office trying to make sense of Robert Stanton's comments. Stanton was one of the "State Boys", but Mc Lauren wasn't sure he was to be trusted to even try to understand how things traditionally had been in Thompson County, as well as in other counties throughout the State. Maybe Stanton himself had been involved in similar real estate deals, he thought to himself. Had Stanton already started his investigation; and what had he found out? If Stanton's investigation led him to J. P., would J. P. talk? Was the letter just a hoax and had been sent to no one but him? These and other questions bounced around in Mc Lauren's head as he began strategically calculating his options and plotting his moves.

He was tempted to call J. P. But what if his phone were bugged? Will Stanton have him tailed? And, what about Gordon Clark over at State Justice? Has he launched his own investigation based on the information in the letter? Who were Clark's contacts in Thompson County? And, what did they know? These were other questions that tugged at Mc Lauren's mind relentlessly. He attempted to banish them from his present memory, but they refused to go away.

Mac Mc Lauren checked the window blinds in his office to make sure they kept out unwelcome eyes. He then went to the wardrobe across the room from his desk and pulled out an automatic golf ball return tee and some balls. He nervously walked to the far side of the room, and plugged the tee's power cord into the electrical outlet. He came back across the room, dropped several golf balls on the floor and began to putt one ball after another toward the tee. He often did this to reduce anxiety and fear. This time, he was having little luck with his putting, and less luck with reducing his anxiety and fear. He attempted to shrug off genuine concerns that pervaded his thoughts. In spite of his best efforts, they held on tenaciously.

Mac Mc Lauren grew up in Thompson County and was on familiar and friendly terms with all those who mattered there. He was chosen as Chairman of the State Board Ethics because of his connections and influence in Thompson County and throughout the State, rather than for his personal ethical standards and morale rectitude; and he had a reputation for playing both sides of the political street and currying the favor of anybody whom he thought he could trust. Mac Mc Lauren's recommendation by and support from State politicos from Thompson County made his nomination to the position a fait accompli. He was adept at cultivating trusting relationships, primarily because his spindly stature did not convey his false sincerity and belied his capacity for ruthlessness. His jocularity and witticism had a way of seducing the unsuspecting into many of his webs of questionable activities and practices. Nevertheless, his appointment to the position went virtually unnoticed by all except those who clearly would benefit from the protective cover his tenure in the position could provide them.

Prior to his appointment to the position, Mac Mc Lauren had represented the moneyed interests on numerous business and real estate transactions in Thompson County and the surrounding counties. He brokered some of the deals, and was brought in as a partner on others.

Therefore, he had first-hand knowledge of how business and real estate deals were accomplished, and who all of the players were. While he suspended his legal activities in the law firm he helped to establish many years before accepting the appointment, he was still listed as a partner and, technically, could provide consulting services for the firm. And, he often did.

The person who sent the anonymous letter to him, along with his discomfort with the weakness he perceived in his long-time friend J. P., were annoyances he preferred would go away. He knew they were distractions that would consume more time than he wanted to devote to them, unless he could find ways to have them silenced or to have them eliminated altogether. J. P. knew too much. He had concluded that the anonymous letter writer was speculating on what had happened in Thompson County, but knew too much for his own comfort and the comfort of those he earlier had represented, and now had to protect. Mc Lauren reasoned that J. P. could be taken care of, but he was unsure who the writer of the anonymous letter was or what could be done about her or him; and he was not sure that those he was protecting could or would help him. He was sure, however, that some of them had to meet to discuss what had to be done next.

16

Kaye walked into her condo unit and went directly to the phone to check her messages.

"Hi, Cuz. We got a problem," the voice said hurriedly. It was John. "Call me as soon as you can. Before Thursday," he added with fear and panic in his voice.

Kaye mumbled a few words to herself and continued to retrieve her messages. When she finished, she pulled her electronic organizer from her shoulder bag and punched a few buttons to bring up John's phone number. She continued to mumble to herself as she dialed the number and waited for a ring on the other end.

"Hey, this is Kaye," she said. "What's up?"

"I think we got a problem," John said dejectedly.

"What's the problem?" she asked as calmly as she could. She had learned that if she showed any signs of deep concern or sounded panicked, John would pick up on it and follow her lead.

"We got a summons about the land. I think we have to be at a hearing at the courthouse in Thompson County two weeks from tomorrow," John said with a sound of weariness in his voice. Several other unintelligible sounds lurched from him, but Kaye made no attempt to decipher them.

"Great! This is what we've been waiting for," Kaye said with enthusiasm.

"We have?" John asked in disbelief.

"Yeah. We want to get this thing into court. I didn't think it would ever happen. You know, it's been almost six months since Zorn got the last letter."

"I'm scared," John admitted out loud. Kaye had known it from the beginning, but never expected he would actually say it.

"Don't worry. I'll take care of it," Kaye assured him. "Get it to me as soon as you can. You may have to go to court for the hearing. I'll get an attorney to go with you. I won't be there, but everything will work out okay. The attorney will take care of the whole thing. You just be sure you're there for the hearing," she instructed him. "Do you know who it's going to be?'

"We have several options. Freeman can't do it. He told me when he wrote the letter that he wouldn't be able to do anything but write some letters for us. It might be Victor Glover from Windsor, or Jason McNair from Church Hill. I'll let you know who it will be. Don't worry about it; I'll take care of it," Kaye assured him again. John agreed to meet Kaye at *Mamma's Dining Room* the next morning so he could give her the papers the Thompson County Sheriff had delivered to him. After talking with John, Kaye attempted to reach Victor Glover and Steve McNair, but had no success. She called a couple of acquaintances to inquire about engaging some legal assistance on short notice. This effort yielded nothing very promising. So, she stilled herself at her desk and sifted through her mind searching for options that could get her over the immediate obstacle she was facing. As a result of the summons John had given her, she was preoccupied with it and not with the work she was being paid to do. The entire day there was a waste of her time, and a total drain on her attention and her mind.

Kaye sat slumped at the corner desk and contemplated what she was going to do. She knew that her moments of discouragement could be soaked away quickly by a long, hot tub bath filled with lavish amounts of bath beads. And, the body oils and after splashes would give her the pampering she needed for a deep, restful sleep. Just the thought of it was enticing, but she needed something more at that moment. Kaye Webster had to infuse her mind with a different process, a procedure that would transform her spirit and elevate her mind beyond how she felt emotionally and what she knew intellectually. Uncovering and getting to the nub of the land issue was looming ever larger in her thoughts, and the process or procedure for doing it would require her to take an unorthodox approach. Kaye Webster feverishly searched among the items on the desk, found a pad of ruled paper and began to scribble on it. Echoing in her head time and time again were these words: "It is from our greatest challenges that we often discover our strengths." This was a challenge like none she'd ever had. She thought about what she was facing and compared it to the process used to obtain the essential oils from plants, blending them with fixatives and converting the combinations into sweet odors and fragrances that defied olfactory logic. The comparisons intrigued her and she started writing hurriedly as she talked in a didactic fashion, like she was explaining it to a room full of novices.

Many essential oils are extracted or obtained from plants by steam distillation. The first step in this process is to pass steam through the plant material. The essential oil turns to gas, that is then passed through tubing and cooled to make it liquid again. Essential oils are obtained from some flowers by boiling the petals in water.

She stopped talking and writing, closed her eyes for a few moments, then looked at what she had written and smiled. She continued.

Another important process of obtaining essential oils from flowers is by way of solvent extraction. This is a procedure in which petals are dissolved in a solvent, which is a liquid that can dissolve other substances. The solvent is distilled from the solution, leaving a waxy material containing the oil. This material is placed in ethyl alcohol. The oils dissolve in the alcohol and rises with it to the top of the wax. Heat is applied, and the alcohol evaporates, leaving concentrated perfume oil.

Kaye Webster was pleased at her knowledge of the processes, and proud of her ability and facility to recall them without much thought. As she looked at her notes and tapped her pen on the pad of paper, she began to smile and resumed her lesson in perfumery.

Enfleurage is another method of extracting flower oils. Through this method, glass plates are covered with fat, and flower petals are spread over the fat. The fat absorbs the oils from the petals, forming a greasy pomade. The pomade, in turn, is treated with alcohol to dissolve out the oil.

She thought again about the challenge she was facing, and felt resolved that she had to succeed. She was up against the powerful and the well-connected in Thompson County, and she knew it. But, she also knew that, like the ingredients in perfume, she could determine the final results and smell of this injustice. She was never surer that it was within her power to determine the ultimate outcome. Like the eighty or ninety percent of alcohol content in perfumes, she would hold it all together; and like the animal substances included to slow the evaporation, she would be the stabilizing force, holding it all together until the magnitude of the problem was exposed. She would extract all the information she needed and use it in a way that would be hard to refute. "Perfume!" she said several times to herself. "In Latin, it's *per*, meaning through, and *fumus*, meaning smoke." She thought there was a certain irony in it. "But, first, I've gotta to bring some fire!" she said quietly to herself several times. Then, and only then, would she be able to smell the sweet aroma of her success. She dropped her head on the desk as if she had been overcome by mental and physical exhaustion. When she felt herself about to go to sleep, she jumped up, hurried to the bathroom, started filling the bath tub with water and dropping in dollops of bubble baths. For some reason, the animal secretions and substances did not seem as repulsive now, as she had always imagined them to be.

17

Kaye arrived at *Mamma's Dining Room* much earlier than she and John had agreed. She and Mamma Sylvia exchanged their usual rituals and Kaye positioned herself in her usual seat. A few minutes later, Mamma Sylvia came out with Kaye's usual breakfast. "Why the long face, Honey?" Mamma Sylvia asked with genuine concern. "Is it that bad?"

"Oh, goodness! I didn't realize it was bothering me that much."

"What is it?" she asked with genuine concern.

"Just a minor legal problem. I need an attorney to do something for me in Thompson County. Do you know a good one?"

"There's one sitting back there in the corner. He practices in Thompson County. I don't know how good he is though," she said without looking toward the corner where a man was sitting with a cup to his mouth and looking in their direction.

"What's his name?"

"Matthew Crenshaw. I'll call him up here if you want me to. Maybe he can give you some advice or point you in the right direction. I think he's good for something," she said with a chuckle.

"I guess I don't have anything to lose," she replied half-heartedly.

Turning toward the back of the room, Mamma Sylvia yelled, "Hey, Crenshaw, come up here a minute," she demanded. "This wonderful lady needs a little advice."

The man cautiously stepped forward, and Kaye immediately thought she had seen him before. In fact, she had seen him before. But, she didn't remember exactly when or exactly where. At least one time she had seen him, she kept telling herself, but, where?

Mamma Sylvia introduced them and went back to her usual hiding place. Kaye invited the man to sit, and began to explain to him the kind of legal help she was trying to secure for her cousin John two weeks from the day. The man, who had been sitting calmly holding a coffee cup to his lips, now was obviously agitated.

"Oh, I'm sorry I can't do that," he said. "Uh…I don't do those kinds of cases," he stated emphatically, as he labored and stammered to explain himself. "That's not in my area of expertise, and it would create a conflict for me; and…." He stopped in mid-sentence, put the coffee cup to his mouth thoughtfully, like he was searching for another excuse for not getting involved, and looked as though he was intrigued with what he was hearing.

"Could you just go for the hearing? Or file a restraining order? Or get a continuance? Or whatever we need to do to get more time?" Kaye questioned as she was making suggestions and, at the same time, keeping him from giving her any additional reasons he could not help her.

The man removed the cup from his lips, looked at Kaye very seriously and said, "If I go to the hearing, the judge will think I'm involved with the case; I can't have that, you see."

Immediately Kaye realized that she had seen him in *Mamma's Dining Room* once before, alone, sitting in the corner holding a cup to his lips with both hands, just staring into space, almost like he was comatose or transfixed. She remembered that she thought it was a little strange at the time, and dismissed it as an idiosyncrasy or ritual, or he was a really deep thinker. He leaned forward and began to whisper, "Whatever you do, don't use any attorney from Thompson County. They won't look out for your interest." He looked around stealthily and again leaned closer to Kaye and said, "Somebody should take on the land issues here as a cause." He then leaned back in his chair and said, "Why don't you try Norman Winfield over in Evans County. He's good and he's not afraid." "The little weasel is actually scared," Kaye thought to herself, and looked at him with eyes that were penetrating his vacant stare, trying to find the fight in him that was not readily apparent. She couldn't find it. However, she decided not to hold that against him.

The man eased his cup down on the table, then got up abruptly, said, "Good luck," and quickly walked, or almost ran, out the door. Kaye was stunned and unsettled. She sat quietly and thought about everything Matthew Crenshaw had just told her. She was somewhat disappointed because he could not help. Maybe he would not help. Maybe he did not want to help. Maybe he really was afraid to help. There was something odd and strange about him that reminded her of a past relationship that had gone terribly wrong. It was almost like she knew him from somewhere in her distant past. But, that wasn't likely. Yet, his secretive behavior and cautious and closed manner were reminiscent of one Douglas Morgan, the name of a man she wished and hoped she had banned from her memory permanently. It was strange that it would surface now and interfere with her mission and play with her mind. "It's just the devil messing with me," told herself. But, the thoughts of him would not go away.

It was a relationship that never should have happened. She knew that from the beginning, but refused to honor her common sense and to heed her intuition. They were from totally different worlds, going in totally different and opposite directions. The power of this presence was intoxicating and the subtlety of his personality was both magnetic and repellant at the same time. That was a mysterious side of him that would have signaled caution under normal circumstances. However, their chance involvement did not begin under a normal set of circumstances, and there should have been no surprise that it would end the same way. Kaye began to re-play the experience in her mind, almost like she was transfixed and reliving it. It was as if she enveloped herself in her past and called up the person she was fifteen years earlier.

She walked slowly along the promenade that gently hugged the bank of the river. Occasionally, she would stop, look into the muddy waters, look behind her, and shuffle along again. Her eyes frequently filled with tears as her throat swelled with grief. She occasionally would gnaw at the fingers of her right hand and shake her head to and fro. After several minutes of this ritual, she reached the end of the promenade, sat on the edge of it, and stared into the murky water that rolled sleepily by.

Winter, by the calendar, had not come yet; but the locals said it was fast approaching. They offered no empirical evidence to support their prediction, but they sounded as if they knew it was a certainty. "I can feel it in my bones!" was the explanation most often offered. However, there had been several days of blustery winds, and light dustings of snow had fallen three or four times during the past week. The temperature was well below freezing, but it seemed not to matter to her. She wore only a light cardigan over a see-through blouse; and her head was bare. The bottom of her pants legs barely revealed that she had on no socks or stockings. Her well-worn sneakers clung tightly to her dainty feet as she swung them methodically over the water below. An aura of quality covered everything she wore; and her manicured fingered and stylish hair-do set her apart from the typical woman in this quaint mid-western town, just a few miles west of the metropolitan center.

She was a virtual stranger there, even though this was now her home. Its charm and romanticism had drawn her there; and it was there that her past would keep her. She longed to forget it and to hide from the eyes of the world. For the past few months now, the daily walks along the river always brought back to her mind every detail like never before. It seemed that her core existence wanted to remember, and she wanted the world to feel her in pain. However, she was careful to never let her distant relatives and colleagues know of her loneliness. Even if she had walked along the river with them, as she often did earlier during the day, she would always return alone later and think about the life she had escaped in Thompson County and Humphries. This daily cleansing and renewing of her soul seemed to give her the strength she needed to begin another.

This ritual did not escape the notice of Douglas Morgan, who had watched her for weeks as he stood in the distance and thought about how he was going to approach her. Her natural beauty captivated him and her tastefully simple style fascinated him. He had determined her routine and decided that he would sit on a bench near the end of the promenade, at a time he thought she would be there, and attempt to engage her in an innocent conversation. She would have to pass by him to get to the spot where she usually sat. He followed her approach through his peripheral vision, simply said "Hi" as she drew near, and pretended to be noticing several other people who were sitting nearby. She sat down with her back to him and transported herself to another plane. Without looking at her directly, he eventually commented on the crispness of the temperature. "It's a bit chilly, huh?" he said with a question.

After turning around to make sure the stranger was talking to her, she said, "I like it; this is my best time of the year," and thought about his apparent indifference to her presence. "Maybe he's not even talking to me," she told herself and resumed her search for solitude in the midst of a cacophony of sounds. He did not respond, but thought about the next thing he would say to her. Minutes passed without him looking directly at her, but keenly observing every move she made.

Kaye stared into the river as it gently flowed by, and its tranquility seemed to course through the recesses of her mind, like it coursed through the middle of town. Morgan noticed her seemingly oneness with it and said, "You love the river, don't you?" She quickly looked in his direction and saw that still he was not looking at her, but obviously was talking to her.

"I think that is a fair assessment; how did you know?" That was an opening he was looking for, an opportunity for him to feel her out, to learn about her and to show the affable and discerning person he knew himself to be and wanted her to see.

"I know because I can see it in your peace with it." He was certain that the oblique comment would provoke her to ask him to explain himself, or at least it would make her take note of him. And it did. The comment surprised her and she wasn't exactly sure what he meant by it. She turned around, stared at him for a few moments, then asked, "What does that mean?"

He looked passed her, as though he was focusing on something miles away, and finally said nonchalantly, "I've seen you here many times before; and it seems like you're always at peace, looking into the water and swinging your legs." He really wanted to say "pretty legs" but thought that it would be pushing his subtle boldness too far. She thought that was quite perceptive of him, and wondered how he knew. She had never seem him before, and wasn't sure how to take his comments. She looked at him askance momentarily, turned back toward the water and re-focused her attention on it cascading over the rocks below.

Douglas Morgan had played this game before, and knew he had piqued her curiosity and was waiting for the appropriate moment to engage her again. It was a cat and mouse game he relished in playing, "putting out the cheese," as he called it, and then taking it away, but leaving it in sight.

"My, my! Still in deep thought I see," Mamma Sylvia said as she poured Kaye Webster another cup of coffee. The comment startled her and jolted her back into the present. She had gotten lost in her own thoughts and wasn't sure how to respond. She shook her head and said, "Girl, if you only knew!"

"Oh, I've been there before," she said and left Kaye to her private musings.

In an instant, her thoughts were back on the first time she met Douglas Morgan, on what she initially believed was a meeting by chance, and their subsequent romantic involvement. She thought about how she was mysteriously drawn toward him after finishing what she called her time of reflection.

She was walking pass him, intending to walk briskly to her apartment a few blocks away. "Had enough for the day?" he commented without looking at her. She involuntarily walked toward the bench on which he was sitting and stood looking at him for several moments without saying anything.

"My name's Doug Morgan," he said while looking at her squarely in the face. "I know you might think this is very forward of me, but you are such a classy lady."

She was a little amused by his comment, and not knowing exactly what to say, replied, "I try to take care of myself." "You're doing a mighty fine job of it," he said, without giving her an opportunity to respond, and, "I do see you quite often, you know; many more times than you've seen me," he said with a bit of mystery in his voice. Again, he did not give her time to respond, "Do you have a name?" he asked while smiling at her.

"Oh, I'm sorry. My name is Kaye. Katherine Webster.

"Nice to meet you," he said as he stood up and extended his hand toward her. Kaye was surprised by his manners, shook his hand and automatically sat on the bench almost as soon as he did. "Nice to meet you too," she said, and quickly asked, "And, where have you seen me before?" "Here and there," he replied nonchalantly, but never gave her a specific answer. That was the beginning of a friendship based on Kaye's need for acceptance and understanding; and it was also the beginning of a tragic, romantic relationship that lasted three months that eventually felt like an eternity. From that first meeting, Kaye realized that she and Douglas Morgan were almost like complete opposites, and lived and operated in completely different worlds. She was open, honest and giving of her thoughts and feelings, and he was closed, protective of and not very forthcoming with his. He would either answer her questions with a question, or would answer around the edges of them, but never answer them directly. She had grown up in a small town and had been nurtured by family and friends, people who cared about her and her welfare, a town where everybody in her neighborhood knew everybody else. He admitted to growing up in a nearby city, but claimed no close relationship with anybody, not even his parents. While she never could determine exactly what he did, she knew from places he said he had been and things he hinted that he had done, that it was a world she had only dreamt of or could only imagine. Their short discussion that day left Kaye with the feeling that, despite their differences, they made a personal connection, a base for a respectful friendship. It was a feeling that their different ethnic and racial backgrounds naturally drew them together out of a mutual curiosity and defiance of certain social taboos.

On subsequent days that Kaye walked on the promenade, she went with an anticipation that Morgan would be there. He suspected that she would and purposely would not go there. After not seeing him for several days and giving up on the possibility that he would come there again, he quietly walked up behind her one day and sat next to her on the end of the promenade. She was both startled and surprised by his sudden appearance. Her broad smile and light slap on the leg signaled to Morgan that she was glad to see him. In his own way, he was glad to see her again before going back home for a few weeks. After exchanging a few pleasantries, Kaye inquired about what he had been doing and where he had been. "Oh, I've been out of town for a few days, trying to close a deal I've been working on for sometime," he answered dismissively, and immediately asked Kaye about her times on the promenade since their first meeting. "You know me, I've been here everyday," she answered as she chuckled. "That's a part of my regular routine," she added. "I usually stay a lot longer on Saturday afternoons."

Morgan already knew it was a part of her routine. He had seen her each day because he, in fact, had been in town all along. When he was there, he was out-of-town, at the apartment he stayed in while he was there, which was one to two weeks out of each month. He had told her during their first meeting that he lived nearby but never said where. The apartment was located only a block from the river and was in direct line of sight to the promenade. The first time he saw her was through a pair of binoculars he often randomly used to bring objects in the distance closer to him. He didn't consider it spying or a violation of personal privacy, but merely a way to enhance his viewing experience.

For several moments they sat swinging their legs over the water, but verbally saying nothing to each other. However, there was a silent harmony between them, echoing in rhythm with their swinging legs. Suddenly, Morgan said, "I'm a bit hungry. Will you join me for something to eat?" Kaye, taken off guard by the invitation, responded, "Okay, if it's Dutch treat?" "If you insist," he replied. Morgan wanted to insist that he pay for it, but sensed that if he did, she probably would not accompany him. "Ready when you are," he said with a sense of a major accomplishment and personal satisfaction. They got up from the end of the promenade in unison, slowly made their way back to the main street and crossed it directly in front of Morgan's out-of-town apartment. As they walked non-purposely down the street and talked with no specific focus in mind, Kaye, for the first time, became aware of how pedestrians looked at them with apparent disdain. They were looks she could feel, even when she could not see them. Morgan was busy pointing out eating places and restaurants where they could get a good meal. "I'm flexible in terms of food, so the choice is yours," he offered numerous times.

"I like Thai," she replied. "There's a Thai restaurant a few blocks from here." Are you game for that?" she asked.

"I'm game for almost anything," he said with self-assurance. When they walked into the small restaurant, it seemed that people stopped what they were doing and all eyes focused on her and Morgan. Kaye initially thought it was her imagination or her acute sensitivity to the forbidden social taboo of inter-racial couples in friendly conversation or interactions. She calmed herself and looked around the restaurant again. Yes, all eyes were focused on them. She wanted to scream, "What are you people looking at? We're not a couple; we're just having a meal together. We're not even friends." Then she thought to herself, "Well, we are friends. We might be friends." All of her thoughts became a jumble of disconnected themes, slowly vanishing into the dimness that permeated the room.

Morgan noticed the look of confusion on her face and asked, "Is there something wrong?" "No, no," she replied. "Just had some weird thoughts." "Are they thoughts you can share with me?" he asked.

"Maybe I shouldn't," she said as the hostess motioned for them to follow her as she moved swiftly toward the back of the restaurant.

After their causal dining and becoming familiar conversation, Kaye and Morgan retraced their steps, heading in the direction from which they had walked to get there. Upon reaching the entrance to the promenade at the onset of dusk, Morgan asked, "Are you up to walking back down to the river?" "I think I have enough energy for that."

"I thought I should at least take you back where I found you," he said with a chuckle and a slight hint of sarcasm. "Unless I can walk you home," he added almost in the form of a question.

"How sweet of you!" Kaye said sincerely, turning herself in the direction of the river.

"That's because you're such a sweet lady," he said as he gently placed his arm around her shoulder and slightly squeezed her. He expected her to wince or somehow show her disapproval. She did neither. Morgan gradually removed his arm from around her shoulder, moved it downward between them and hesitatingly clasped her petite hand in his. They approached the end of the promenade and Morgan pulled Kaye close to him in a bear hug and kissed her gently on the cheek. She wasn't sure she wanted him to hug her, and she wasn't sure she wanted him to stop. So, she held her breath and stood motionless. Morgan wasn't sure exactly what to do because he had not anticipated that non-response. "Well, I think I have to go; I have a busy day tomorrow," he said as a way to get himself out of an awkward situation. "Are you going to be okay?" he asked as he released her and backed away.

"Oh, yeah, I'll be fine," she said while trying to regain control of her breathing.

"It was really great to see you again. Maybe I'll see you again soon," he said as he turned to leave.

"Maybe so," Kaye said with a doubtful sound in her voice.

Morgan got to the main street, crossed it, looked back and saw Kaye looking at him. He waved at her and started walking in the direction away from his apartment and disappeared as quickly as he had arrived. Kaye stood at the end of the promenade for a few minutes, looking down into the water and reflecting on the advances Morgan made toward her and her inability to resist him or to draw him close to her. She thought about the looks of disapproval that were thrown in their direction, and the intense discomfort they caused her to experience. She smiled to herself and hurriedly made her way off the promenade and went home.

Several weeks past before she saw Morgan again. He was sitting on the end of the promenade when she got there. It was as if he was expecting her. "I thought you'd be here soon he said."

"Why did you think that?" she asked with a mischievous smile.

"I just knew it was about that time," he stated with confidence and laughed.

That Saturday afternoon was essentially a repeat of the last one they'd spent together. Talking, walking, having dinner, standing on the promenade and trying to establish a comfort level that was suitable for each. The one major exception was that Morgan held her closer and longer, and kissed her lips and face passionately. Kaye found herself willingly participating in his advances toward her and tenderly encouraging him with her own seductive responses. They concluded the evening as before, with him leaving rather abruptly and disappearing, and with her walking longingly and hurriedly back to her apartment.

Several subsequent Saturday afternoons they spent together were similar to others. Kaye began to realize that she was becoming emotionally attached to Morgan. It was something she had not expected to happen. But, it had. And, Morgan knew it because he had planned it that way. He made several overtures to her about them having a physical relationship, and how he could take care of all her financial needs. This line of discussion always gave her a feeling of uneasiness and caused her to become standoffish in her interactions with him. She usually laughed at the suggestions and said, "People say a lot of things during lustful moments that they don't mean under normal circumstances." "No, I'm serious. As serious as I can be," was his usual reply.

Kaye always seriously considered his suggestions but never would let him know that she had. She thought back to what she knew about him and determined that she knew very little. She had shared many of her ambitions, fears and innermost feelings with him, but he had shared very little of his with her. It was like he did not have a past, and was forever avoiding the present. She didn't even know what he did or where he lived. Even though they had spent several days together, he was still a mystery to her. She could never get a direct answer to the simplest question. It was like he always had something to hide. She realized that he could put on a warm and friendly façade when he needed to, but he had a cold, impenetrable exterior that would not let her in nor let him out. She believed she knew the form of the man but she was certain she had never seen his substance; and she didn't know if he had any. The last time they met, Kaye gracefully told him that she was considering his proposals but demanded to know more about him and the secrets he obviously was keeping from her. Morgan understood pressure, subtle or obvious, and that the look on Kaye's face said he could not escape telling her everything she needed to know.

"There's really not a lot to tell. We'll have a long talk the next time

I see you," he said. "Promise." Many weeks went by and she sat at the end of the promenade expecting him to surprise her with his sudden appearance. She never saw him again. Kaye chuckled to herself and said, "Dudes, dawgs, dead-beats and low-lifes." But, she still wasn't sure in which category Douglas Morgan belonged.

As she mentally wiped him out of her mind again and processed her brief exchange with Matthew Crenshaw, her mood quickly changed. She became almost ecstatic because she realized that he had given her another piece of the puzzle. In fact, it was probably the most important piece. He had just confirmed for her what she had always suspected. She had said as much in her letter, but she had no way of proving it. "Did he give it to her by accident, or did he give it to her on purpose?" Kaye asked herself. She wanted to believe that he had given it to her on purpose and trusted it to her care.

John finally arrived, obviously frustrated and harried. Spotting Kaye sitting in the usual place and rushing straight toward her as soon as he opened the door, he said loud enough for all to hear, "Do you believe it, a traffic jam in Humphries?" It seemed like he glided across the room, threw himself into the seat next to Kaye, waving a piece of paper at her "This is it, he said as he shuffled it across the table toward Kaye and said, "This is the summons!" She grabbed it and motioned for John to follow her. "Let's get outta here," she commanded as she grabbed up her belongings and hurried toward the cashier. "Gotta run, Sylvia," she yelled as she searched her purse for change to pay her tab and leave a tip. She dropped her purse in her favorite shoulder bag and headed for the door. She stopped momentarily and yelled, "Oh, thanks Sylvia. Crenshaw is a smart ol' dude." She bounced with confidence as she rushed toward the door, with John tagging behind and struggling to keep up with her.

"Well, it looks like he is good for something after all," Mamma Sylvia yelled back and laughed heartily.

18

"Hi, this is Monica. Se habla Espanol! This is Attorney Winfield's Office," the perky voice chimed with a slight accent and sounded as if it had given that greeting thousands of times before.

"This is Kaye Webster. May I speak with Attorney Winfield, please."

"I'm sorry, he's not in. May I help you with something?"

"No. I need to talk with him."

"Can one of the other attorneys help you?"

"No. I need to talk with Atty. Winfield," Kaye insisted.

"Would you like to leave a number and have him call you, Ma'am?"

"Yes. I think that will work." Kaye left her number, but two days later Norman Winfield had not returned her call. Feeling a sense of urgency and having a need to feel in control, Kaye drove thirty miles to Pleasantville, in Evans County, to park herself in Norman Winfield's office until she could see him. When Kaye announced her presence and her urgent need to see Atty. Winfield, Monica did not appear too pleased to see her. She hastily picked up the phone, pushed a button and a buzz could be heard somewhere in the distance. She put the phone back on the cradle after a minute or two and asked Kaye to fill out a form, front and back, and returned it to her as soon as she finished. "Oh, by the way," she said, "there will be an initial consultation fee of $60; I can take that now"

She reached into her shoulder bag, searched and found the money, gave it to the receptionist and settled in to complete the form. *Name.*

Address. Social security number. Home telephone number. Driver's license number. Kaye stopped suddenly, flipped the form over, scanned her eyes down the page and mumbled to herself, "The same damn form." She finished filling in the information and gave the form back to Monica. The perky young woman examined it front and back, then disappeared for a few minutes.

While Kaye waited for Atty. Winfield, she paced throughout the reception area examining the paraphernalia attached to walls and laying on tables. Newspaper clippings about community activities, golf outings, and a 30th birthday celebration. Certificates of Achievement. College Degrees and Law School Diploma. Family Photos. It appeared that Matthew Crenshaw was right. Norman Winfield was probably good, and he appeared not to be afraid. Norman Winfield was a forty-something, slightly graying man with a springy walk. His wire-rimmed glasses conveyed a notion of scholarship and his firm handshake telegraphed clues about his strength. He led Kaye back toward the area where earlier the buzz could be heard in the distance.

Kaye immediately handed him the folder containing the Promissory Note, Deed of Trust, and summons for the court appearance. "This is the documentation related to what I am about to tell you," she said and began to tell the story as she had understood it from John, Jr., and the way she had told it several times before.

Winfield asked some of the same questions that had been asked by Jarvis Freeman. He too shook his head and chuckled as he examined the documents.

"Do you know if your cousin John Jr. borrowed any money from these people?' he asked Kaye.

"No, not that I know of."

"What do they mean by `value received' him then?" Winfield wanted to know as he pointed it out on one of the documents. She knew it was a rhetorical question, but she felt obligated to offer some kind of response. "Your guess is as good as mine," Kaye replied.

"They knew he didn't know what he was signing," he commented as he continued to examine the documents.

"If you can't take on the case now, can you at least show up for the hearing, or try to get a restraining order or an injunction, or whatever can be done to buy more time?" Kaye asked with a sense of desperation.

"Hell, no. We won't worry about an injunction, a restraining order or any of that stuff. We'll just show up for the hearing and see what they have to say. This is a case I would love to get into court with anyway," he said with obvious joy. "We can win this thing, hands down."

That was exactly what Kaye wanted to hear. She wanted Winfield to know that he would be representing John Wilkinson, Jr., but that she would be personally responsible for all of the legal expenses on his behalf. She also did not want her name associated with the case at all, but she wanted to be kept informed of the progress. Her anonymity was important to her for reasons she did not explain. Winfield agreed to honor Kaye's request and assured her that John would be well represented. His office would have John to come in before the hearing date to provide any additional information he might have about the case and to go over what to expect during the hearing. John would have to accompany Winfield to the hearing, however.

"Attorney Whitfield, I have confidence that you know the ins and outs of the law and will represent John well," she said respectfully. "But, I have to tell you, you're dealing with some real crooks here."

"Thanks for the warning," he said seriously. "Remember, I deal with *real* crooks almost everyday." They both laughed.

Kaye pulled out her electronic organizer, punched a few buttons and called out John's telephone number to Winfield.

"I'll tell John to expect a call from you," she said as she prepared herself to leave.

Winfield accompanied Kaye back to the reception area, and again assured her that John's case was in good hands. Each extended a strong arm, gave a firm handshake and went their separate ways.

19

Katherine Louise Webster had learned early in life that she had to ensure her own success, but unwittingly had abdicated that belief to others after receiving some modest measure of it. She learned that she couldn't leave her success to chance or let it depend exclusively on the good graces and generosity of others. Norman Winfield undoubtedly would represent John well; but he probably wasn't aware of the forces Kaye was certain were lined up against him. She had determined that he was smart with the law in the books, but she wasn't sure that he was smart about the law of the streets and the criminal intentions and mentality of some high-ranking officials in Thompson County. She was afraid he would not know how to play their game without knowing their rules, and without knowing who was playing in the game and which positions they held. She also wasn't sure he was willing to twist their arms if he got them in a vulnerable position, or to hammer them into submission, or into a position where they had no choice but to relinquish any hold they may have on her interests. But, she would soon find out.

When Kaye got home, she thumbed through her file cabinet and found the unnamed folder containing a copy of the letter she had sent to only four other people. She pulled the folder out and carefully checked it to be sure the letter was still in it. It was time to use it again. Using several facial tissues to conceal her fingerprints, she carefully pulled an envelope out of a box of envelopes, took it to a typewriter on the corner desk and began typing something on it. After she finished, she used the blade of the arts and craft knife, surgically removed one stamp from a book of stamps and placed it on the envelope. She then stuck the envelope inside the folder with the letter, took it to the living room and placed it on the table by the door leading outside. She did not want to forget it the next morning. This was a tub bath day for her, and she could hardly wait to enjoy it. Thoughts of the hot, soapy water caressing her delicate body ran freely through her mind. The phone rang before she could draw her water and begin her ritual. It was her cousin John.

"What's going on, Cuz?" he asked as soon as she answered the phone.

"Hey, John, I was going to call you later tonight. Here's what's happening: Expect a call from an Atty. Norman Winfield from Pleasantville. He's going to go with you to court. You won't have to say anything. He'll do all the talking. Now, the attorney will probably have you to come to his office to ask you a few questions. It's nothing to be concerned about. He's assured me that he can win this case if it goes to court. He also knows that I will pay whatever the cost is, so you don't have to worry about that."

John was somewhat relieved, but he wanted to know if Kaye would be going to court with them. Kaye sensed his anxiety and assured him that if she could be there, she would, but she had another appointment she had to keep. "Winfield has assured me that things will go well. I have confidence in him," she said enthusiastically to him, but reserved some reservations about Winfield for herself.

Kaye allayed whatever fears John may have had and coached him to expect a favorable ruling for himself, with the possibility of getting back all the money he had paid Zorn and his father. She then drew her water, pampered herself and settled her soft, voluptuous body into her king-sized bed for a peaceful night's sleep.

The land issues in Thompson County preoccupied Kaye's thoughts as she busied herself early the next morning trying to get out of her condo long before her usual time. She grabbed the folder from the table by the door when she was ready to go and hurried down the steps, through the parking lot to her car. After letting it warm for just a few minutes, Kaye drove in the opposite direction from where she worked, trying to remember the exact location of an all-night copy center she had seen in Thompson County. As she got closer to her destination, she remembered that a self-service copy center was near the place she had planned to mail the letter.

She entered the door with a fierce determination and went straight to the self-service copy machine. She pushed the "Start" button and watched as a blank sheet spewed from the copier. She then opened the folder, used tissues from her shoulder bag to grasp the letter from the folder, and then put the letter on the glass. She pushed the "Start" button again and actually made one copy of the letter, took it off the glass then carefully put it back in the folder. Then she pushed the "Start" button again and watched another blank sheet come forth. She removed the three sheets from the copy holding bin, took them to the cashier and paid for three copies. She then hurried to her car, carefully removed the copy of the letter which was sandwiched between the two blank sheets, meticulously folded it with a handful of tissues and inserted it into the envelope without leaving any of her prints. Reasoning that the letter would not fall out during processing and delivery, she stuck the flap inside the envelope, walked up the street from the copy center and dropped it in a mail box and went back to her car. Kaye smiled to herself as she drove back toward Humphries. She thought of how she really wanted to share her adventures with Mamma Sylvia, but she knew she couldn't. But, she would stop at *Mamma's Dining Room* for breakfast. The minute she entered the door and headed toward her favorite table, Matthew Crenshaw abruptly lowered the cup from his lips, looked at her quizzically and quickly got up from his perch and stealthily eased out the door. Kaye got the impression that, based the way he looked over his shoulder at her as he left, it was a clear indication he was avoiding her. After exchanging her routine pleasantries with Mamma Sylvia, Kaye mentioned Matthew Crenshaw's behavior to her, primarily to see what kind of response it would elicit. "It was like he was afraid of me," she said as she looked at Mamma Sylvia to detect any messages that were not verbalized.

"He's a little strange, a bit jumpy at times," Mamma Sylvia said. "But, he's a pretty good ole dude. He eats here almost everyday. Usually comes in here either after you've gone, or before you get here," she said matter-of-factly.

Mamma Sylvia's demeanor gave her no reason to be suspicious of anything she said. Therefore, she could accept her words at face value and relieve her own mind of the tendency to look or scrounge around for meanings and messages that were not readily apparent.

Kaye sat calmly eating her breakfast while trying to bring herself down from her adrenalin high. She replayed in her mind, step-by-step, what she had just done, trying to assure herself that she had made no mistakes and that what she was doing had to be done. There was no other choice. She would not allow thoughts that it was a coward's act to enter her mind, no matter how hard they tried. She finished her breakfast with renewed, natural energy and headed to work with a self-assurance that her latest letter would cause some more fireworks and somebody to scurry about trying to figure out what it all meant and where it was leading.

20

It had been two days since the hearing was scheduled; but Kaye had heard nothing about the outcome from her cousin John or from Norman Winfield. She wanted very badly to call John or Winfield for an update, but her instincts persuaded her not to. She would wait it out. Kaye sat at her desk with an intent look on her face as she carefully examined a sheet of paper with names circled and connected with a network of arrows and lines. She often spent her lunch period working on cross-word puzzles or reading up on an area in which she had an interest. Occasionally, she would surf the Internet and download information she found interesting. No matter what she wanted to do, lunchtime always provided her an escape from the typical office gossip and the plethora of complaints about life's trivial matters. During the past few months, she had spent this time digesting the case. Her anger and emotions had dragged her deeper into it as she uncovered more of the facts. Her preoccupation with it helped her to intensify her efforts as a Claims Adjuster, and forced her to evaluate what else she wanted to do with the rest of her life and what it was that she had a real passion for doing. She had worked in the Claims Adjuster profession for more than twenty years and was a top-notch performer. Anything new on the horizon she learned before it was implemented, and she usually ended up teaching it to others. There were very few challenges in the profession for her. There were even fewer for her in Humphries. She had found her sleuthing to be challenging and exhilarating, and a calling that was tugging at her like nothing she had done before. She often found herself daydreaming about what life would be like investigating and researching bits and pieces of obscure information that appeared to be unconnected, and forming a comprehensive picture only she was able to see and to put together. She could become as good at that as she was as a

Claims Adjuster. She was confident of that, but now claim adjusting was losing its allure, becoming pedestrian, and not giving her the sense of accomplishment and satisfaction she desperately needed. As Kaye was doodling and connecting points on her paper, the phone rang, startling her from an intense and focused look at what was emerging from her work.

"This is Ms. Webster," she said in her best telephone voice.

"Ms. Webster, this is Norm Winfield," the voice on the other end said authoritatively.

"Oh, how you doing, Atty. Winfield?"

"Did your cousin John tell you what happened at the hearing?" Winfield asked gleefully.

"No, I haven't heard from John."

"Well, a curious thing happened that puzzled me. Zorn and his attorney did not show up for it. The judge didn't seem to be too upset, but it caught me by surprise," Winfield said, and waited for Kaye to respond. She said nothing, but was thinking about what could have happened. After determining that she was not going to respond, Winfield added, "I'm not sure what to make of it."

"That's very interesting," Kaye finally said after a long silence between them. "Who was the judge?"

"Let's see," Winfield said as if he were searching for a name. "A fellow named Francis Wilcox. I think he goes by Frank Wilcox." Kaye quickly wrote down Francis/ Frank Wilcox on the paper and circled it. Immediately, she knew she had to send out another letter. "And who is Zorn's attorney, again?" Kaye asked as she closed her eyes and stroked her forehead.

"His name is Chadwick Pollard; I think he goes by Chad."

"Well, what's next?" Kaye asked as she jotted down his name also.

"Something else curious happened the day after the scheduled hearing. I got a call from Zorn's attorney wanting to know if we are willing to settle this thing out of court."

Kaye leaned back in her chair and smiled. She could hardly contain her emotions.

"What do you think that means?" she asked as emotionless as she could, and bracing for an answer that made sense to her.

"I'm not sure, but I said no; we want to take this to court. I hope that was okay," he said with a question in his voice. "We've got a good case here," he said with growing confidence.

"That's great. We don't want to settle out of court," Kaye assured him.

"I think John might be a little puzzled about all of this, but he'll be better off in the long run."

"I'll talk with John. Let's keep it going," Kaye instructed Winfield. "Keep me on board."

Kaye gently put the handset in the cradle and said, "We got the bastards on the run now," She said to herself, then laughed out loud and started thinking about her next move. She thoughtfully picked up the pad of paper, gently tapped her forehead with the pencil, then started doodling again, connecting more points and drawing arrows and dotted lines in many different directions.

21

Mac Mc Lauren and J. P. Sellers hovered over a table in a private room at The Belmont Club. The room attendant had been instructed to leave plenty of ice for them on the credenza, along with the best bourbon, bottles of water and condiments. They also insisted that he did not disturb them for at least an hour. Before the attendant could finish the set up and get out of the room, they both had finished their first drink and were well into their second. They had not seen each other for several months, and the last time they had talked had been just as long. This meeting was supposed to be one of the "get to-gathers" they usually had about twice a year. They would have a few drinks, laugh and talk about pranks they had pulled as boys, update each other on things they needed to know and generally enjoy each other's company. This one would be different.

After looking nervously around the room, Mac Mc Lauren placed his briefcase on the table. He opened it, pulled a letter out of a folder and pushed it across the table in J. P.'s direction. "Better not touch it, unless you want your prints on it," he said. J. P. stood slightly and leaned over to get a better view. He shook his head as he struggled to read it.

"You're right, this is hot. Hell, Anders Zorn has been dead for years. I'm not sure who inherited his estate," J. P. said as he continued to read. "I've just assumed that it was divided between his children," he added after a few moments. "Damn, they even know what Dent Madden was up to when he was working for the County. Wow! This is serious stuff," he exclaimed.

"Yeah! I know. And look who it went to," Mc Lauren said with resignation. J. P. stretched his neck and scanned the paper carefully to see who had received a copy of the letter. "Man, this is real serious," he said eventually as he eased back down into his seat.

"You find out anything?" he asked.

"Not a damn thing," J. P. replied as he took another gulp, leaned forward and looked at the letter again. "Nobody knows a thing. At least they ain't saying if they do." "You check all your sources?" he asked in a way to suggest that maybe J. P. wasn't thorough enough for the gravity of the issue at hand.

"All I know to check without raising too many suspicions," J. P. replied with a tone of disappointment.

"I had a chance to feel out Bob Stanton over at the Bureau. Didn't pick up any vibes there either," Mac Mc Lauren offered mournfully. "I'm not even sure he got a copy of the letter," he added wishfully. "Hell, it's been about five months and I haven't heard a word," he continued. "You think it went to a Federal judge?" J. P. asked and looked at Mc Lauren to see if he could detect an honest reply.

"Beats me!" he said, as he rattled and swirled the ice in his glass and got up to go fix himself another drink.

J. P. was not sure what to make of Mac's response. He fixed his eyes on Mac as he moved across the room, still looking for a hint of honesty or any equivocation.

While Mc Lauren was plunking cubes of ice into his glass, there was a firm, steady rap on the door. He looked exasperated and reached to open the door as he was saying, "I told that stupid..." He didn't finish the sentence. He looked shocked.

"Hey, what's up, ole buddy," the man said. "I was told I could find you back here."

Mc Lauren thought for a few seconds and realized that he had seen the man before but he still wasn't sure he knew who the man was. Mc Lauren's legal mind began to churn: Who was he and why was he there? What kind of trouble was he in? Did he write the letter? He was slightly disheveled and appeared to be under the influence of some kind of intoxicating substance.

"How you doing?" Mc Lauren asked as he stepped toward the man and extended his hand. He then peeked out the door and asked him in. Mac still wasn't sure who he was.

"I won't bother you now," he said. "I understand you have a little pow-wow going on right now. I just wanted to let you know I'll get back to you later."

"No, that's alright. Come on in. I'm just here shooting the breeze a little bit with J. P. Sellers." J. P. had walked up toward the credenza. He had heard the entire exchange between Mc Lauren and the man from the beginning, and he too had begun to ask himself similar questions. J. P. knew the man was Bennett Zorn, but he wasn't sure that Mac knew it. J. P. knew Bennett fairly well, but he knew Bennett's father even better. Mc Lauren knew Anders Zorn but, but apparently did not know Bennett Zorn and was suspicious of his presence.

"You know J. P. Sellers?" Mc Lauren asked Zorn as he stepped into the room. "Sure I do," Zorn said as he and J. P. exchanged greetings and shook hands as Mc Lauren finished making his drink. "How is Mrs. Zorn doing?" J. P. asked as he smiled obsequiously at him.

Bennett Zorn did not reply to J. P.'s question. J. P. wasn't sure if Zorn didn't hear him or was simply ignoring him. Either way, J. P. took it as a personal slight, one of many he had learned to ignore and overcome.

Then it became clear to Mc Lauren who the man was. "Better fix yourself a stiff one and sit for awhile," Mc Lauren said as hospitably as he could under the circumstances, and moved quickly toward the table. As inconspicuously as he could, Mc Lauren put the letter back into his briefcase as soon as he got there, and set the briefcase under the table. "Maybe I'll do that," he said while moving toward the credenza. Zorn and J. P. quietly made their drinks and awkwardly joined Mac Mc Lauren who sat patiently at the table. The three men sat silently and stared at each other a few minutes as they sipped their drinks. There was a quiet tension in the room that they could sense but could not explain. Each could feel it but neither dared to talk about it. Mc Lauren and J. P. knew a lot, but what did Zorn know? Bennett Zorn attempted to break the silent awkwardness by turning to Mc Lauren and saying, "I understand you've been at the State a few years now." Mc Lauren wasn't sure if Zorn was asking a question or making a statement. "About three years now," Mc Lauren stated.

"You must see a lot of stuff come across your desk these days," he said with a slur. Again, Mc Lauren wasn't sure if Zorn was asking him or telling him. J. P. gave Zorn a quizzical look and Mc Lauren appeared to be intrigued with Zorn's questions or comments; he wasn't sure which. "This bastard knows something," J. P. said to himself as he looked at him suspiciously. "Is this s.o.b. trying to get money out of me? " Mc Lauren asked himself.

Mc Lauren and J. P. looked at each other, then they both looked at Zorn; but they said nothing. Zorn appeared to be self-absorbed. It was certain that he was being consumed by his drink. He had had only one drink with Mc Lauren and J. P. , but his actions and behaviors told them he was already intoxicated. He rambled for a few minutes about his father and his adoration of him. He also talked incoherently about somebody trying to sabotage him. This piqued J. P.'s interest and prompted Mc Lauren to ask Zorn to explain himself. Mc Lauren and J. P. sensed that Zorn knew something and was anxious to tell somebody. Zorn stuttered and stammered, and hemmed and hawed. It was clear that he was agitated and frustrated about something. He looked at J. P. as though he was irritated at his presence. Mc Lauren sensed Zorn's reluctance to talk and injected, "Anything you can share with me, you can tell J. P." Zorn thought for a second then chuckled. He finally reached into his coat pocket and pulled out a crumpled, folded envelope. Zorn gracefully unfolded the envelope, wiggled his hand in and snatched out a letter. He unfolded the letter and slightly tossed it onto the table.

"Do you believe this shit?" he said to nobody in particular, clearly agitated at the situation in which he was finding himself.

Mc Lauren slowly backed his chair away from the table with a confidence that said he knew exactly what it was. J. P. leaned forward to get a closer look. He began to read the letter, then jumped up from his seat, knocking it over, and said, "Holy Crappoly!" This was an expression J. P. apparently also had perfected for moments of great distress and total surprise.

Instantly, Mc Lauren knew the letter was no joke, and J. P. knew that the letter was not one of Mac's legal tricks. Or, was it? "Maybe this whole thing with Zorn showing up had been planned by Mac and Zorn," J. P. thought to himself and headed to get another drink.

"Somebody knows too much," Zorn said and looked at Mc Lauren with suspicion. "They obviously got the goods on a lotta folks."

Mc Lauren wasn't sure if Zorn's comments were meant as a threat to him or comments of genuine concerns for Zorn himself. J. P. paced the few feet of floor space that were available in the private meeting room. He mumbled to himself and nervously gulped his drink. Mc Lauren sat quietly and said nothing. He had not even looked at the letter. He didn't have to; he knew what it was. He stared at Zorn with growing suspicion, trying to detect what he was attempting to do, or exactly what he was trying to say.

Zorn looked at Mc Lauren seriously and finally asked, "You get a copy of this thing?" nodding his head toward the letter that was still on the table where he had flung it.

"Yeah, I got a copy about four months ago," Mc Lauren responded reluctantly. "Four months ago!" Zorn said with surprise. "I just got this a week or so ago."

"Plain, white envelope and no return address?" Mc Lauren asked and stated at the same time.

"Yeah, you got it," Zorn said. "It came in a day or two before we had a hearing on calling in a loan. Whoever sent it had to know all about it. But, I can't figure out who it was."

J. P. continued to pace and to think. The word "loan" had really gotten his attention and he was now ready to sit down. J. P. Sellers and Anders Zorn had witnessed the signing of legal documents for each other. Mc Lauren had navigated many of the documents through the twisted record keeping process in Thompson County and had gotten them stamped "Official." He was legal counsel on many other business and real estate deals that apparently were questionable and subject to legal challenge. J. P. was curious about what happened at the hearing, and asked Zorn rather forcefully, "So, what happened at the hearing?"

"We, my attorney and I, never made it to the hearing," Zorn said with a degree of both disappointment and relief. Pointing to the letter that was still laying on the table where he had tossed it, he said, "That damn little piece of paper stopped us," he said with a chuckle. The answer was not sufficient for J. P., but he had gleaned enough information from it to determine what had happened. For the first time, James Preston Sellers was convinced that it was not a legal trick Mc Lauren was attempting to pull. He reasoned that if Zorn had inherited his father's estate, his own level of distress was bound to increase with time. The anonymous letter was just laying the ground work. He was amused that he had figured it out. J. P. was fond of saying, "I might not be well-educated, but I'm not stupid, either." He chuckled to himself because the letter implicated many of Thompson County's "Big Mucks," the same people whose official positions and community standings were measures he unconsciously used to define his own manhood.

Mc Lauren also wanted to know why they never attended the hearing, and decided to ask again the same question J. P. had asked earlier. "I took the letter to my attorney, Chad Pollard, as soon as it came in. He called Judge Frank Wilcox, who was supposed to hear the case, and told him about it. Wilcox thought it was best that we just didn't show up until this whole thing could be sorted out," Zorn explained. Mc Lauren knew Pollard and Wilcox, but he didn't know how to use the information Zorn had just shared with them. He was concerned that State officials may have gotten to both of them already, and if he tried to use the information, he could get himself into deeper legal trouble. There was a stunned silence among them as they sat drinking and avoiding looking at each other.

Mc Lauren was certain that the letter was real, but he still was uncertain about what the Federal Judge might do. The uncertainty was expressed through his squinting eyes and by his solemn facial expression. J. P. Sellers was relieved, but he had a nagging and unsettling feeling in his stomach and a slight flutter in his heart. A slight rap on the door broke the silence that permeated the room. The door opened and the attendant stuck his head in then stepped cautiously into the room. "Anything for you gentlemen?" he asked and hurriedly said, "It's been about an hour."

"No, we're 'bout ready to leave," Mc Lauren said. The three men continued to sit in silence for a few minutes, finishing their last drink. Then, almost in unison, they picked up their belongings and quietly walked out of the private meeting Room, stealthily traversed the main parlor, quietly walked toward the main entrance; and quickly left The Belmont Club in their separate cars that were waiting for them.

22

Indeed, Matthew Crenshaw was a little strange--at least by some people's standards. It seemed that he always showed up just when he was needed and that he was always lurking in the shadows somewhere when he wasn't. The few people in Humphries who knew him, knew him only as an attorney in Thompson County. They couldn't tell you exactly where he worked or tell you exactly what he did. Anybody who spent any time talking with him usually came away with the feeling that he was smart. However, they just didn't know how smart. Crenshaw graduated number one in his law school class, was on the *Law Review* and passed the bar without really studying for it in a consistent and methodical manner. It seemed that he just showed up from nowhere, set up his own law office and practiced alone in it for a few years. But, he had a difficult time making it successful in Thompson County. He didn't run with The Belmont Club set, and for many years he could not even become a club member. He recognized early on that the big, lucrative cases were not going to come his way, no matter how smart he was or how arduously he pursued them. His smartness was not going to get him in with the power elite, and he understood that. Rather than beat up himself over the situation, Crenshaw took on some of the overflow work from a few of the other attorneys in Thompson County. After a few years of this arrangement, he realized that the money he made did not and could not outweigh his integrity. He decided to give up his private practice and to take a job as an assistant district attorney. Matthew Crenshaw had studied the law with a passion as a student and he had practiced it with a passion as a private attorney. His job as an assistant district attorney gave him a different passion about the law that he had not experienced before. Thompson County could not adequately compensate him for the long, arduous hours he spent preparing for and prosecuting cases. But, he was there for a more noble purpose. Crenshaw was the assistant district attorney who was usually elected to prepare the briefs, opening and closing statements, and prosecuting strategies for the more notorious and sensational cases. However, the district attorney would either prosecute those cases himself or he would assign them to two other assistant district attorneys in the office. Crenshaw understood the game that was being played, but chose to say nothing. Crenshaw was totally consumed by and with his work. He was always at work early, and he was usually one of the last to leave. On Wednesdays and Fridays he was usually walking out the door no later than 6:00 pm, almost without exception. When he wasn't preparing cases, he was reading up on arcane cases or examining the arguments of recent U.S. Supreme Court decisions. The often diametrically opposed majority and dissenting opinions of the Justices always intrigued him. He called his case preparation and reading "research," but his colleagues jokingly called it "getting smart." When Crenshaw was often teased about not having a real life, he would just smile, affect an accent, and express his sentiments with an appropriate foreign language, or with a foreign phrase, interspersed with an aphorism and quotes from Shakespeare. Common among his foreign expressions were: Cogito ergo sum! (I think, therefore I am.) "Je pense, dont je suis!" (I think, therefore I am.) "Primus inter pares!" (First among equals.) "Comme il faut!" (As it should be.) and "Ab igne ignem!" (As you sow, so shall you reap.) "Quod erat demonstrandum!" (Which was to be proved.) He would often chuckle to himself and say, "I love it!" Occasionally he would say with a tinge of sarcasm, "It's real enough for me," but never say what he really meant by the expression. That was an indication that a verbal battle was about to ensue, and time for the average person to leave him alone, or look on speechlessly while he gave them a good tongue-lashing. His verbal ability and facility with languages were marvels to some people and confounding to others. There were rumors that Crenshaw had been married at one time, but nobody knew for sure. At least nobody was willing to talk on the record about it because they had no proof. There were also rumors that the only reason he had left the Northeast, where he was from originally, and had come to Humphries, was because he had a child somewhere in the area. That rumor was laughed at by many and doubted by most.

In fact, Crenshaw had been married before, but the marriage was snatched from him after suffering through five painful years of it and producing one child. Humphries was not a place he normally would have elected to be, but his circumstances left him little choice. Always protective of his personal privacy and that of his son, he had learned to keep his business to himself. The less people knew about him, he believed, the better it was for them and for him. He was a mystery to most people who knew of him, and he preferred it that way. But, these are the facts:

He had been married to Lorna, a "society girl" who had lived a life he had only heard about or read about, a kind of life he wanted to live. She had traveled to several countries and had moved among people of enormous means and influence before she was twenty years of age. Her father was a doctor who had grown up poor, but who wanted his daughter to have the very best he could give her. Lorna was stunningly beautiful and obviously schooled in class, culture and sophistication. In spite of her beauty and worldliness, she was extremely insecure and unsure of herself. She needed constant reassurance that she was beautiful and worthy of love and affection. When she couldn't trust the reassurance she received from those who said they loved her, she resorted to prescription drugs, and was addicted to them at the time Crenshaw met her. Her stunning beauty and his love for her blinded him to a problem that was in the making for several years, a problem that would grow uncontrollably with the passage of time. Crenshaw met her while he was in his last year of law school, and she was finishing her last year of college. He learned of her insecurities shortly after he met her, but didn't learn of her dependency problems until after the birth of their son two years after they were married. He assumed that his unconditional love for her and his devout dedication to her would undo the damage she suffered during her first two years of life in an orphanage. She had all the classic symptoms of a person suffering from reactive attachment disorder, which is a disruption of social interaction between a child and a caregiver due to neglect of the child's basic emotional and physical needs. Some of her symptoms were manipulative behaviors, difficulties trusting others, grandiose ideas about herself, lack of cause and effect thinking, temper tantrums and rejecting friendships. She had become masterful at masking her problems by abusing drugs, and by employing her practiced and trained behaviors whenever she needed to. In many ways, she was a bundle of contradictions.

After numerous stays in treatment facilities and his efforts to help her to overcome her problems, Crenshaw finally came to the realization that in addition to him enabling her in her drug addiction, he did not have the skills to help her reconstruct those critical aspects of her childhood development that she never received. He also came to realize that the primary reason she wanted to get married within months of their graduations was that she saw him a means of ensuring her a life style that she wanted but could not trust, and maintaining a way of life that was getting out of her control. Her prescription drug addiction developed into one of illegal drug use, and began to drain them financially and to strain the foundation of their relationship. Crenshaw had the idea that he was going to show her some "tough love" and demanded that she transform herself or he would walk out on her and take their son. For weeks she was the model wife and mother, giving her husband uncompromising attention and doting endlessly on their baby son. Crenshaw was impressed with her and was sure he had finally gotten her attention. He was even looking for ways to reinforce the positive changes he had seen in her, and had inquired about possible weekend getaways through a travel agency. Crenshaw returned home one evening from a busy day at his office, feeling excited about his life and yearning to spend a relaxing evening with his wife and son. Her car, which was usually parked in the driveway, was not there; and he assumed she had parked it in the garage. He couldn't explain it, but as soon as he opened the door there was a eeriness about the silence that was engulfing the house. He examined all of the bedrooms and discovered that all of their clothes were gone. He entered the family room and found none of his son's toys. There were no signs found of her or their son, and he instinctively felt that they were not coming back. He found it difficult to believe, but she had walked out on him and taken their son with her. Trying to cope with his shock and to suppress his anger, he made his way to the kitchen and found the following letter attached to the refrigerator door, meticulously placed and secured with several small magnets:

My Dearest Matt:

I realize I have been a big disappointment to you; and I've been a disappointment to myself and my family. I know you are really pissed off, now that you've learned that Tony and I are gone.

It's better this way. I took him with me because kids love unconditionally. I need that now, more than anything else. I know that is hard for you to understand, but you will in time. Don't worry about him or me; I can take care of us. I took the half the money out of the bank accounts. That is enough to give us a good start back in Humphries. We will be with Momma until we are able to be on our own. I told Tony we were going to see his Grandma, and that you will be coming to get us soon.

I beg you not to attempt to contact me for at least three months. That will give me time to get myself straight. I wouldn't wish this problem I have on my worst enemy. When we get there, I'll call to let you know. Give me two days to get there. Will you please try to understand?

I know that there is nobody who will ever love me the way you do. I love you.

Forever,

Lorna

Crenshaw was devastated. His profound sense of loss was almost more than he could bear, and his anger felt like it was seething throughout his body. A flood of tears welled up in his eyes, as he managed to stumble to the family room and threw himself into his favorite recliner rocker. He looked around, trying to focus through the anger and tears, and attempted to recount the events that had brought him to that moment in time. Upper most in his mind was how he had tried to be the perfect husband and dad, providing the best for them that he could, and being everything to them that he knew how to be. His mind quickly led him to see himself as a failure, in spite of his best efforts. Those thoughts were troubling to Matthew Crenshaw. He had a proven track record of personal accomplishments and successes, he told himself. But, the thoughts of failure would not relinquish their hold on his mind. He struggled to lift himself from the recliner rocker and started pacing throughout the house, looking at all that he had gained and realizing all that he had lost.

Nearly two years in the making, the house was built to Lorna's requirements and furnished to her taste; she called it her dream house. The house was post and beam constructed with a three-quarter, wrap-around deck and built-in pick-nick seats. It was a house built for comfortable living as well as classy, unpretentious entertaining. The family sleeping quarters on the third floor allowed for privacy out of the presence of guest sleeping quarters on the main or first floor. The guest sleeping quarters were down the hall from the living room, and set off by French doors. Tony took great delight in his task of putting dirty laundry in the laundry shut of the third floor, then going to the basement later to ensure that the dirty laundry was there, laying neatly in the basket next to the washer and dryer. Although it was nearly a daily routine for him, it seems that he was still amazed that the laundry always ended up there. Laid out comfortably in the basement were another sleeping room that doubled as an office, a large play area with a pool table and big-screen television, a wet bar and a full bath. The mere presence of the fireplace in the basement gave the area a feeling of comfort, safe and warmth; and the large sliding-glass doors leading directly outside gave the feeling of a direct connection to the cold, dangerous woods just a few feet away.

Their evenings together in the family room were times of easy laughter and playful lounging, watching television, competing in video games, reading to Tony and just being in each other's presence. Crenshaw walked into the living room and thought of all the times they had together, entertaining family and friends, standing or sitting around the wood-burning stove discussing local, national and world events. While they were wonderful times, they were also times of great concern for Matthew Crenshaw because he was never sure how Lorna would act or react to some of the topics under discussion. He was also preoccupied with thoughts about her and who among the crowd knew of her problems. It was a kind a torture that slowly ate away at him, little by little.

Although she was not there, the remnants of her presence were. He wandered aimlessly about, taking in all of the material things that were supposed to make her happy and to increase her capacity to give and receive genuine care and unconditional love. There were paintings, a high-end sound system, fine clothing, designer furniture, and expensive jewelry, all the things she wanted and believed she needed to plug the psychological holes and wounds she had that were exposing her to bouts of depression and moments of self-doubt. Crenshaw recognized somewhere along the way early in their relationship that Lorna found in him what she couldn't find in herself. And, she looked to him to give her a healthy sense of herself, and the assurance that she was a person worthy of love and affection. These were some of the things that drew him to her but none of the things he eventually realized he could do for her or give her. Crenshaw approached the steps leading upstairs, visualized his son Tony running up them to the sitting area overlooking the living room, sat on the bottom step and began crying. He thought of how Tony loved to look up at the skylights in the sitting area while it was raining and ask why the rain drops splashing against them did not come down on him. It was baffling to him because he loved to stand outside and look up while it was raining. Crenshaw knew that his wife loved him; and he knew that Tony loved both of them. But, there was a force more powerful and destructive than all their love for each other. It was a force that she would not deny and could not escape. It was a force that destroyed her and turned their world on end. It was a powerful force that would change their lives forever.

Within 2 months of Lorna's leaving Crenshaw, he received a phone message from his mother-in law informing him that he needed to come to Humphries as soon as he could. He didn't bother to call back to ask why, but gathered a few items, threw them in an overnight bag and drove all night to reach his wife and son. He was greeted with the sad news that Lorna had taken an overdose of illegal drugs and died from them. She apparently had spent most of the money she took from their accounts on drugs. For the second time in as many months, Crenshaw was completely devastated. When she had called to let him know they had arrived in Humphries safely, they talked at length about him allowing her time and space to find herself and their prospects of reuniting sometime soon and being the family they both knew they were destined to be. They would work tirelessly at making the marriage work; their son Tony deserved no less from them. Lorna was optimistic that she could overcome her problems and Crenshaw was confident that, with his understanding, love and support, she would. But, that was not to be. His immediate concern was Tony and how he would react to his mother's death, and then how to proceed with life as normally as possible, under the circumstances. His son had been left in the care of her mother, who had become quite emotionally attached to him, and taking him away from her would have been double tragedy for her. She had just lost her only child. She literally begged Crenshaw to let Tony stay with her, pointing out all the advantages of such an arrangement and the role she could play in helping him to rear the boy. He would always be the major influence in his life and could come to see him and take him for visits upon his requests. Matthew Crenshaw pondered the requests many days as he familiarized himself with Humphries, thought about what life would be like for his son there, and how his life would change if he had neither his son or Lorna in his life every day. He came to the decision that he would let his son decide where he wanted to stay. When Tony decided that he wanted to stay with his grandmother, Crenshaw decided that he could not leave without him. Therefore, he decided to stay in Humphries also. Close enough where he could see his son when he wanted to, but far enough away so he would not unnecessarily interfere with his life. He could spend time with Tony every Wednesday and Friday evening, and maybe take him to church some Sundays He could establish a practice or find a job there, and start a new life. The more he thought about those possibilities, the better they sounded. He immediately turned over all of his personal matters to a trusted friend to handle, and his pending cases to respected colleagues to resolve. He stayed in Humphries, never return to the place where he was trying to build a family life for his wife, his son and himself. The beautiful house, with all the trappings of success, didn't matter anymore. The memories of it would be unbearable and his feelings of personal failure would loom larger than they probably were. The "society girl" wife was a trophy he never deserved, but an albatross he would always love. He was determined to move beyond what had seemed like a continuous nightmare that lasted for three years, and try to regain an assurance that the quality of our lives is determined by the choices we make. This time, he had not chosen wisely. Those are the little-known facts about Matthew Crenshaw and how he came to be in Humphries and Thompson County.

23

Kaye Webster sat at her corner desk relaxing and examining the diagram she had drawn on the legal note pad that she seemed to always have somewhere nearby. This was an ideal time for her to relax, because she had taken off the afternoon to spend time doing some research in the Thompson County Register of Deed's Office and the Records Office. Kaye found the clerks helpful, but she found the research taxing. After studying the diagram for a few minutes, she turned the page and turned the note pad at a ninety- degree angle. Across the top in capital letters was the word "CHARACTERS." There were five columns across the page with the words, also in capital letters, "BENEFICIARY," "TRUSTEE," "ATTORNEY," "ACREAGE," and "BOOK/PAGE#," in that order. She smiled at what was written under each column, flipped the note pad to the second page titled "CHARACTERS" and examined what was written under the five columns labeled "TRUST," "ATTORNEY," "BENEFICIARY," "ACREAGE," and "BOOK/PAGE#." She then flipped the note pad to the third page titled CHARACTERS" and examined what was written under the five columns labeled "ATTORNEY," "BENEFICIARY," "TRUSTEE," "ACREAGE," and "BOOK/PAGE#." It was clear to her that the template she constructed of the characters was almost all that she needed to expose them. But, there was another piece that was missing. Anything else she could get would only make the evidence more convincing.

Kaye flipped through all of the pages again and carefully laid the legal note pad in the desk drawer. She sat for a few minutes looking out the window, sensing that the sun was visibly plunging over the horizon. She thought about the information she had printed from the Internet during her lunch hour that day and searched on the desk for a stack of folders she brought home, and found it. Kaye then leaned back in her chair, opened the folder and quickly scanned each sheet. She pulled a yellow marker from the pen and pencil caddy, read each sheet carefully and highlighted information she found insightful. Some of the items she highlighted were:

- In 1786, Thomas Jefferson declared, "It may be regarded as certain that not a foot of land will ever be taken from the Indians without their consent. The sacredness of their right is felt by every thinking man."

- In 1795, just nine years after Jefferson's pronouncement, the Indians were forced to sign the Treaty of Pleasantville, ceding most of the Ohio Valley to the United States. The Louisiana Purchase, which was negotiated by Jefferson in 1803, added 828,000 square miles to the U. S. Some of the newly acquired territory was designated "Indian Territory," and was used to resettle Indian from eastern tribes as they were cleared from their homelands.

- On May 28, 1830, President Andrew Johnson signed the Indian Removal Act that called for the resettlement of all Indians east of the Mississippi river. The sum of $500,000 was appropriated by the U. S. Congress to compensate the Indians for the land and to pay for the resettlement. The Act authorized the president to set up districts within so-called Indian Territory for the reception of tribes agreeing to land exchanges.

- By 1850, the federal government had concluded 245 separate Indian treaties, by means of which it had acquired 450 thousand acres of Indian land at a total estimated cost of $90 million.

- The treaty of 1854 with the Omaha Tribe contained the first comprehensive provision for the division of Indian land into individual holdings, and provided a model both and for the general allotment act that followed in 1887.

- The Homestead Act was signed into law May 20, 1862, providing that an American citizen, or a person who had announced his intention of becoming a citizen, could get title to a farm of 160 acres of public land for use as a "homestead." The homesteader was required to build a house on the property and to begin farming on it. The person had to live on the property five years, then a small registration fee of $26-34 was required to file the necessary papers to transfer the title to them. If they wished to acquire the title earlier, they could do so after six months by paying $1.25 per acre. Between 1862 and 1900, about 80 million acres were "homesteaded." The Homestead Act specifically excluded blacks.

- On February 2, 1887, the U. S. Congress passed the Dawes Severalty Act, in an apparent attempt to replace the Indian Reservation system parceling out tract of land (40, 40, and 160 acres) to families, individuals and orphaned children. The action was taken on the supposition that this would provide Indians with greater incentives for success. However, surplus lands were to be opened to white settler only, who thus acquired the best land within the reservation.

- On February 10, 1890, some 11 million acres of Sioux Indian Territory, ceded to the U.S. in 1889, were opened for general settlement.

- On May 2, 1890, the Oklahoma Territory, the last territory in the contiguous United States, was created by an act of Congress. It was established by redefining Indian Territory and creating an area for settlers within Indian lands.

- By 1934, when Congress overturned the Dawes Severalty Act with the Indian Reorganization Act, Indian lands had dwindled from 138 million acres to 48 million. The Act was passed to halt the allotment policy, and efforts were made to restore tribal organization and to recover lost land.

Kaye read the material, re-read it as she highlighted some of it, then sat and thought. Some of the issues of land began to make more sense to her, but she thirsted to learn more. Kaye asked herself, "If people will steal hundreds of thousands of acres of land, or a whole continent, why should I be surprised when I've discovered they've stolen or finagled a few or a few hundred acres?"

Armed with information she could find in the library and on the

Internet, she would continue to sit for hours reading fascinating and intriguing pieces if history that were never taught or talked about and examining old documents. The more she learned, the angrier she became; and angrier she became, the more she had to know.

During her lunch hour she started developing a spreadsheet from the angles, lines and arrows she had doodled and played with it for several days. All of the information was now coming together in a way that would give the average person looking at it a clear and concise understanding of what she had uncovered.

24

Judge Frank Wilcox did not want to meet with Bennett Zorn and Chad Pollard in his office in the Thompson County Courthouse, or anywhere in public, and he was reluctant about meeting with them at his house. However, he knew that he had no choice but to meet with them in an attempt to assess what they were dealing with and what they had to do next. The three men examined the letter very carefully and concluded that it could be explosive, with the potential of sealing the fate of each of them. They speculated about who may have written it, but could not come up with a likely suspect. Bennett Zorn admitted that the person was rather clever, having unraveled a scheme that his father's legal mind, along with the minds of his father's cronies, had put together. "Person or persons," Wilcox interjected dramatically. "Look at the how they wrote the date. Probably somebody who was in the military or knows how military people usually write dates," he added.

Neither Zorn nor Pollard had thought that maybe more than one person could be involved. They weren't quite sure what he meant by the date, and weren't interested in knowing at that moment.

"Who showed up at the hearing?" Pollard asked.

"John Wilkinson and his attorney. Some fellow named Winfield, I believe," Wilcox replied. "Never seen him or heard of him before," Wilcox added. "Over from around Evans County I believe."

"You think Wilkinson wrote the letter?" Pollard turned to Zorn and asked.

"Are you kidding me! Wilkinson's not that smart," Zorn said condescendingly. "I doubt that he can even write a decent sentence," he added angrily.

"You think his attorney wrote it?" Pollard asked.

"Gosh no," Wilcox said. "I don't think he's that type. I believe he likes to take you head on. He's pretty cocksure. Almost a little arrogant; but he's strictly by the book," he said with assurance. "If it's not in the book or by the book, he won't even see it or believe it," he said with a broad grin on his face.

"What do you think about this one, Judge?" Pollard asked deferentially.

Wilcox looked at Zorn and asked, "How much land's involved with it?" "About 25 acres," Zorn responded without hesitation.

"How much land are you sitting on that might get exposed?" Wilcox wanted to know.

"Somewhere around 800 acres," Zorn said with a look of concern on his face.

"Are you ready to roll the dice on all 800?" Wilcox asked in a manner to suggest the obvious answer.

"No, I don't think so," he said half-heartedly. "But, that doesn't say anything about what's on the land," Zorn interjected to make clear the magnitude of the issue.

"You might want to think about letting this one go, if you can strike a deal with Wilkinson and his attorney."

"I already tried that once and they turned down our offer to settle this thing out of court," Pollard injected.

"I don't think he's the type to give in," Wilcox said. "But, you could hang tough on it and see what happens."

"Yeah, he was adamant about getting this thing into court," Pollard said with disdain. "Just a little too anxious for me," he added. "I don't think they'll back down."

"I think he's trouble," Wilcox said. "Under the circumstances, that's probably where you don't want to be," he said advisedly.

"Yeah, it's a big risk now. If he loses, there's no telling where he'll take it. If he wins, there's no telling where he'll look next," Pollard said.

"You saw who this thing was supposed to go to, didn't you?" Wilcox asked.

"We know it went to at least one of the people listed there," Pollard said.

"How do we know that?" Wilcox asked.

Zorn, who had been quite for several minutes, said, "I ran into Mac Mc Lauren in The Belmont Club last Saturday afternoon, and he shared with me that he got a copy of the letter about four months ago."

"If the date on the letter is right, that's about the same time it was sent out," Judge Wilcox observed. "I didn't know Mac was in town," he added with a hint of anger and surprise in his voice.

A look of disbelief swept over Chad Pollard's face. He was surprised that Zorn had not shared that piece of information with him. Wilcox was surprised that Mac Mc Lauren had come to town without calling him or dropping by to say hello. That was unusual, and he wasn't sure what to make of it. Zorn was careful not to reveal the details of his meeting with Mc Lauren. He was embarrassed by the way he showed his true weakness to Mc Lauren and J. P. Sellers. And he didn't mention J. P. Seller's name at all. In fact, Zorn preferred to forget about the meeting completely and he wished he could take back his decision to call in the loan. He wanted to blame the trustee of the *Deed of Trust* for giving him bad advice. It was too late.

It was clear to Judge Frank Wilcox that he was implicated in the letter. He worried that any future actions he took and decisions that he made would be scrutinized by somebody, and he didn't want an Appellate Judge or anybody from the State looking over his shoulder. Chad Pollard realized that any missteps he made could damage his legal career and diminish any hopes he might have for a political career.

Neither man wanted to have anything to do with Bennett Zorn and his case, and neither man knew how to tell him that they didn't. After a few minutes of idle talk, Judge Wilcox stood to signal to Pollard and Zorn that their time was up. Nobody mentioned specifically what the next step was, and Zorn wasn't going to ask. Wilcox showed Pollard and Zorn to the door and went to his study to weigh his options. As Pollard and Zorn walked hurriedly toward their cars, Pollard asked Zorn to think about what he wanted to do and to call him with a decision the next day. Bennett Zorn drove home thinking about the problems his father Anders Zorn had created for him by trying to help him. Although he had always had some doubts about how his father had acquired his vast land holdings and wealth, he had no need to question it. He now reasoned that whatever his father did was none of his business and that, after all, he personally had nothing to do with it. What he had inherited was rightfully his and he would do whatever he could to protect it because Anders Zorn would want it that way. His father had told him to always stand up and be a man. He could hear his father bellowing, "Find what you want, boy, and go after it. Don't let nobody stop you!" The stern and commanding voice made him still quiver, more than fifteen years after his father's death. Bennett Zorn also knew that if he didn't make the right decision about one contentious transaction, he possibly could lose everything his father left him. He knew the right thing to do, but he wanted to do it for the right reason.

After riding and thinking for what seemed like hours, but were in fact only a few minutes, Bennett Zorn finally arrived home and promptly went to bed, knowing that morning would come too soon, and that the day could bring more anxieties and uncertainties than he wanted to think about. But, the certainties of the past few days and months would not let release him and let him sleep in peace. There was queasiness in the bottom of his stomach that signaled desperation and despair. Unable to imagine what his life would be like without his power and wealth, he began to sum up where he was and how he got there.

It was often said that he would make something of himself because his mother held him up and his father pushed him. Bennett Zorn was an average student, but his mother was always advocating for him with his teachers, professing that he was a superior student; and his father made sure he had everything he needed to satisfy his material wants. They reasoned that their involvement with his education ensured that he was going to have significant academic successes. "It's about exposure, Ben," his mother was fond of saying, "It's all about exposure." Bennett Zorn wasn't exactly sure what she meant by that at the time, but relished in her effusive praises of him. She went to great lengths to introduce him to people in positions of authority and influence, and talked volubly about what a find young man he was. She also gave him as many learning experiences as she thought he could handle, and even gave him some she knew he couldn't. His mother felt that was her job, and that his job was to be polite, look intelligent and say nothing. He did his jobs very well. It was expected that his only sibling, Rachel, would observe it all and say nothing; and she did. However, she was a superior student, and everyone knew it without her mother professing it; and she also was a gifted athlete. She set her own directions and never gave in to her parents' status-seeking pressures to be in the presence of and to be connected with the power elite in Thompson County or anywhere else they could find them. When Bennett Zorn enrolled in a local Prep School during his junior year in high school, he was envied by some students and admired by others. In either case, they knew he was on his way to accomplishing something big. He was an average student who was fortunate enough to attend a prestigious university. Most who knew him said it was not because of his smarts but because of his father's connections. In any event, he applied to a specific medical school at Anders Zorn's urging, and was admitted. Most people who knew him didn't understand how or why; but he was graduated and was actually in practice on his own for a few years. Sensing that he could not make it successful, and that he could make much more money following in his father's footsteps, Bennett Zorn gave up his practice and moved back to Thompson County. He teamed up with his father and operated several businesses, including apartment complexes, car washes, office buildings, gasoline station, self-storage facilities, all on land his father got under questionable circumstances. After Anders Zorn's death, Bennett became the administrator of his father's estate and the inheritor of most of his holdings. What would Anders Zorn think of him if he loss everything his father had acquired and left to him and his sister? Even the respect accorded them because of who they were?

25

G ordon Clark, Attorney General, and Robert Stanton, Head of the State Bureau of Investigations, discussed their letters with each other as soon as they received them. Ignoring the advice of the author of the letter, they did not discuss the letter with Mac Mc Lauren because they did not trust him. Clark and Stanton were critical of Mc Lauren's phony, fixed smile and knew that his political connections, not his integrity or competence, got him the job as Chairman of the Board of Ethics. They did not discuss the letter with Federal Judge Enos Elliston because they didn't want the Federal government interfering in State matters. They also reasoned that if they got a Federal Judge involved, it would appear that they were not doing their job. They wanted to uncover what the letter was about before the judge had an opportunity to act; and they agreed that, if the judge contacted them, they would cooperate, but they would not call him, if they elected to call him at all, until they had investigated the allegations and prepared their findings. Neither knew Elliston personally, but both had heard of his reputation as "carrying a big stick and using it."

Robert Stanton and the State Bureau of Investigation had already dispatched two teams of agents: one team, designated Special Task Force--Thompson County-1 (STF--TC1), to try to find out as much as it could about who wrote the letter; and the other team, designated Special Task Force--Thompson County-2 (STF--TC2) to check into the allegations. STF--TC1 examined the letter, postal stamp, fingerprints, paper, envelope, printer ink, typewriter ribbon ink, and font size and impression, but came up with nothing that was helpful. No saliva on the envelope flaps. No fingerprints on the backside of the self-adhesive stamps. There was nothing unusual about the envelopes, paper, and typewriter ribbon ink, font size and impressions. They were standard, off-the-shelf office supplies that could be purchased anywhere. No clean DNA fingerprints that could be matched against an existing data bank. STC-TC1 had no luck.

Robert Stanton, following the advice offered in the letter, had instructed STF—TC2 to go over to Thompson County to conduct one or two title searches on properties owned by Bennett Zorn and Dent Madden. The only other specific instruction was that the properties searched had to be randomly selected. Special Agent Rebecca Burke, one of the agents assigned to the team, simply walked into the Thompson County Tax Office, found a computer, sat down at it and quickly determined how to retrieve a listing of properties on which the property taxes had been paid. Several workers in the Tax Office came by; she smiled and spoke to them and continued working until she got what she wanted. It was like she belonged there, and she was there long enough to get what she was assigned to do, but not long enough to raise any suspicions. The next day she went to the Register of Deeds Office and announced that she was thinking about buying a piece of property and needed help in conducting her own preliminary search of the title; she just needed to understand how the information was filed. She assured the clerk that if she decided to purchase the property, she would be sure to have one of the local title companies to conduct an official title search for her so she could get title insurance. The agent asked the clerk to give her a little guidance in backtracking the ownership of any piece of property and in identifying any encumbrances that may have been placed on it. The clerk was more than happy to help, explaining in great details how that type of information was generally tracked in Thompson County.

Special Agent Burke assured the clerk that she had the basic understanding of what she needed to do. Then she opened a folder that had been secured under her arm and turned to a blank page and began to jot down notes about what she was finding.

"May I make copies of anything?" Agent Burke asked the clerk as she began to discover documents she thought Stanton might be looking for from her.

"Oh sure, Honey. All of this stuff is public information," she replied. "Just let me know when you're ready. They're supposed to be fifteen cents a copy, but I'll just make you a few copies, if you don't have too many."

"I really appreciate that," Rebecca said. "You're so helpful."

The clerk went about her tasks and left Rebecca to do hers. Special Agent Burke found numerous irregularities in the first searches she conducted on properties once owned by Dent Zorn, and now owned by Bennett Zorn. She also found some irregularities in the second and third properties randomly selected for searches. There were enough irregularities for the agent to draw the conclusion that some of the transactions probably were fraudulent. She found paper trails that led nowhere, and documents showing transfers without the proper signatures. She also found what appeared to be potential conflicts of interests with land transactions because Zorn's name was on land documents as Thompson County Clerk of Court and later appeared as the owner of the same land a few years later. Special Agent Burke didn't know specifically what she was looking for, but what she found alarmed her. She knew that the land record keeping process in Thompson County had serious problems, and she had copies of documents to prove it. The special agent on STF-TC2 prepared a detailed report, along with copies of relevant documents, and forwarded them to Robert Stanton. When Stanton read the report he also knew there was a serious problem. Only Stanton knew what he was looking for and he had found it. He was surprised, however, at how accurately the anonymous letter portrayed what was happening in Thompson County. He called Atty. General Gordon Clark and arranged a meeting to discuss the findings. "Gordon, this is Bob Stanton."

"Hey, Bob. How's it going?" Gordon replied.

"Not much. Got some information I think you'll find interesting," Stanton said. "What do you say we get together to discuss it?"

Gordon knew this was a cue that the information had to be discussed in private face-to-face, not over the phone. "Sounds like a winner to me," he replied. "I got a few snippets myself," he said. "Great! How about the usual place tomorrow for an early lunch?" Stanton requested.

"That'll work. Eleven fifteen. I'll be there," he said in a concise, direct and unemotional manner.

Gordon Clark and Robert Stanton met at a small shop about five blocks from the State Government Office Complex. They entered the sandwich shop from opposite directions, and they each carried a folder. It was clear that they had met like this many times before and they knew the routine well. The greetings were perfunctory but cordial, and they had an unmistakable ease with each other that communicated respect and trust. They placed their orders at the service counter, walked to a table in the back of the shop and took seats that did not allow their faces to be seen. They exchanged folders but did not open them, as they waited for their food and looked casually around them.

"That letter was right on the money," Stanton said eventually.

"I had a feeling it was," Clark replied.

"Some crooked shit's been going on over there that's about to get exposed," Stanton said softly.

"It's probably about time," Clark responded.

"The report and copies you have there are probably just the tip of the iceberg," Stanton said. "If we do a full-scale investigation, there's no telling what we'll turn up."

"I put out some feelers over there and picked up on some stuff that doesn't look too good for a few folks in the profession," Clark said. "You got some notes and a couple of names in the folder that I think you'll find interesting, but not surprising. I'm sure it all fits together."
"The letter hints at going to the press. We gotta keep the lid on this thing until we can determine the depth and scope of what we're dealing with," Stanton said with some worry. "I'm concerned about time," he added with a sound of worry and frustration.

"I believe we can circumvent the standard process if we can get a little cooperation," Clark assured Stanton. "If we can't get the cooperation we need, I have a good source that might give us a hand if we play it right."

Before Stanton could pursue Clark's line of discussion, the server arrived with their food. While plopping the plates, glasses and check on the table, he asked, "Can I get you gentlemen anything else?" "No, we're good to go," Stanton said. He was curious about what Clark had in mind, but felt confident that Clark would share his plan with him at the appropriate time. "I put a few things in motion already," Clark said, "and if I'm right, the net is going to snare a big fish." Stanton was more curious than ever, but he knew Clark well enough not to ask him to explain himself. He had an idea what Clark had in mind, but he wasn't sure.

"Yeah, I think you're right about that," Stanton replied. He started piecing together all that Clark had said.

"How are you on resources?" Clark asked.

"I put together two teams to work this case. I redeployed the one that came up with nothing on the letter," he said. Pointing to the folder, Stanton said, "The one that came up with this is standing by."

"I might need them to do some decoy work for me somewhere along the way. I'll let you know," Clark said.

"There're only two of them, but they're damn good," Stanton stated.

"That's great. They've got to be good. People are going to get a little cagey over there, so we might have to go right into the den with them to get what we need."

Both Clark and Stanton found the analogy quite humorous. They laughed out loud for the first time, and looked behind them with looks of embarrassment. Noticing that the sandwich shop was getting busy with the lunchtime crowd, they quickly finished their food and prepared to leave.

Stanton turned the check over, looked at it and he declared with a question, "This one's on me?"

"You sure?" Clark asked instinctively, as if they had played out that routine many times before.

"Yeah, I got it. You get the next one." Stanton left the money on the table and the men carefully maneuvered their way around the crowed tables and left the sandwich shop. When they reached the sidewalk, the men simply smiled, nodded at each other and walked in the same directions from which each had come.

26

J. P. Sellers had not rested well since the letter showed up out of nowhere and became the topic of secret discussions and growing concern. He knew from the beginning that the information in it could be disastrous for him, and he felt almost helpless about doing anything to protect himself. But, he couldn't just sit around and do nothing. Besides, he had gotten where he was by making things happen and by making connections with the right people. It didn't matter that he considered the right people "The Big Mucks," and often mocked them by acting haughty and pretentious. He also knew they were the movers and shakers in Thompson County, and made the key decisions about what would or would not happen in the county. It was curious to J. P. how he spoke of them disparagingly at times, even though he was proud to be associated with them; but he did not see himself exactly the same way he saw them. In his mind, their ways were contemptuous and vulgar, while they had developed the art of placid decorum and refinement. Although he was of both minds about them, he thought that this contradiction was humorous; and he knew from personal experience that their dichotomous ways were meant only to deceive. He was both detested by it and was drawn to it, and needed it to feed his sense of belonging and emotional well-being.

J. P. left his office swinging his briefcase and marching briskly down Main Street to the Thompson County Courthouse Building. With focused determination, he entered the building, rushed by the Information Desk, turned right and headed down the corridor toward the wing housing the hearing rooms and the judges' chambers. He threw his briefcase and keys on the security conveyor, patted his pockets and stepped hurriedly through the scanner. Apparently, this process was not new to him. J. P. grabbed his keys and briefcase from the conveyor, as they came out the over end, and continued down the corridor and went directly to the office of Judge J. Francis Wilcox.

When J. P. walked in, the assistant said, "Come on in Mr. Sellers, the judge is waiting for you. You may go right on back," signaling with the direction of his hand.

J. P. knew exactly where to go and walked in that direction with preternatural confidence. He stepped into the Frank Wilcox office and asked, "How you doing, Judge?" as he sat in a plush armchair placed diagonally across from the judge's desk. The armchair was lower than normal, requiring J. P. to look up at the judge.

"Not too bad, J. P. Seen better days, and I might even see some worse," Wilcox said dejectedly, while looking down worriedly at J. P.

J. P. was a little puzzled by those comments because they were uncharacteristic of Judge Frank Wilcox. J. P. did not want to appear too sensitive, but he knew those fuzzy comments meant something out of the ordinary. He wanted to understand exactly what Wilcox meant, but he decided to state the purpose of his business and leave.

"You probably haven't heard about this, Frank, but there's a letter floating around that's got some pretty damaging stuff in it if it gets in the wrong hands."

Wilcox perked up and asked, "What kind of letter are you talking about?" as if he already knew the answer.

Without telling Wilcox where he had seen the letter, J. P. started describing some of the details of it. Wilcox said, "Hold on for a second." He opened his briefcase, took out an envelope, slipped his fingers in and pulled out a letter. Wilcox then held up the letter for J. P. to see, and asked, "Is this the letter you're talking about?"

J. P. looked shocked. "Yeah, that's it. Where did you get it from?"

"It came in the mail a couple of days ago," Wilcox said. "It was real strange," he continued. "I saw a copy of the letter just a day or two day before this one came."

"Where did you see it?" J. P. asked.

"I believe you know Bennett Zorn."

"Yeah, I do," J. P. replied.

"Well, he and his attorney, fellow named Chad Pollard, came by with a copy. It seems that Bennett got a copy a few days before we were supposed to have a foreclosure hearing on some property his old man left him."

"Were you supposed to be hearing the case?" J. P. asked.

"Yeah, I was, but I told them they probably shouldn't show up, unless they could figure this thing out," Judge Wilcox stated with an air of caution.

J. P. thought back to the meeting he and Mac Mc Lauren had with Bennett Zorn at The Belmont Club. The things that Zorn told them then began to make more sense now.

"Who do you think is behind this whole thing?" J. P. asked nervously.

"I be damned if I know," Wilcox said. "But, it's making me a little skittish right about now," he added with a weariness in his voice.

J. P. wanted to say, "Me too," but he wasn't exactly sure what skittish meant. So, he said nothing.

"Bennett told me Mac Mc Lauren was in town asking questions the other week," Wilcox said. "Strange he didn't give me a call or come by to see me. I wonder what he was up to," he stated out loud and with no apparent expectation of an answer from J. P.

"Oh, I don't think it was much of anything," J. P. assured Wilcox, feeling an obligation to respond to him nonetheless. "We had one of our regular get-togethers and we got into a discussion about the letter. Zorn came by with a copy of the letter, and it just added to the discussion." Wilcox was surprised because Zorn had not said J. P. Sellers was at the meeting he had with Mac Mc Lauren.

"Bennett is a little upset about this, but I think he did the right thing,"

Wilcox said with some hesitation in his delivery. "What was that?" J. P. asked anxiously.

"On the advice of his attorney, he decided not to accelerate the maturity on that loan," he said. Recognizing that J. P. may not have understood, given his blank stare, Wilcox said, "He decided not to foreclose on the *Deed of Trust* he's holding on that property. He'd be a fool if he did, given the circumstances."

"What's he gonna do?" J. P. asked.

"If he's smart, he'll set aside the judgment and hope the whole thing blows over.

Hell, I could never rule in his favor now, even if I wanted to."

Satisfied that he had heard enough, J. P. told Wilcox he had just wanted to give him "a head's up" on the letter, but Wilcox knew that was not the real purpose for J. P.'s visit. Similar to Wilcox, J. P. was worried, but he tried his best not to show it, at least not to Judge Wilcox.. With a little less bounce in his stride and a little more concern on his face, he walked nervously back up Main Street toward his office, looking round and about him all the way, and worried more as soon as he got there.

27

J. P. Seller, in fact, knew the security routine at the Thompson County Courthouse Building very well because he had been there many times before and in Judge Frank Wilcox's chambers more times than he could remember. After he returned to his office and thought about the discussion he'd had in the judge's chambers, there was one occasion that was resonating loudly in his mind and causing him the greatest worry. The incident came back to him as if it had just happened moments ago, rather than many years earlier.

"Mr. Sellers?" a gravely voice asked on the other end of the phone.

"Yes sir, this is Mr. Sellers," J. P. said with pride.

"This is Frank Wilcox."

"Yes sir, Judge, what can I do for you?" J. P. asked with a burst of confidence.

"I have a business proposition I think you might be interested in," Judge Wilcox offered in the form of a recommendation and a command.

"You know me, Judge, I'm always looking for a good proposition," J. P. replied gleefully.

"If you have no lunch plans, why don't you drop by my office and I'll fill you in on the details," Judge issued in the form of an order. "And, J. P., keep this one under your hat."

"You betcha, Judge, I'll be there." He gently put the receiver back into the cradle, feeling quite good about himself and the fact that Judge Wilcox was taking him into his confidence. For a fleeting moment, he thought about the proposition and guessed that it had to be very good for Judge Wilcox to be offering it to him. J. P. did have lunch plans, but he could not deny Judge Wilcox his wishes.

Because of his connections and in his position to know and hear many things, Judge Wilcox acquired a treasure trove of information, and knew how to use it to his advantage and to others' disadvantage. He had heard that one of the Thompson County's elderly citizens had recently died without leaving a will. He had heard that there were approximately ten heirs who would inherit an equal interest in the dead man's estate, including one hundred and fifty acres of land. He had also read the same information in the local newspaper, but he couldn't rely solely on those sources. So, he requested that his clerk search the County records looking for a will and any information on personal property, but never stated why he needed it. The clerk could not find that a will had been filed with the Register of Deeds or with the Estates Division of the County Clerk's Office, and that the only personal property of any real value was the land. From his personal knowledge and informants, Judge Wilcox developed a list of the potential heirs to the estate. He saw an opportunity to do what he reasoned that they could not do, and was setting in motion a plan to accomplish it.

J. P. Seller arrived at this appointed time, and was greeted by Judge Wilcox with a hearty handshake and a slap on the back. Wilcox engaged in no small-talk, that was customary for J. P., and got right to the purpose for J. P. being there, not even allowing him an opportunity to sit.

"I believe you know a lot about what goes on in the County, J. P.," Judge Wilcox said quietly and in a tone that solicited trust. "I know you know a lot of the people here and what they're up to and how they think."

"Yes sir," J. P. chimed in proudly.

"Well, here's a list of people who are about to inherit an estate. I think you know, or know of, most of them," Wilcox said as he handed J. P. a paper with the words "Benjamin Fuller Heirs" printed across the top.

Judge Wilcox watched J. P. intensely as he studied the list and nodded his head.

Wilcox continued, "I think you'll find that one or two of them are ready to sell their interest in the estate, with a little coaxing," he said and winked. "For a fair price, that is" he added almost as an after-thought.

"Yeah, I know the Fuller family," J. P. assured him.

While handing J. P. a folder, Judge Wilcox said, "Here's a copy of the deed for the land in the estate and a copy of the plat for the land."

J. P. quickly scanned the contents and placed the list of names in the folder.

Wilcox instructed J. P., "Try to buy out as many of the heirs as you can. Go by Chad Pollard's office and get copies of Purchase Agreements he has for you. They're the basic agreements you deal with all the time," Judge Wilcox assured J. P. He added, "After you've made your first share purchase, you need to give Pollard a call," Judge Wilcox instructed J. P. "Make sure they understand they're selling their share of the estate, they're not selling the land," the Judge emphasized.

"I will, Judge," J. P. promised.

"Now, if you need any money for these transactions, let Pollard know.

"I think I'll be alright, Judge," J. P. replied with a bit of boastfulness in his voice.

"This is going to be a great deal for you, J. P.," Judge Wilcox assured him. "It might take a little time to get all the details worked out. But, you won't be sorry." Judge Wilcox then gave J. P. a slight slap on his back, shook his hand and gently nudged him toward the door.

J. P. Sellers left Judge Wilcox's chambers puffed up with pride and overflowing with unearned confidence. He wasn't exactly sure where Judge Wilcox's plan was taking them but he was ready for the ride. Before he even left the Courthouse Building, he started letting anybody whom he thought might know the Fuller family that he was interested in talking with them, and handing out business cards to pass on to them.

Within a week, J. P. was certain that at least half of them were aware of his inquiry. At the end of two weeks, his efforts had gained him nothing.

Early the following week, J. P. received a call from Judge Wilcox instructing him to contact Jake Fuller because he might be interested in selling his interest in his father's estate.

"See how much he wants for his interest in the estate,'" he instructed J. P. Then added, "I understand there's little of anything of value in it except the land. You must know how much land is worth in that part of the county," he stated in the form of a question. "If he wants less than his ten percent interest is worth, give him a few hundred dollars more, and he'll be happier than a pig in the mud," Wilcox said with a chuckle, as if he were amused at himself and his humor.

"Sure, Judge, I'll get right on it."

"When you get it all worked out with Jake Fuller, get the agreement back to Chad Pollard and get in contact with me," he continued to instruct J. P.

"Sure thing, Judge." J. P. was pleased that Judge Wilcox was sharing so much with him and, apparently, was steering him through some real estate maneuvers he had heard about but had never done before, and didn't fully understand. Now, it was beginning to make sense.

Judge Wilcox was sharing with J. P. only that which he wanted him to know. He didn't tell him that Jake Fuller had applied for a loan at the local bank and was denied because he had no collateral in case he defaulted on the loan. The estate he and his sisters and brothers would inherit was owned in common, with each getting an equal share, and with neither owning any specific part of the estate. Therefore, it could not be used as collateral. The bank president suggested to Mr. Fuller that he might want to consider selling his interest in the estate. When Mr. Fuller indicated that was probably what he would do, the president immediately called Judge Wilcox to inform him.

Within minutes after talking with Judge Wilcox, J. P. was driving to the western part of the county in an attempt to locate Mr. Jake Fuller. J. P. made several stops, once he got to the western side of the county, and asked several people where he could find him. After a few more stops and small talking with a few more people, J. P. closed in on Jake Fuller at the local *Mom 'N Pops Store*. He introduced himself, tried to impress him with his small talk and seemingly I'm-your-friend familiarity, then awkwardly stated the true purpose of his business.

"Mr. Fuller, I've heard you might be interested in selling your interest in your Dad's estate. Uh, uh, am I right about that?" J. P. knew of Mr. Fuller and also knew that his friends called him "Uncle" Jake Fuller. However, J. P. thought giving him a proper handle would be the respectful thing to do.

"Yeah, that might be right," Mr. Fuller said without looking at J. P. "Well, if you're selling, I'm interested in buying," J P. said with a broad smile. "I'll give you a real fair price for it, too," he quickly added while trying to gauge Mr. Fuller's response. A person more perceptive than Jake Fuller probably would have seized on J. P. Sellers' use of the word "too" and become skeptical of any dealings with him. That piece of seemingly innocuous information completely escaped Jake Fuller.

"What do you think is a fair price?" Mr. Fuller asked with great sincerity.

"A fair price is whatever it's worth," J. P. retorted, feeling that he had scored a direct hit in his negotiating prowess, proving to Mr. Fuller his trustworthiness without revealing his real intentions. Mr. Fuller stood motionless for a few minutes, as if he were thinking, and finally said, "I guess that makes sense." Then he added forcefully, "I'll need at least $10,000 for my share," and looked directly at J. P for his reaction.

"You're in the driver's seat," J. P. said and laughed. "I think an estate way out here is worth that kind of money." Then he added in the form of a question and as a way to confirm what he believed from Judge Wilcox and the list of names he had, "Is your interest ten percent?" J. P. asked in a manner that telegraphed he already knew the answer.

"Well, there are ten of us children, so I guess I'm supposed to get one tenth of the estate; that's about ten percent the way I figure," Mr. Fuller said with confidence and chuckled. "That sounds about right to me, too," J. P. said. Then he added, "I'll tell you what Mr. Fuller, if you're ready to move on this now, I'll throw in another $2,000 and we can close this thing out in less than a week."

Mr. Fuller looked at J. P. in disbelief and a gaze that said, "This is too go to be true." Sensing that he had Mr. Fuller's attention, J. P. quickly added, "I can give you $2,000 now to close the deal and you'll get the balance after the attorneys do their thing. You know how they are?" he said with a hearty laugh. "And, if you have any questions or change your mind, you can get in contact with the attorney who will handle the closing; his number is right here in the agreement," J. P. said as he pushed the Purchase Agreement toward Mr. Fuller. "Read this and if you agree with it, sign right here," he said while pointing to the signature line. Before Mr. Fuller could begin reading, J. P. pulled his checkbook out of this back pocket and said, "How should I make out the check?"

"Jacob Lee Fuller," he said proudly. Mr. Fuller looked at the agreement momentarily and wasn't sure what it was stating. He stared at it blankly, indicating that he wasn't sure what to do. J. P. sensed that Mr. Fuller was in a quandary and reached over to point out to Mr. Fuller that he was not selling any property, but was only selling his interest in his Dad's estate.

"You don't have anything to worry about, Mr. Fuller," J. P. said and momentarily placed his arm around his shoulders.

Those words were reassuring to Mr. Fuller, exactly what he wanted to hear, and the added measure of a friendly hug was what he needed. He signed the Purchase Agreement immediately and reverently gave it back to J. P. He smiled broadly and reached out to shake J. P.'s hand, feeling assured that he had made a great deal.

28

"Ms. Webster?" the voice asked as soon as Kaye answered the phone.

"Yes, this is she," Kaye said with a confident and pleasant smile in her voice.

"This is Norm Winfield. I just got a call from Chad Pollard offering to set aside the judgment against your cousin John's twenty five acres of land. I told him we had to think about it, and asked if he had anything to offer," Winfield said.

"What else did he have?"

"That was it," Winfield replied. "What about giving his $15,000 back to him?" she asked with a chuckle and a smile.

"I was alluding to that with Pollard, but I don't think they want to budge on it," Winfield responded cautiously.

"I think we need to get it all, or we go to court," she said without hesitation.

"I think we probably could win this one in court; but you never know how the judge will rule on an issue like this because of the statute of limitations," Winfield cautioned.

"Yeah, you never know," Kaye responded as she smiled. "The judge would be stupid to even hear this case," she thought to herself.

"I know you're paying the freight on this, but what do you think your cousin John will say about it?" Winfield asked.

"I know John wants his money back," she said with apparent

irritation. "Why don't you get back to Zorn's attorney and let him know that John wants an offer on the refund of the money, in addition to setting aside the judgment on the land; then he'll consider it," Kaye instructed Winfield.

"That sounds good to me. At least they'll know we're flexible," Winfield said.

"Yeah, we are," Kaye said sarcastically. "We'll find out just how serious they are about getting this little biddy monkey off their back," she added to let Winfield know this was not a joking matter. Winfield chuckled and said, "Yeah, we'll find out. I'll get back to you the minute I hear from Pollard."

When Kaye hung up the phone, she buckled over laughing. "We really got the bastards running now," she said aloud. "They better hurry up and get this little biddy monkey off their backs because there's a great big, ugly ape 'bout to jump on." Her initial impulse was to get up and dance in the middle the floor, clapping her hands and swinging her hips. Instead, she composed herself and forcefully stuck up her thumbs and, uncharacteristically pumped her fists several times. She was confident she was winning the battle of nerves, but wasn't sure Winfield knew it, or could even appreciate what she had done.

She called her cousin John and told him about the negotiating that was going on. She assured him again that, if they play it right, his land will be free and clear and he will still get all or some of his money back. John thanked Kaye numerous times and, before he hung up, said, "I can't thank you enough, Cuz."

"That's what I'm here for," she replied. "I'll keep you in the loop."

Attorney Winfield did not tell Kaye that Judge Frank Wilcox had also called a day or two before Chad Pollard, introducing himself and asking questions about the land issue between her cousin John and Bennett Zorn. He implied that if the case went to court, he would have to hear it, and didn't feel that it warranted the use of his time. Winfield thought it was out of the ordinary that a judge would be calling about such matters before a hearing. However, Winfield explained some of the details to the judge, who listened quietly until he finished. Judge Wilcox listened carefully as Winfield rattled off the essentials of the case, and would occasionally interject, "Un-huh." He was actually trying to detect any connection to what Winfield was saying and the wording in the letter that was floating dangerously around. After Winfield finished his tutorial, Judge Wilcox cautiously advised that John Wilkinson and Bennett Zorn try to reach an agreement to keep the issue out of his court. With those words of advice, Winfield realized that he probably didn't have a friend in the Thompson County justice system. However, he did decide that he would not take Judge Wilcox's advice, just to see where the legal maneuvering would lead him. He told the judge he had to discuss the issue with his client and try to get him to settle the issue. If things did not turn out satisfactorily, he could always say John Wilkinson wanted to pursue the matter in court.

Kaye knew when she first got involved with helping John Wilkinson, Jr., to get the issue on his land resolved, that the issue was larger than his twenty five acres. She didn't know how big it was. Even if she resolved it, and she had no doubt that she would, she also knew that could not be the end of the story. She still could not share her grand plan with anyone.

The laser printer spewed out seven copies of a chart titled "CHARACTERS," containing an alphabetical listing of names. Then it printed out seven sets each of charts titled "CHARACTERS," with the words "BENEFICIARY," "TRUSTEE," "ATTORNEY," "ACREAGE," and "BOOK/PAGE#" across the first page; the words "TRUSTEE," "ATTORNEY," "BENEFICIARY," "ACREAGE," and BOOK/PAGE#" across the second; and the words "ATTORNEY," BENEFICIARY," "TRUSTEE," "ACREAGE," and "BOOK/PAGE#" across the third. Each set had names listed, and most of the names appeared on each set, as well as on the chart simply titled "CHARACTERS." Satisfied that she would not need another copy of the information again, Kaye deleted the file she had named "CHARACTERS." As she had done before, Kaye carefully removed the pages from the printer using tissues to keep the pages from collecting her prints. She then put a set of four pages each of her master plan inside six of the seven mid-sized, brown envelopes she had already prepared for mailing. Inside of the seventh mid-sized, brown envelope she stuffed her last copy of the original letter, along with the set of four pages. She then put all of the envelopes inside a larger brown envelope and placed it at the very back of her corner desk drawer, saying, "I'll come back and get you when I need you, baby."

Kaye sat looking out the window, as she often did when she had to make critical decisions, or when she played out in her mind the outcomes of her actions and the likely resulting reactions. She wondered what, if anything, the original recipients were doing but she had no way of finding out. She had given them everything they needed, but she still wasn't sure they would take the information seriously. Kaye couldn't wait for them. In fact, she was confident that Bennett Zorn's change of heart was a direct result of her intervention. She hoped that Judge Wilcox realized somebody was looking over his shoulder, but she was certain he didn't know who. If he didn't get the message loud and clear this time, she would be sure he got it the next time. Moments of deep thought and reflection gave Katherine Louise Webster solace. Her mind invariably would wander far beyond the present and take her to sometimes long forgotten and to other times longed for. Her thoughts not only connected her to the ups and down of her past, but they also connected her to the future she knew she would make for herself. In spite of her sauciness and verve, cowering within her would always be the compassionate, kind and sensitive little girl her father always called "Sweet Kaye."

Kaye awakened herself from this moment of contemplation and sentimentality and went to draw water for a long, hot bath. The day had drained her physically and emotionally, and she realized she needed pampering like never before. She ran the water a little hotter than usual, and sprinkled a few extra bath beads into the tub to make the water feel silkier, emptying the container and putting it aside to be placed later on a shelf along with the others in her collection. She gracefully lit the two candles that always adorned the side of the tub and smiled as she gently blew out the long stemmed match perched between her dainty fingers. As the tub filled, she slipped out of some of her clothes and pulled and pushed at some. Before long she was free. She turned on the whirlpool attached to the foot of the tub, and rested comfortably on the edge of it, stroking the water and feeling the suds. At the perfect moment, she turned off the gold faucet, stepped into the tub and gently sat as the silky water and cottony suds consumed her delicate body. She leaned back in the tub, closed her eyes and draped one foot on each side of the tub. The slow, melodic whine of the whirlpool motor soothed her mind and the steady, gentle swirl of the water flowed lazily toward her, caressing every inch of her body along the way. During moments like these, she would try to forget the world, and pretend that she had no past; and that she had no future. There was only the moment, and that was all that mattered to her. Kaye knew that these moments did not come often, and she knew once they did, they never lasted long enough. Her biggest challenge had always been not to let the normal travails of life steal those moments. This time, there was no contest. After staying in the tub for more than an hour, she was still torn between staying in longer and getting out now. Her need to go to sleep outweighed her desire to stay longer. She hoisted her delicate body out of the tub and methodically patted herself dry with a large, fluffy towel. After searching the shelf where she kept her moisturizers, she found the container she was looking for. She twisted open the top with a slight tug, put her nose to it and inhaled deeply. Then she gingerly rubbed the moisturizer all over her body and stood before the full-length mirror admiring herself, gently feeling her breasts, messaging her hips and legs, occasionally turning herself so she could see her buttocks in the mirror, and carefully and seductively feeling and pinching the insides of her comely thighs as she crouched to gain access to them.

Placed along the top two shelves in the bathroom were several empty bottles and containers, beautifully displayed in obvious patterns by size, shape and color. Each was a masterpiece in its own right, creatively and innovatively designed and presented to make a unique statement about its essence and presence. Included among them was a flowery bottle decorated with graduations of bright reds and tender pinks. There was one with rounded curves, lending a nuance of feminine sexuality and crowned with a glass stopper resembling a dewdrop. Placed immediately behind it was a tall, black phallic-shaped bottle, collared in a wide golden band and capped with a frosted blue oval. Another bottle resembled a frosted oyster shell and was adorned with a black pearl stopper. There was a diamond shaped glass bottle with a golden stopper, shaped like a bud on the verge of blossoming. One was a frosted oyster-shell like, with an inverted heart shaped stopper, striped with a few thin lines of lavender. The bottles and containers were infused and impregnated with colors that were breathtaking. They ranged from light aqua to deep blues, from light snow whites to midnight blacks, from velvety cream to shocking yellow, and from candy-apple to grassy green. Kaye had the philosophy that each bottle or container and its packaging had to be extraordinary; and that the structure of the fragrance had to be in a class of its own. Each had to be uniquely different, yet comfortably familiar. If not, she wouldn't buy it. The fragrances powerfully awakened her sense of smell and the bottles sensually excited her imagination. The fragrances, their bottles and containers and their tops, all conspired to transport her to another world.

Kaye finished admiring herself in the mirror, searched casually about the bathroom and found the container she had emptied of its bath beads. She then carefully placed it on the top shelf in her collection, nudging and tapping it gingerly to ensure that it occupied the exact space she had designed for it. She backed a few inches away from the shelves, admired her artistic accomplishment and scanned all the shelves ritualistically. She was then ready to brush her teeth, to go to bed and to renew her mind for another battle that was sure to present itself the following day.

🐚 **29** 🐚

Mac Mc Lauren and J. P. Sellers had not talked since their meeting at The Belmont Club. After the meeting with Judge Frank Wilcox, J. P. felt that he should call Mc Lauren and give him a "heads up" about the letter Wilcox also had received. On his way home several days later, he stopped at a convenience store and called Mc Lauren at home from a pay phone. "This is Mac Mc Lauren," the voice said hesitantly.

"Mac, this is J. P. Did I catch you at a bad time?" he asked.

"Make it a quick one," Mc Lauren snapped, as if he wanted J. P. off the phone as soon as possible.

"Mac, I thought you might wanna know that Frank Wilcox got a copy of that letter."

There was a long silence on the other end. Mc Lauren finally asked, "How do you know that?"

"Frank told me," J. P. replied. "He was wondering why you didn't call him when you were in town the other week." There was a long silence again. Mc Lauren was wondering how his name had come up in connection with the letter, J. P. Sellers and Frank Wilcox. "Did Wilcox say why he got a copy of the letter and what he makes of it?" Mc Lauren asked.

"He didn't say exactly, but I know he was supposed to hear that case Bennett Zorn was talking about. I believe he thinks it was somehow related to that letter," J. P. added, feeling that he was passing on to Mc Lauren information he needed but didn't have.

"Looks like somebody's got a bead on him, too," Mc Lauren said with a chuckle.

"Yeah, it looks like that," J. P. said. "I believe the old boy's a little skittish," he added without really knowing what the word meant, but thought it sounded good because Judge Wilcox had used it.

"He'd better be," Mc Lauren said.

"Why do you say that, Mac?" J. P. anxiously wanted to know.

"Instincts, J. P., instincts."

"What the hell do you mean by that?" J. P. asked with a serious demeanor.

"Something's going on, but I'm not sure what it is," Mc Lauren answered. "The "State Boys" have been talking to each other. They act like nothing is going on when they're around me. I saw them huddling in a sandwich shop the other day, but they didn't see me," Mc Lauren said with worry. "I've asked a few more questions," J. P. said, "but nobody seems to know anything."

"Better be careful. If Wilcox got a letter, there's no telling who else got one," Mc Lauren advised J. P. "If they know anything, they're not going to tell you now," he added. Mac Mc Lauren began to wonder if he could trust J. P., but he knew he couldn't trust Gordon Clark and Robert Stanton, the "State Boys". J. P. wondered if he could continue his allegiance to Mc Lauren, if Mc Lauren was going to be the focus of an investigation and some bad publicity. They both thought about how to distance themselves from each other without making it obvious. They gave their usual good-byes and promised to talk soon.

After his discussion with Mc Lauren, J. P. dropped by The Belmont Club to have a cocktail and to see if he could pick up on any gossip. There was none. At least there was none anybody was willing to share with him. For the first time, he felt out of place at The Belmont Club. There was a coldness about the place that he had not felt before. There were people there who gave him hard, cold stares he had not experienced before. People he knew. People he knew when he worked at the feed and hardware store. People who once had done business with him through his real estate business. People he went to church with and prayed with and prayed for; who professed to do good deeds and who declared themselves to be good and decent people. They were people who were upstanding citizens of Sawyer Village and Thompson County, yet harbored a seamy side of their human qualities they assumed only they understood and that no one else could ever see. These were people he thought he knew, and in many ways idolized, but he realized that he really didn't know at all. It appeared that their faces scowled and sneered at him every time he looked at them. They were faces that smiled with genuine, brotherly love and Christian intentions, but concealed the ugly truth of a collective guilt that none was willing to acknowledge and to accept that any of them was capable of owning. The menacing looks on their faces and the deafening sounds of their silence reduced James Preston Sellers to quiet tears, tears that his cocktail could not comfort and tears that his trappings of success could not extinguish. He sat quietly and stared intensely into his glass as though he was searching for answers to all that pained him. He suddenly started having flashbacks of his meeting with Mac Mc Lauren and Bennett Zorn and seeing images of himself in Zorn. The more effort he exerted at staving them off, the more fluidly they reverberated through his mind. He soon decided that he could endure no more of himself and what he had become, summoned the wait staff to bring his check, and hastily left The Belmont Club. J. P. drove around Sawyer Village thinking like he had never thought before. He was quite certain that, if there were any problems they all potentially faced, Mac Mc Lauren and Frank Wilcox probably would look out for themselves and "The Big Mucks," and leave him to fend for himself. He was preoccupied with that thought. Somebody was tightening the noose around a lot of necks in Thompson County, he reasoned to himself, and he didn't want his neck to be one of them. J. P. worriedly pulled and tucked at his shirt collar without being aware of it, and twisted and turned his head as though he was trying to free himself from some menacing and phantom force that was gradually choking him. J. P. knew intuitively that the dynamite had already been set, and that somebody was just waiting to light it. Sure, he had cut a few deals with "The Big Mucks" that might be questionable, but he could always plead ignorant of exactly how the whole thing worked. After all, they are the experts;

he was just following their advice. They're the educated ones; he's not, he rationalized to himself. He just made a decent, honest living. That's exactly what he could say, and he could say it convincingly. He had heard the expression "plausible deniability," and he thought that it might work to his benefit in this case, although he didn't know exactly what it meant. He wasn't well educated, he told himself but he wasn't stupid, either, a refrain he knew well.

J.P. didn't know about the depth of all the land issues, but he had an idea. He had been intimately involved with only one, and thought his involvement was justifiable. While he was a small-time player in the real estate business in Thompson County, he knew some of the heavy hitters like Mac Mc Lauren and Frank Wilcox. He also knew of people like Dent Madden who had used their positions as county employees to facilitate their real estate acquisitions. Many of them, like Anders Zorn, had helped to write the book on illegally and unethically acquiring real estate and making it all appear legal and ethical. They had made millions of dollars doing that. In many instances, some had sold their real estate holdings and used the money to go into other businesses in an attempt to cover their tracks. J. P. Sellers had seen it happen; Kaye Webster had figured out how it happened.

30

Matthew Crenshaw's phone rang just as he entered the door of his modest apartment. As usual, he was reluctant to answer it. Very few people had his number, and almost nobody called him at home at night. His number was unlisted and unpublished. Thinking that maybe it was his son, he answered the phone.

"Hi, this is the Crenshaw residence," he said casually.

"Hey, I don't believe it. This is Double E," the voice said and waited for a response. Crenshaw thought he recognized the voice and the term "Double E" registered somewhere in his distant past, but a name and face would not come to him immediately.

"Excuse me?" Crenshaw said with a question.

"Lighten up Matthew. This is Enos Elliston," he said.

"I be damned, E Squared," Crenshaw said with genuine surprise and obvious delight. "How the hell are ya?" he asked. "About as well as I can be, being in the judging business these days," Judge Enos Elliston said jokingly.

"Yeah, I've been reading about you. Man, it looks like you're moving straight to the head of the class," Crenshaw said in a complimentary way.

"It's been a good career, but I don't know if I want that or not."

"I'm curious to know how you got up with me?" Crenshaw asked.

"You know us judges; we have our sources," he said nonchalantly, without saying specifically how he had gotten the number. In fact, it only took a two telephone calls and Judge Elliston had all the public information he needed on Crenshaw. Crenshaw knew that too, but wanted to get any information Judge Elliston was willing to give him.

"Man, it's been years," Crenshaw said, without pursuing further what he knew was a useless line of discussion.

"It sure has, Matthew," Elliston agreed and moved immediately to the purpose of his call. "Look, I got something a few months ago that I've been sitting on," clearly moving right into the real purpose of his call. "I need to run it by you for your thoughts on it."

"Yeah, what's that?" Crenshaw asked while trying to figure out how it might involve him.

"I need you to keep this under wraps, okay? Judge Elliston said and waited for Crenshaw to reply.

"Sure, unless it is a matter of life or death," Crenshaw said and laughed.

"It was an anonymous letter with a lot of allegations about some shenanigans going on in Thompson County. If they're true, it's going to spell real trouble for some of the county officials and some of your colleagues," Elliston said seriously.

"That sounds pretty serious to me," Crenshaw said, but not with surprise.

"It's very serious, if it's true," Elliston countered.

Matthew Crenshaw wanted to say, "All of it is very true," but he couldn't. Instead, he asked, "Am I implicated somehow?" "Oh, no, not at all," Elliston said quickly. "If I thought you were involved Matthew, I wouldn't be talking with you right now." Crenshaw knew that, but he wanted Elliston to say it. "Man, I'm glad to hear that," Crenshaw said, affecting a sigh of relief.

"Matthew, it's been a long time since we clerked together early in their careers, and litigated against each other only once, but when I found out that you were an assistant DA in Thompson County, I knew there was at least one person over there that I knew for certain I could trust."

"I appreciate the vote of confidence, Judge" Crenshaw said deferentially.

"It's a touchy situation, because the State AG, and SBI got a copy of the same letter. The issue really is in their bailiwick because it is a local matter, possibly involving fraud and misuse of public office and misappropriation of public resources. Some land issues," Judge Elliston said cautiously, not revealing all that he actually knew.

"Wow!" Crenshaw exclaimed. "Sounds like pretty serious stuff.

"Yeah, pretty serious stuff," the judge repeated.

"What's the State doing?" Crenshaw asked.

"I'm not sure. I thought one of the State guys would have called by now, but they haven't. Oh, by the way, there was another State guy involved who was supposed to get a copy of the letter." Elliston said; then added, "I believe he has something to do with Ethics." Immediately, Crenshaw knew Judge Enos Elliston was talking about Mac Mc Lauren. Crenshaw and Mc Lauren practiced law during the same time in Thompson County; and he was aware of his position with the State. Crenshaw simply said, "That's interesting and quite ironic." Crenshaw had heard about some of the questionable deals involving real estate, but he was disappointed that Mc Lauren may have been involved with them.

"I thought so too," Elliston replied.

"So, where do you think it's headed?" Crenshaw asked.

"I don't know. But, whoever sent the letter obviously got the goods and knows how to get them to the right people. Even named some names."

"Sounds like somebody involved probably got a short-shrift, or there's a big, gapping hole in whatever they're doing."

"I've figured it about the same way," Elliston replied.

Crenshaw wanted to know the names Elliston mentioned but he wasn't going to ask. They were probably names of people he knew. Elliston had told him a lot, but he hadn't said what he thought Crenshaw could do. Therefore, he thought that was an innocuous question if he asked it tactfully. "You want me to clean this thing up for you so you can help me get a federal judgeship?" Crenshaw asked jokingly.

"You haven't changed at all, have you?" "I hope not," Crenshaw said.

"Seriously," Elliston said, "I need somebody I can count on if I have to get involved over there. The letter leads you to believe there's nobody over there who can be trusted," he said.

"I'll do whatever I can without getting myself fired," Crenshaw said with a chuckle.

"Glad I can count on you, Matthew. I'll definitely call if I need you," the judge assured him.

"Man, or should I say Judge? It sure has been good talking with you, after all these years."

"You can call me E squared if you want. You just stay clear of the suck holes over there."

Matthew Crenshaw was surprised to hear from Judge Enos Elliston. And, he was very surprised to hear him allude to problems involving land in Thompson County. However, he was not surprised about the problems themselves. He was still curious about the names that appeared in the letter; but he was more curious about its contents. Crenshaw had always thought somebody should take on the land issues in Thompson County as a cause, almost every time a question about land was raised. But he was cautious to whom he would actually say it. He had said it to few people over the years, but to nobody he thought could actually do anything about it. Did somebody actually take his suggestion seriously, he thought to himself. He paced through his small apartment and thought about all the people he may have made the suggestion to; but he could not think of anybody who would have acted on it. He dismissed those thoughts from his mind, read awhile and went to bed.

31

Kaye received a call from Norman Winfield saying that Bennett Zorn was willing to refund $5,000 and to set aside the judgment. Kaye thought about the offer for a few seconds and calmly said, "Why don't you tell'em John has to think about it for a few days, and will get back to you with an answer." Winfield was a little puzzled by Kaye's response, but figured she was going to get her cousin John to accept it. "That shouldn't be a problem; they got time," Winfield said thoughtfully.

"We got time, too," she responded immediately. "If they'll refund $5,000, they'll refund all $15,000," she said with a serious tone. "I'll make sure of that," she added with emphasis and in a no-nonsense tone that was unmistakable.

"How're we going to do that?" Winfield asked, wondering what other demands she might press him to place on Zorn and his attorney.

"Oh, I just had a thought," she said in a dismissive manner. "Something I think they'll like," she added with a tone of mystery.

"You're the boss," Winfield said with a resignation, "You're paying the bill."

Kaye detected what Winfield was really saying because of the way he said it, even though he didn't voice it.

"They know we caught them with their fingers in the cookie jar and we're about to slam the lid on them good and tight," she said and laughed heartily.

"You're right about that," he said as he forced out a laugh too, not confident that he understood where she was leading him. "Talk with John and let me know what your answer is," he instructed her while trying to escape from that moment of discomfort for him.

"Sure will," Kaye said compliantly, but knowing that she had already given him the only answer. She didn't have to talk to John. Winfield was right; she was paying the bill.

Winfield hung up the phone wondering what Kaye had in mind. He thought he understood her negotiating strategy, but now he wasn't sure. Kaye hung up the phone feeling more confident than ever about what she was doing, and knowing that her last delivery would have a maximum impact. She figured that the delivery would either develop a siege mentality among all the players, or it would create an atmosphere of distrust among them. It would permanently rattle some of them and it would completely seal the fate of others. Kaye felt that, no matter the outcome, she couldn't lose on the gamble she was about to take. Her resolve would not allow it.

Kaye pampered herself with a ritualistic bath and a gentle oiling, then went to bed knowing that she had to get up early the next morning for the 30-mile trek to make her special delivery, once again, crisscrossing, doubling back, ensuring that nobody was following her.

Upon returning from Perkins City after making her delivery the following morning, Kaye drove directly to *Mama's Dining Room* for breakfast before going to work. She arrived much earlier than she normally did and was quite surprised to see Matthew Crenshaw sitting in his trance-like position at a table in the back of the restaurant. She had not seen him since the time he looked at her suspiciously over his shoulder as he hurried away. She had thought about him often because he gave her a critical piece of information in a few seconds that would have taken her months to figure out on her own. When she walked in and Crenshaw recognized who she was, he suddenly leaned back in his chair. His reaction communicated that he was just as surprised as Kaye. Crenshaw instantly remembered that she was one of the people to whom he had said that somebody should take on the land issue in Thompson County as a cause. Maybe she's the one who sent his old friend Enos Elliston the letter, he thought to himself. She did have a land issue she was trying to resolve, and he had referred her to an attorney in Evans County for help with the problem. He could always pick up the phone and call Winfield, but he did not want his name associated with the issue in any way. He then told himself that if she took his advice, Norm Winfield represented her and got the problem resolved. He had seen her several times and had talked to her only once, but she didn't look like the type to do such a thing. He could always call Winfield to ask if his referral ever got in contact with him, and what was the disposition or status of her case. That was not Matthew Crenshaw's style. He preferred to stand back, observe and determine through his own intellect what he wanted to know.

Kaye exchanged her ritual with Mamma Sylvia as she moved briskly toward her favorite table. As she prepared herself to sit down, she turned to look in Crenshaw's direction and discovered he was not there. It was almost like he had vanished. Shrugging as she sat, it was as if she wasn't surprised.

She sat eating her breakfast and thinking about the range of reactions her last delivery would probably get from the recipients. This time, Bennett Zorn should have no doubts about whether he wanted to set aside the judgment against John's land and refund all of his money, she thought to herself. She also thought that it should be clear to Judge Frank Wilcox that somebody knew about the depth of his involvement with the land issues in Thompson County. Kaye wanted Frank Wilcox to get his personal copy again so he would know for certain that somebody was still looking over his shoulder. She chuckled to herself as she thought about the reaction Dent Madden would probably have when he got his delivery. From what she had determined, he had been one of he major players and had used his official position as the county land attorney to steal land for himself and to help his buddies do the same. It appeared to her that he might have used the Register of Deeds to help make it all appear to be legal. Kaye was not able to determine if Estelle Madden was related to Dent Madden. It was her hunch that she was, however. She did not ask any questions about the possible relationship for fear of raising suspicions about her inquiry, and possibly meddling in the personal lives of people not of her economic and social standing. However, she did not think it was coincidental that many of parcels and tracts of land Dent Madden owned were acquired during the time Estelle Dent held the Register of Deeds position. If Dent Madden had not seen a copy of the first letter she had sent, she wanted to make sure he received his personal copy.

Kaye Webster was certain that if the four recipients of the first letter had not acted by now, the next delivery they received was bound to spur them to do something. The last letter pointed them in the direction they should look. This time, they would have everything they needed--a list of names and diagrams showing all of the connections. If they didn't act, they had no intentions of doing anything. She would sit back and see what would happen. She finished her breakfast with feelings of accomplishment and wholeness, a serenity and internal peace that fulfilled her like nothing else had done before. The adventure she had been involved with recently excited her and made her feel alive again. The feelings gave her indescribable pleasure, an excitement and exhilaration that seemed to be bubbling inside her. Her work as a Claims Adjuster had become more boring and more routine, like never before. She had to leave and go to work, but she knew she would hate every minute she was there, and would barely be able to focus on what she was being paid to do. It would cause her enormous pain and continue to diminish her ability to force herself to go there. However, Kaye gathered up her belongings, forced a smile upon her face, paid her tab, hollered her usual farewell to Sylvia and walked blithely out the door.

32

All of the letters were delivered the next day. Atty. General Gordon Clark and Robert Stanton, Head of the State Bureau of Investigations were not surprised. It was as if they had been expecting the alphabetical list of "CHARACTERS" and the three accompanying sheets listing the connections among the names on the first sheet. They both knew, from the information written in the first letter, that the person who sent it either had done detailed research on or had first-hand knowledge of the land issues in Thompson County. They had also concluded that the individual who signed the letter "A Person with a Conscious and High Ethical Standards," in fact, may have decided to get a conscious and to identify herself or himself and the role they may have played in the schemes. Or, the person may have been taken advantage of in one of the deals and, now, was seeking revenge. In any event, it was clear to them that the person had a lot of information that they preferred not to see in the hands of the media, at least not until they had time to figure out the true nature of what they were dealing with. That is one of the reasons Gordon Clark and Robert Stanton had already set in motion a plan to uncover the details of what had happened, and probably was continuing to happen, in Thompson County.

Heywood Bradford "Mac" Mc Lauren was stunned again when his mid-sized, brown envelope arrived. It had been months since he had received the first letter. He still wanted badly to dismiss it completely as a hoax, but because Bennett Zorn and Judge Frank Wilcox also had received copies of the same letter, he couldn't, even if he had tried. Mc Lauren still didn't know if Clark and Stanton had received copies of the first letter and he could barely entertain the thought that they also may have received a mid-sized, brown envelope containing the same information. Mc Lauren wondered again if he was being investigated and what he would do if detailed information about his past and current maneuverings in Thompson County became public knowledge. He knew, however, that he had to do something, but he wasn't sure exactly what.

Bennett Zorn called his attorney Chad Pollard immediately and got Pollard's voice mail. He did not leave a message. Zorn counted the number of times the name Anders Zorn appeared on the spreadsheet and, in his mind, substituted his father's name with his own. Zorn began to shake with fear as he carefully examined the names and connections on the three sheets of attachments. As he examined them, he began to shake so badly that he could no longer hold the papers steady enough to read them He dropped the sheets on his desk, fumbled for his keys, unlocked the lower right desk drawer, searched through it nervously and pulled out folders containing instruments involving land he had inherited from his father and dropped them on his desk too. Zorn looked at the stack of wealth with disdain and sat sobbing silently and shaking his head for a few minutes. Suddenly, he grabbed up the stack of folders and the information that arrived in the mid-sized, brown envelope and stormed out the door. Dent Madden left Sawyer Village the day after the mid-sized, brown envelopes were mailed, and he was going away for several days. As was customary, his wife Estelle opened the mail the day it arrived so she could share with him what had come in when he called later that day. Estelle read the letter with a detached interest until it mentioned Dent's name and implicated her by way of the position she held at one time, Register of Deeds. Estelle could hardly believe what she was reading. She read the letter again, trying to digest every word and every nuance of it. Estelle Madden then examined the alphabetical listing of names. She knew all of them. She then examined the attached lists showing how all of the names were connected. Estelle already knew how the names were connected; she was surprised somebody else had discovered how. She wanted to call Dent Madden right away to inform him of the packet of information, but she didn't know exactly where he would be staying or how to get in contact with him; he refused to carry a cell phone. She would have to wait until he called her later.

When Frank Wilcox received his envelope and saw that in the lower, left-hand corner it was marked in bold print and underlined "Personal and Confidential," he had a nauseating and sinking feeling that it was somehow related to the first letter he had received. Wilcox opened the mid-sized, brown envelope with a movement of anger and a demeanor of apprehension. He was torn between pulling them out and leaving them in. He hesitated momentarily before pulling out the pages containing information he felt sure would incriminate him. Eventually, he pulled the stack of papers out and looked at the top sheet labeled "CHARACTERS." Wilcox realized immediately that it was an alphabetical listing and scanned down the page and saw James Francis Wilcox listed near the bottom. "I be damned," he said as he flipped through the remaining three pages and realized immediately what they showed. Wilcox knew, or knew of, all of the individuals whose names appeared, and, for the most part, he was aware of their connections to each other. Wilcox's face showed strain and worry. He was particularly concerned about several of the individuals listed who had received favorable rulings from him on disputes he could not legally justify. Would they sell out in order to protect themselves? he asked himself. Could he claim that their attorney's facts were more compelling and defense was stronger than the plaintiff attorney's case? Was there an attorney involved with writing the letter and sending out the incriminating information? Could he retire before everything was exposed, and would he still receive his pension if he were convicted for any of his crimes? Judge Wilcox asked himself many questions and thought through many different scenarios that might give him a legal leg to stand on. Wilcox knew the seriousness of the situation because there was already enough prima facie evidence to convict him of illegal and unethical conduct and for the abuse and misuse of judicial powers. He also knew that there was much more incriminating information that could send him to prison for many years. However, he didn't know who was releasing the information and he didn't know how to stop it. He also didn't know how much they already knew and with whom they had shared it. He didn't know when he might receive another letter or another packet of information. The more he contemplated the situation, the more helpless he felt about it, and longed for the days when he could have made a few calls and silenced anyone he wanted to. He never had to be directly involved, but the force of his position and his aura of respectability could be felt; and the way he got what he wanted was certain and swift. This was different. It was like a phantom detective had uncovered secrets he was certain had been hermetically sealed and buried forever. Now, something or somebody was exposing them with a methodical and subtle precision that caused him, a powerful and respectable judge, to feel feint of heart. He deduced that those who once did his bidding were themselves in precarious and untenable situations, hoping and wishing the maelstrom slowly and surely engulfing them would quickly and permanently disappear. In spite of the anguish and turmoil slowly but definitely enveloping Judge Wilcox, he finally decided that the damage had been done already, and his worrying about it was not going to help matters. "Whatever happens, happens," was his attitude. After looking around his office and reminiscing about his trappings of success, he settled in to review some upcoming cases assigned to him and was interrupted by a buzz from his assistant.

"Yes?" he asked.

"There's an Atty. Pollard on the phone who wants to talk with you. He says it's urgent," the voice said.

Without responding, Wilcox pushed a button on his phone and said, "What is it Chad?"

"Judge, this thing is getting out of hand I believe."

"What do you mean, getting out of hand?" the Judge asked agitatedly.

"Bennett Zorn stormed over here a minute ago looking like he'd seen a few ghosts."

"Maybe he did," Wilcox said sarcastically.

"Judge, he brought me a list of names and three other pages showing something that I think you should see. I probably need to bring it over," Chad Pollard said.

"Don't bother," the Judge said, "I already have a copy."

There was a long, eerie silence. Pollard said nothing and Wilcox said nothing. "Whoever it is that's doing this, I think they have him where they want him," Wilcox finally said. "By the way, did you all try to settle that case about that land?" he asked.

"Yeah, we tried, but it doesn't look like they're going to give an inch," Pollard said.

"I think you better advise your client to give a mile on that one, or put everything he has in jeopardy," Wilcox advised Pollard. "He doesn't have time to worry about them giving an inch," he said like he was agitated.

"Judge?" Pollard said with a inflection in his voice, and waited for Wilcox to answer.

"Yeah?" Judge Wilcox answered in the form of a question.

"Pollard here," he said cautiously. "Do you think they know about the partitioning of the Fuller land?"

"I don't know what you're talking about," he said angrily and dropped the phone in the cradle without answering the question. The Judge was clearly spooked by Pollard's call coming at a time when too much was happening too fast.

Judge Wilcox then hurriedly rummaged about his desk, scooped up several items, stuffed into his briefcase several folders, stacks of paper and the four pages of information that had come in the mid-sized, brown envelope. He pushed his chair back from his desk, like he was in a fit of anger, stormed toward the door and snatched his coat off the coat rack by the door as he passed by. As he walked from his office and hurried past his assistant, he said without looking in his direction, "I'm gone for the day. I'll let you know if I'll hold court tomorrow."

33

Judge Frank Wilcox did not hold court the following day. But, he did know about the partitioning of the Fuller estate, and he spent the entire day thinking about all the events leading up to it. In fact, he had thought about it all night, and started the day with a few Bloody Mary's in an attempt to help him forget. He continued to drink as the day wore on and was thoroughly inebriated before noon, almost to the point of delirium. Within hours of Jake Fuller signing the Purchase Agreement J. P. Sellers had given him, J. P. called Judge Frank Wilcox to inform him that he had the signed document. Wilcox informed Chad Pollard that J. P. soon would be coming by to see him. Pollard informed Wilcox that he'd already done a title search on the property, and that it was free and clear except for some unpaid property taxes for the previous year. Three days later, J. P. Seller asked Jake Fuller to meet him in Chad Pollard's office the following morning to sign all the paperwork for transferring his interest in his father's estate and getting the remainder of the money due him. J. P. was even kind enough to offer to come to Jake Fuller's place and drive him the thirty miles to Humphries to close the transaction. Jake Fuller assured J. P. that he could get there on his own, but inquired about the exact location of the office.

Chad Pollard was careful to point out to Jake Fuller the details of the documents he was about to sign and asked him several times if he had any questions about them, as he hurriedly leafed through them page by page. Like J. P. had done, Pollard assured Jake Fuller that he was transferring his interest in his father's estate, not actually selling his share of the land. Then, Pollard pointed out to Jake Fuller that with an estate to be divided among so many heirs, it was to his advantage to get rid of his interest now because it would probably take forever to settle it. He even implied that he could be dead before the estate was settled. Chad Pollard explained the settlement statement to Jake Fuller, noting that his portion of the property taxes past due, along with the closing costs he would normally pay, would all be paid by J. P. That was news to J. P., but he nodded in agreement and trusted that Pollard and Wilcox were working in his best interest. Of all the things Pollard told Jake Fuller during the transaction, the things he didn't tell him were the very things that later were going to hurt him the most.

News traveled fast in Thompson County, and it traveled through an informal network that was more efficient than the county's only weekly newspaper and the two weekend shoppers. Two of the other Fuller heirs called J. P. at his office several days after Jake Fuller had sold his interest in the estate, offering to sell him their interest also, if they could get a deal similar. That was great news to J. P. and he was certain Judge Wilcox would be quite proud of him for arranging those transactions. J.P. assured them that he was interested in purchasing their shares and would be able to complete the transactions within a week, at the very most. He took their names, checked them against the list Judge Wilcox had given him, and asked how he could get in contact with them when the Purchase Agreement and their initial checks were ready.

As soon as J. P. hung up the phone, he called Judge Wilcox and relayed the good news. Wilcox instructed J. P. to contact Chad Pollard to inform him of the details, and told him that Pollard would have the $24,000 he needed to complete those transactions. The same day, J. P. got the Purchase Agreements and checks from Chad Pollard and called the heirs to arrange a time to meet them. The next day, he located the heirs, had them to sign Purchase Agreements, and presented each with a check for $2,000. Again, J. P. was careful to point out that they were selling their interest in their father's estate, not actually selling their land. The transactions were completed in Chad Pollard's office several days later, with Pollard pointing out the advantages to them for selling their interest in the estate, and noting that J. P. had agreed to pay the closing costs they normally would pay. In less than two weeks, J. P. had acquired a thirty percent interest in the Fuller estate for $36,000. Technically, he had only $12,000 invested, but all three shares of interests were in his name. Chad Pollard had given him $24,000, and he assumed that he and Judge Wilcox each had invested $12,000, and that they were the ones orchestrating the events in a way that was fascinating to him. Still, he didn't know exactly where it all was leading, but J. P. was still a willing participant in the game. Less than a month after the first transaction had been completed, Judge Wilcox asked J. P. to meet him in his office as soon as he could. As usual, the meeting was short and to the point. Judge Wilcox asked J. P. to contact the remainder of the Fuller heirs and offer to purchase their shares of interest in their father's estate, but to offer them less money than he had paid for the interest he already had purchased. J. P. wasn't sure why Judge Wilcox wanted to offer less, because he knew the word was already circulating about how much he had paid for the other interests. However, J. P. trusted that Judge Wilcox knew what he was doing, and would arrange to have the money available if all of the heirs were willing to sell. Therefore, J. P. didn't ask any questions, because he wasn't sure what to ask or what to say, except to follow the judge's instructions. While ushering J. P. out the door, Judge Wilcox informed him that he should get started on the assignment immediately and call him as soon as he had talked to the last heir.

The ever-persistent J. P. Sellers had talked to all of the remaining heirs in less than twenty four hours. None of them was willing to sell their share of interest in the estate at any price. J. P. had a feeling that he had failed, and was hesitant about calling Judge Wilcox to relay the bad news. When he finally called Judge Wilcox, and Judge Wilcox actually said, "Good!" J. P. was confused. He wanted to believe that Judge Wilcox was not saying it was "good" that J. P. had failed, but he wasn't sure. The judge clarified himself when he instructed J. P. to go back to the heirs and offer to sell them his shares of interest in the Fuller estate for $60,000, since they would not sell him their shares of interest. The picture was coming into better focus for J. P. with each assignment Judge Wilcox gave him to complete. J. P. did as he was instructed and reported back to Judge Wilcox that the heirs were not interested in purchasing his shares of interest in the estate, especially for the $60,000 he was asking. Judge Wilcox sounded elated again, and instructed J. P. to contact Chad Pollard and relay to him that the Fuller heirs had refused his offer to sell them his shares of interest in their father's estate. He assured J. P. that everything was working out as he had expected and that, within a few more weeks, he would get his money back from the first share of interest he had purchased in the estate and an additional large sum of money for his time and effort. He just had to continue following his instructions and taking Chad Pollard's advice. J. P. assured the judge that he was trustworthy, and that he would rely on "the pros" to work everything out.

Shortly after J. P. contacted Pollard, per Judge Wilcox's instructions, Pollard sent each of the heirs a letter informing them that J. P. Sellers wanted them to buy his shares of interest in the Fuller estate. If they could not or would not, as J. P.'s attorney, he would have to advise him to file a petition in the court, asking to have the estate partitioned and ordered to be sold at auction. They could avoid that course of action by purchasing J. P.'s interest. Pollard gave them one week to respond. It was during that period of time that the Fullers contacted several attorneys in Thompson County, seeking their advice on what to do about the dilemma facing them. They all listened to their story, read the letter they received from Chad Pollard, but declined to represent them on that particular matter or to refer them to another attorney. They said it was much too complicated and would require too much of their time. The week went by and they failed to respond to Pollard's letter.

Pollard had been keeping Judge Wilcox apprised of how the Fuller estate issue was unfolding and, when he did not hear from the Fuller heirs in the allotted time, he informed the judge that they had not responded to his letter. Therefore, he would be filing a court petition on J. P. Seller's behalf in a matter of days, requesting to have the estate partitioned and ordered to be sold at auction. A few days later, Pollard filed the court petition requesting the partitioning as he promised, and alerted Judge Wilcox that it had been filed. One of the Fuller heirs read about the petition in the local newspaper and informed the remainder of the heirs. Within days, each of the Fuller heirs received a certified, registered letter instructing them to appear in court for a hearing on the matter. Jake Fuller, sensing that something was wrong with how things were unfolding, suggested that they contact an attorney in one of the three surrounding counties to represent them in the matter. After several visits and calls to the several attorneys, they couldn't find one who was interested in talking with them at all. They claimed it was a complicated case and it would take too much of their time. Therefore, the Fullers appeared in court without legal representation and could not give Judge Frank Wilcox any legal reasons why he should not honor Mr. James Preston Sellers' request. He stated numerous times how sympathetic he was to their position, but he had to follow the law, that is established in every state on these kinds of matters, and base his order on that law. He ruled that the estate must be partitioned and the first half of it had to be sold at auction within forty five days. However, if they wanted to buy Mr. Sellers' interest in the entire estate, they had thirty days to purchase it at fair market value and to pay all the legal expenses Mr. Sellers had incurred to date and the court costs. If those conditions were not satisfied within the specified time period, an auction would be held on seventy five of the one hundred acres, and the land would become the property of the highest bidder. The proceeds from the auction sale would have to be divided equally among the seven heirs who had not sold their interest and Mr. Sellers, who had acquired thirty percent of it. The attorney who brought the petition before the court was entitled to twenty percent of the sale price, but no less than $8,000. If they did not purchase Mr. Sellers' remaining interest in the estate within forty five days of the first auction, the balance of the property shall be sold at auction the following day, and the proceeds shall be allocated as noted above. It was so ordered by Judge J. Francis Wilcox. There was a long silence after the order was issued, an intenseness crept over the Fullers as they stared at J. P. and Pollard, and J. P. and Pollard looked everywhere except at the Fullers.

"You're all nothing but a bunch of crooks," Jake Fuller blurted out angrily, pointing at J. P. and Chad Pollard. "You both lied to me," he continued. "Judge, it's not fair what they've done," he screamed at them with repeated vulgarities. Judge Wilcox asked Jake to be silent or he would have him removed from the courtroom by the deputy. As Jake was attempting to compose himself, Judge Wilcox asked, "Mr. Fuller, do you currently have an interest in this estate?" Wilcox already knew the answer to that question, but was trying to establish the foundation for his next question.

Jake Fuller looked perplexed and said, "I did until these crooks swindled me out of it."

"So, is that a no?" Judge Wilcox asked.

Jake Fuller said nothing.

"I think that is a no." Judge Wilcox said with an air of finality. "Mr. Fuller, according to all the information I have here, you sold your share of interest in the estate; and I can find nothing that says you sold it under duress. I find nothing that says you are mentally incompetent. You voluntarily sold your share of interest and you have nothing to say about it now. In these and all legal matters, I have to follow the law. The law's the law." Judge Wilcox stood and said, "Have a good day ladies and gentlemen."

The Fuller heirs, shocked and stunned about what was happening, contacted the local bank in an attempt to borrow enough money to purchase J. P. Sellers' share of interest in the estate. When they offered the land as collateral for the loan, the bank denied it to them and explained that it was heir property, held in common by seven of the ten heirs and J. P. Sellers. Such arrangements were too complicated for the bank to take a risk on. They contacted several banks in the surrounding counties and received similar explanations as the reason for denying them a loan. The closer to the deadline for purchasing J. P. Sellers' interest in the estate, the angrier Jake Fuller became. He blamed himself for causing the problems for the remainder of his siblings, and vowed publicly to "take care of" J. P. and Pollard. The thirty-day deadline passed and they still had not secured the loan; and they were afraid to use their savings to get all the land back into their possession. Among all of them, they had more than enough money for that purpose; but they never shared that kind of personal information with each other. Judge Wilcox knew they had at least that amount money because the president of the bank had informed Judge Wilcox they had that amount in the local bank. On the forty-fifth day, the property was auctioned on the steps of Thompson County Courthouse, with only one bidder participating. The highest and only bid for the seventy five acres was $80,000 and was submitted by Z & W Real Estate Investment Trust. Judge Wilcox declared that the bid price for the property was fair and ordered the proceeds to be disbursed. Of the $80,000 the auction sale brought for the property, $12,000 was taken for court costs; and the court allocated and distributed $16,000 to Chad Pollard, $5,200 to each heir owning an interest in the estate, and $15,600 to J. P. Sellers. As soon as J. P. received his proceeds from the sale, he contacted Judge Wilcox to inform him. J. P. was instructed by Judge Wilcox to keep all of the $15,600 for his initial $12,000 and the balance was "a modest return" on his investment. He also informed J. P. that he would be receiving a larger share of money later. Judge Wilcox then told J. P. that he thought the remaining seventy five acres would be auctioned because he didn't think the Fuller heirs would come up with enough money to buy out J. P.'s interest in the estate. "They won't do anything but fight among themselves," he said with assurance.

"Yeah," J. P. said, "They can never agree on anything anyway."

"The sooner we resolve it for them, the better off it will be for everybody," Judge Wilcox added. "Even if they kept it, they wouldn't know what to do with it," J. P. said with authority.

"You're right about that," Judge Wilcox said. "Each piece would be too small for each one of them to do anything significant with it. Getting all of it in the hands of a few people serves a higher purpose anyway," he said with a tone of paternalism in his voice. All of the Fuller heirs together had received enough from the sale of the first seventy five acres to purchase J. P. Sellers' interest in the remainder of their father's estate. Although they discussed pooling their money to buy it, some of them were skeptical and thought it might be a bad idea because the judge might force the property to be auctioned anyway. They fussed and talked among themselves, and they asked advice of many people who knew even less about the problem than they did. Therefore, they took no action to avert, impede or stop the court-ordered sale because they didn't know what to do. The forty-five days passed and the last seventy-five acres were auctioned on the forty sixth day after the sale of the first seventy five acres. This time, there were two bidders, but Z & W Real Estate Investment Trust had the highest bid of $80,000, exactly the same as the first bid. Again, Judge Wilcox declared the fair price, and ordered the proceeds disbursed according to his order. All of the parties received exactly the same amount they received from the first seventy five acres that were partitioned and auctioned.

When J. P. received his proceeds from the second sale, he called Judge Wilcox again to inform him. Judge Wilcox thanked J. P. for all that he had done, and instructed him to keep all the money for the time and effort he had devoted to the project. J. P. sat silently for a few seconds, trying to comprehend what he was hearing. He was taken aback and wasn't sure he was hearing the judge correctly. He hadn't thought of what he was doing as a project, and he had not spent a lot of time following Judge Wilcox's instructions. He'd made a few telephone calls and a few trips to the western part of the county, but he considered that just a normal part of his business. He realized the judge had told him that he had a good business proposition for him and that he would be rewarded for his effort, but he found his generosity incredulous. Judge Wilcox interrupted J. P.'s thoughts and said, "You know, there might be other deals we might want to bring you in on."

Again, J. P. tried to understand what he was hearing, and his mind focused on the words "deals" and "we." The judge talked on for a few minutes without J. P. really hearing anything he said. J. P. was trying to piece together all that had transpired in such a short period of time, and to make sure it made sense to him. He was also mentally calculating how much money had actually exchanged hands from the partitioning and court-ordered sale of the property in the Fuller estate.

Immediately after he and Judge Wilcox ended their discussion, J. P. searched through his briefcase for the Disbursement of Funds reports he had received along with his proceeds. He found the reports and began adding them together to determine exactly how the proceeds were disbursed. In a matter of minutes, he had calculated the following:

PROCEEDS FROM SALE OF PROPERTY	$160,000.00
DISBURSAL OF FUNDS	
Court Costs	$24,000.00
Attorney's Fees	$32,000.00
Fuller Heirs ($10,400 each)	$72,800.00
J. P. Sellers	$31,200.00
TOTAL DISBURSEMENT	$160,000.00
BALANCE REMAINING	($0.00)

J. P. was quite pleased with himself and with all that Judge Wilcox had told him. He was equally pleased with how he was brought into the confidence of some of Thompson County's important and respected citizens. He knew he was now playing in the big league.

However, there was much he did not know and would not know. He did not know that the $24,000 he received from Chad Pollard was actually contributed by Z & W Real Estate Investment Trust, which was owned by Bennett Zorn and Sheldon Wilcox, Judge Frank Wilcox's brother. He wasn't sure what Judge Wilcox was getting out of the deal, but he was certain that he was getting something. He was never offered another opportunity to participate in a similar business deal with Judge Wilcox or Chad Pollard. But, he was still connected to the movers and shakers of Thompson County and was brought in on other deals only when he was needed.

By the end of the day, Judge J. Francis Wilcox was falling-down drunk, stuttering and stammering about things that only made sense to himself, and apparently talking to himself and laughing, or laughing and talking with an imaginary person that only he could see. From all appearance, he was teetering somewhere between delirium and insanity, or perhaps hanging precariously on the narrow lip of feebleness. When he was in this state, Judge Wilcox displayed all the characteristics of simply being a man, a mad man, a possessed man, unable to hide behind his title or his position, and too out of touch with his tendencies for being in charge and control to know or to care. The natural protuberance of his big, bulbous, and bright red nose got in the way of his narrowly cast face when he was sober, and nearly consumed his entire face when he was intoxicated. It wasn't often that he found himself in such a state. But, when he did, it usually meant that somebody or something was gnawing at him and forcing him to look at himself, to face the internal contradictions that belied the outward appearances of incorruptibility and invincibility he labored arduously to perfect. He was forced to evaluate his actions or to look at himself, and the result was usually a day or two of uncontrollable drinking and more than a few moments of trying to rid himself of an accumulation of guilt. Afterwards, Judge Wilcox justified whatever he had done that was ethically, morally or legally questionable, and would come to the convenient conclusion that it wasn't his fault that people weren't smart enough to keep themselves out of situations where others could take advantage of them. They should have known better, or they should have asked for help if they didn't know what they were doing. It wasn't his job to look after them. Judge Wilcox eventually went to sleep, still holding a Bloody Mary in one hand and the remote control for the television in the other. His last coherent thought was that he would be at work the following day, carrying on the business of the court as usual. For after all, life had to go on. However, ricocheting in his mind was the thought of that woman who, many months earlier, had been examining documents and asking questions.

34

Dent Madden was back in town the same day he left. His trip scheduled for several days lasted barely more than eight hours. He was looking forward to a week of golfing and fraternizing with several buddies. This was an annual event where they would enjoy each others' company, talking about their business exploits and sharing their latest secrets about facilitating deals. Upon his arrival at the resort, he called his wife Estelle and learned about the packet of information he had received. She screamed, "You gotta get back here as soon as you can," without returning his pleasant hello. "My god Estelle, what's wrong?" he demanded to know. "You don't really want to know," she assured him. "But, you got a packet of information in the mail today that's going to expose a lot of people and put us to shame."

"What kind of information?" he asked in a way that said he really didn't want to know, just as Estelle had said. But, her customary over-dramatization had an edginess about it that said he'd better pay attention.

"It's about those land transactions," she said with a sigh of disgust and resignation. Madden appeared almost apoplectic, clutching at his head and rolling his eyes simultaneously.

His vacation would have to wait. Without informing his buddies of his problem, Madden checked out of the hotel just as quickly as he had checked into it and went directly back to the airport to get the next flight that would get him anywhere close to Thompson County. Madden arrived back in Sawyer Village about 11:00 p.m. and stayed up all night studying the packet of information. Although Estelle had told him his name appeared in the letter that was dated several months earlier, he was still dismayed to see it in print. He was named specifically as a person who undoubtedly had used his office as a conduit to get real estate transferred to some of his relatives and friends, and then had the real estate transferred to him after he retired as a Thompson County employee. Dent Madden was also amazed that the alphabetical listing and attachments showed the connections between numerous people and some of the real estate issues in Thompson County. Madden had sold much of his real estate holdings, but whoever researched the information had done an excellent job tracing and compiling the various land transactions that had occurred over many years and had tied him to many of them. He knew all the individuals whose names appeared on the listing, but he decided immediately that he would not contact any of them to determine if they had received the same packet of information. Instead, he would wait and see what happened. Nobody from the State had gotten in contact with him, not even Mac Mc Lauren. Then, Madden thought that maybe the reason Mc Lauren had not contacted him was because Mc Lauren was concerned about himself. Mc Lauren had been involved with several real estate deals with Madden, but Madden had been the architect of them. If Mc Lauren received a copy of the letter and the information packet, maybe he was trying to figure out how to cover himself. "Mc Lauren is Head of Ethics for the State; how would it look if he were convicted for some of his past transgressions?" Madden asked himself.

Dent Madden examined the alphabetical listing again and said, "Judges, lawyers, county, developers, commissioners, real estate brokers, and me, the former county land attorney. That would make a some story," he said aloud. Madden started thinking about ways to deflect any negative fallout from the information the pages revealed. He knew the ins and outs of Thompson County's land records and the record-keeping process. He also knew the current Register of Deeds and thought about how he could get her to allow him access to records that may have to be altered again. "Too late for that," a voice seemed to be reverberating around him. Madden's concern was that whoever wrote the letter and compiled the listings may have already made copies of documents that incriminated him. He looked at the attachments again and felt certain that was the case. For many years, Dent Madden was the man to know in Thompson County because he knew more about real estate transactions than anyone else there, and he knew more about the history of transactions. If there was a problem of almost any type, the locals' favorite expression was, "Get Dent Madden to work the issue for you." For those well connected, that was a code for, "If you pay him the right kind of money or give him a piece of the action, he'll fix it for you." Madden had become adept at working with attorneys to create documents and paper trails that appeared to be legal. Madden was a Thompson County employee, but he used his office as a private enterprise to help himself and his relatives and friends. Once as Director of the Farm Stabilization Program and then as Clerk of Court, he rigged his offices and the Register of Deeds Office against the very people they were established to help and to protect. As Director of the Farm Stabilization Program, he decided how many acres of various crops could be planted and who would plant them. Often sensing an opportunity to capitalize on someone's lack of understanding how the system worked, Madden would encourage them to lease their land to one of his friends or associates, or to allow them to plant their crop allotment. A deed would be prepared, transferring to the friends or associates the leased land or the acreage for the crop allotment. When the lease period or planting was over, often the land was not deeded back to the rightful owner. As Clerk of Court, Madden interpreted and applied laws, and implemented policies and procedures to benefit himself and his associates and friends. Whatever he said became the law, and he was in a position to enforce it or to have colleagues legitimize it and enforce it for him. Madden had done that for many years without any latent feelings of remorse and shame.

When Mac Mc Lauren got home that evening, he called J. P. Sellers and told him about the latest packet of information he received that day. "Holy Crap-po-ly!" J. P. exclaimed. "Do you know who sent it?" he asked franticly. "Where was it mailed from?" he continued without giving Mac Lauren time to answer the first question. Before Mac Lauren could answer, he asked, "Whose names are on the list?" With a tone of exhaustion from all of J. P.'s questions, Lauren said, "It's a list of Who's Who in Thompson County," and randomly called off names and emphasized the name James Preston Sellers. "This thing's gonna explode, Mac," J. P. said worriedly.

"I believe it has already. We just haven't heard it or felt it yet," Mc

Lauren replied sardonically. "I wonder who else got it?" J. P. inquired, worried even more after Mc Lauren's comment.

"You can bet Bob Stanton and Gordon Clark got it, but those bastards are as tight-lipped as sour grapes and green lemons will make you pucker up," Mc Lauren ranted. "You think Wilcox'll tell you if he got a packet?" he asked.

"I can feel him out, if I can get a few minutes with him," J. P. responded.

"I'll bet that federal judge got a packet, too," Mc Lauren added with a sense of frustration.

"If he did, the Feds are going to be swarming all over the place pretty soon," J. P. said. "Pretty much like a pack of hyenas after a wounded animal," he added after a moment of reflection. It was difficult to tell if J. P. was aware of the symbolism of what he just stated or the analogy he just used. But, it was clear that he was grasping the severity of what was about to happen.

"Yeah. They're probably already here."

J. P. said to himself, "The Feds could already be in Thompson County." A look of desperation flashed across his face and suddenly he was anxious to hang up the phone. "Let me see what I can find out, Mac, and get back to you tomorrow evening," he said. He sat for a few moments looking at the phone as though he was expecting it to do or say something. J. P. eventually left his house and went to the Meadows Square Shopping Mall, taking a circuitous and indirect route. He backtracked several times, crossing several streets and roads he had just traveled moments before. He entered the main entrance looking around and admiring one of the projects in which he was a partner and of which he was most proud. Comprising more than 950,000 square feet of retail space and 1,500 parking spaces on 75 acres of land, it was also one of the most profitable of the projects in which he had been involved. Besides, the Mall, along with the project's 75-acre office complex that followed immediately, had helped to transform Thompson County, along with four counties that adjoined Thompson, providing employment for some residents and the only form of entertainment for many more.

Arrayed adjacent to or parallel to four large anchor stores were several fashionable boutiques and high-end shops, occasionally interrupted by a spat of low-end kiosks offering anything from jewelry to sunglasses, and banners to tee-shirts. The entertainment center was always busy, catering to anyone who was drawn into its clutches. Electronic games barked, whistled and twirled, inviting the curious and the gullible to drop a mere quarter into their innocent slots and challenge a dumb machine to have a little fun. After sucking in and devouring quarters as soon as they were dropped and thrashing the challenger, the game machines repeated their invitation to have fun. J. P. always marveled, during his infrequent visits to the Mall, at how simple it was to get people to part with their coins. And, he delighted in seeing shoppers gorging themselves at the Food Court. All of it meant money for J. P. and his partners, "easy money" they often said among themselves, praising themselves on their business acumen and ability to seize on an opportunity that was there for the taking.

How the 150-acres of land was acquired involuntarily entered J. P.'s mind, though he wished that it hadn't; and it interfered with his memories of the Mall's grand opening. He chuckled at the festive nature of the occasion, and the secrets that were precursors to the event. He could still see the stone, cold faces of people he knew were somehow involved in making it all happen; but, he never understood, nor did he really care, what role they played. He had his suspicions, but he never voiced nor entertained them. He reasoned that there were some things he was better off not knowing. "City Fathers; Pillars of the Community," he whispered to himself, "and they are bigger crooks than me." He chuckled, but this time said aloud, "Lawyers, elected officials, judges, county employees, business men; a regular rogues gallery." That, apparently, was humorous to him, as he repeated the words, "a regular rogues gallery." He liked the way it sounded, and repeated it several more times. Then he became serious when the words Jake Fuller hurled at him and Chad Pollard many years earlier began screaming at him again, "You're all nothing but a bunch of crooks." He tried to silence them by repeating what Judge Wilcox had said to justify and rationalize what had happened: "Each piece would be too small for each one of them to do anything significant with it anyway. Getting all of it in the hands of a few people serves a higher purpose," he pontificated as though he was the ultimate authority on such matters and his pronouncements were sacrosanct.

J. P. walked, looked and thought. He thought about all the events that had transpired during the past few months. He thought about how close somebody was coming to exposing what had been happening with land in Thompson County. He thought that maybe Mac Mc Lauren was right and the Feds were already in Thompson County and, in fact, were watching him. He turned around periodically to see if he could observe anyone watching him. Off in the distance, ensconced between two kiosks, he observed three men standing, talking and, apparently, looking toward him. J. P. was certain that one of the men was Frank Wilcox. One of them appeared to be Dent Madden. J. P. wasn't certain that he had ever seen the other man, but he was more than certain that he didn't like his appearance. He maneuvered himself closer to the trio to get a closer look. One man was Madden, but the other man was unknown to J. P. "I wonder if he's from the Feds," he asked himself. "What are those guys up to?" he questioned. "Why are they here?" he wondered.

The three men turned and walked away as J. P. was deciding if he would join in their discussion. He followed them, staying far enough back for them not to detect him, but close enough to be sure they would not get out of his sight. The three men headed toward the center of the mall where a large waterfall and a wishing well rested comfortably under the domed ceiling.

35

ontrary to his initial impulse, Dent Madden called Mac Mc Lauren after receiving his packet containing the letter and lists, and chided Mc Lauren about not contacting him after he received his letter several months earlier. "You know how it is, Dent. I'm in one helluva predicament as Head of Ethics," he said in a manner he thought would evoke some sympathy. "I hope you can understand that," he added apologetically.

Without allowing Madden an opportunity to accept his attempted offer of forgiveness, Mc Lauren shifted the discussion away from himself. "Why don't you get together with Frank Wilcox and let him know I believe the State is about to shake up some things down there," he unintentionally demanded. "What do you think is going on?" Madden demanded to know.

"Whatever it is, it can't be too good for any of us," Mc Lauren said with a heavy note of fear and a tinge of fatalism in his voice.

Wilcox was one of the silent partners in the Thompson County Meadows Square Shopping Mall Project and had been instrumental in helping them to get the land issue resolved for the mall and to bring the project to fruition. For his "legal" help, Wilcox was rewarded with a 10% stake in the project. Only Mac Mc Lauren and a few others knew that.

Dent Madden, as he was instructed, told Judge Wilcox that Mc Lauren believed the State Atty. General and the State Bureau of Investigations were investigating the allegations made in the letter, although he had no proof they ever received it. He assumed that they had also received the mid-sized, brown envelope containing the same information he and Madden had received. Mc Lauren could do nothing at the moment because he believed he was being watched. He suggested that Madden, as the former county land attorney, and Wilcox, a smart judge, get together and determine what had to be done to thwart any investigation and, if possible, to clear up any loose ends that might incriminate them. Mc Lauren had no knowledge or proof of an investigation in progress, but his instincts told him something was in the works. Things were too quiet. J. P. Sellers was also a partner in the project, with just a fraction of a percentage stake. Judge Wilcox recommended to his brother Sheldon that they include J. P. in order to help ensure his silence. He had to invest several thousand dollars of his own money. However, they did not need his money and they did not need him at this point. He had served their purpose well, but now they needed him where they could watch him. Judge Wilcox had surmised that if J. P. earned a few thousand dollars a year without doing anything to for it, he would gladly accept it and be quiet. Judge Wilcox was right.

Immediately after the Fuller estate land was transferred to the Z & W Real Estate Investment Trust, the land was being prepared to build the shopping mall. Jake Fuller, more certain than ever, knew that he was targeted by J. P. and Chad Pollard to steal their estate. He also knew he had been duped into a scheme that forced selling the land far below its true value. Therefore, he filed a lawsuit against J. P., Pollard and Z & W charging fraud. Jake Fuller did not prevail because Judge Frank Wilcox ensured that he didn't. Judge Wilcox also refused to issue an injunction delaying the construction of the mall, as Jake Fuller's attorney had requested. The attorney Jake Fuller had hired from more than a hundred miles away did not understand how things were done in Thompson County and he didn't know enough to ask. Jake Fuller issued several threats for J. P., Pollard and Wilcox. He also threatened to appeal Wilcox's decision to the State District Court and to the State Supreme Court if that was necessary. Two weeks later Jake Fuller disappeared and was never heard from again. It was rumored that he drowned while fishing from his boat in the Allen River, which runs through Thompson County. Only his boat was never found.

From time to time, Madden and Wilcox, representing the investors, had to resort to outside assistance to help them achieve their objectives.

They always used a go-between to arrange to take care of problems they could not take care of themselves. Those problems were rare. They never knew who provided the assistance and how it was provided, and they didn't want to know. It was simple. They stated their problem, the go-between stated the price. Half of the investment up front, and the other half after the problem was eliminated. Everybody was happy. Nobody ever talked about it, but everybody speculated about what happened. Madden and Wilcox had to meet with the go-between again, and they had to meet with him immediately. The Thompson County Meadows Square Shopping Mall was the most convenient location for each of them on such short notice. They thought it was a safe place to meet because it was a very busy place. Three well dressed, middle-aged men walking casually and stopping occasionally to look around them would raise no suspicion, they believed. They had not noticed J. P. Sellers watching them from afar and following them and trying to determine the nature of their assemblage. They finished their negotiating and left the mall separately.

J. P. thought perhaps the third man was from the Feds, and Madden and Wilcox were trying to strike a deal for themselves. But, he was wrong.

36

Three days after mailing her last packets, Kaye Webster received a call from Norman Winfield. "Ms. Webster, I think I got some good news for you," he said jubilantly, allowing no time for the usual chitchat. "I could use some right about now," she replied and waited anxiously for his response.

"Well, I think we finally got them to give up completely on that land issue involving your cousin John," he said with obvious delight.

"Oh, yeah. What's going on?" Kaye asked.

"Well, I got a call from Bennett Zorn's attorney. They're going to set aside the judgment and refund all of his money, instead of just the $5,000 they offered initially," he reported enthusiastically.

"That's mighty great of them," she said contemptuously, as she rolled her eyes toward the ceiling. "But, what about the interest on all the money John paid Zorn and his old man over the years?" she asked in a calculating manner. "Does he get that, too?" she quickly added to make sure there was no mistaking her sincerity. Winfield was speechless momentarily. "I don't believe this," he was saying to himself. They had not discussed it and Winfield had not negotiated it with Bennett Zorn and Chad Pollard, but he was embarrassed to say it. He finally said, "We didn't talk about it specifically, but since they've come this far, I don't see it as an issue."

"Let's be sure it's not an issue," she said, "so we can close this thing out. It's not an issue for me, so I'm sure they don't want to make it an issue," she said with a hint of derision. With a sound of exasperation, Winfield said, "I'll get back to you. I believe those boys are ready to move on."

Kaye knew that Madden, Wilcox, Zorn and the rest of the gang were ready to move on, but she wasn't. She had ensured that her cousin John would get the judgment against his land set aside and that he would also get his money refunded. Now, she wanted to expose the breadth and depth of the land issues in Thompson County. Her sense of justice, of what was right and fair, would let her do no less. Kaye called John and told him the news.

"I don't believe it, Cuz," he said.

"I told you we would. They'll come up with the interest, too," she assured him.

"We'll have to celebrate when this whole mess is over," he offered.

"That sounds good to me," she said, knowing that it would probably be months, if not years, before the whole mess was over. Zorn had gotten a little too greedy, and his greed helped to expose the greed of all the others. Kaye still could not tell John what she was doing, but she knew that getting John's land issue resolved was just the beginning. Kaye decided to spend her lunch hour surfing the Internet searching for and collecting additional facts that helped her to continue putting the Thompson County land issue into a broader historical context. She found the following facts interesting but not surprising:

- The Georgia legislature, in 1795, enacted a law selling 35 million acres of its western land, comprising the present states of Alabama and Mississippi, to four land companies for $500,000. The sale was considered corrupt because nearly all of the Georgia legislators who voted for the law had been bribed by agents of the land company. Known as the Yazoo Fraud, a year later a new legislature repealed the law denying the sale of the 35 million acres to the speculators.

- Between 1850 and 1871, operators of railroads got 176 millions acres of public land from the U.S. Government, free of charge, and millions of dollars in loans from state legislatures. Many of the railroad executives went to the Federal and to state capitals with free railroad passes, money and shares of stock to get favorable decisions.

- In 1850, when the proposed railroad scheme for Illinois was made intersectional by a plan to extend to the Gulf of Mexico, Congress gave Illinois, Mississippi, and Alabama a right-of-way through the public lands for a distance of six miles on both sides of the road, amounting to 3,840 acres for each mile of railroad.

Kaye had always wondered how some people had acquired huge tracts of land and others had difficulty acquiring and retaining small parcels. The more she educated herself, the more sense it made to her. When land was not acquired legally, it was taken illegally. Those in power and control found ways to make it appear that illegal land acquisitions were legal. "It has always been about land because land has always meant wealth; and wealth has always meant power and control," she said to herself. "That also means economic freedom." She wondered how the gross, unearned economic gains affected their consciences. After some reflections, she thought maybe they were conscienceless. Then, she mumbled to herself, "Everybody got in on the act back then, and they're still doing it today." She sat in a state of disbelief, as though she was consumed by the anger that was welling up inside her. She realized she was hungry, but could not bring herself to get anything to eat. She also sensed that she was very tired, mentally drained and fatigued, but could not find the strength to enjoy a moment's rest. She was a bundle of contradictions at that moment, and felt all powerful and powerless at the same time.

Kaye was snapped from her near catatonic state by the sudden and continuous ringing of her telephone. She looked at it momentary, deciding whether to let it continue ringing or to answer. Expressing her irritation at it, she answered uncharacteristically, "Yes, may I help you?"

"Is this Ms. Webster?" asked the voice reluctantly on the other end.

"Yes, this is Kaye Webster."

"Did I catch you at a bad time?" asked the familiar voice.

"Oh, no! I was just in deep thought."

"Great!" answered the man. "This is Norm Winfield," he said. "I have something else for you to think about" he said jubilantly.

Oh, yeah! What's that?" she asked.

"I just got a call from Zorn's attorney. They are going to give Mr. Wilkinson interest on the money he paid them."

"I bet they will," she said facetiously. "I told you they would," she added with a tone of anger in her voice.

Winfield wasn't exactly sure what to say to Kaye. He could sense that she wasn't completely pleased with the news he had just relayed to her, but he wasn't sure why. There was an uneasy silence between them for a few moments, with Winfield thinking about all that had happened since he took her case, and Kaye thinking about all the things she had to do before declaring victory. Winfield broke the silence by saying, "We should have the money from them within a couple of days. Why don't you and your cousin call and arrange to come by to close out this matter."

"Okay, we'll do that," she answered with a lack of enthusiasm. Kaye Webster hung up the phone with a feeling of emptiness. In spite of her unrelenting battle with Zorn and Pollard, she was expecting and wanting it to last longer. In fact, she was hoping that they would not give in so easily and so soon. She was sensing that the fight was too easy and did not allow her to expose and defeat them the way she wanted to and needed to. She was disappointed. She had initiated other actions that she knew would raise the stakes, but she didn't know how their caving in now would affect how she wanted things to play out. Her initial impulse was to write another letter and spell out in more detail how the pious and upstanding citizens of Thompson County, and specifically Sawyer Village, were robbing the poor, unsuspecting people of their land. She even thought of writing a letter to the editor, but abandoned that idea after speculating that the owners of the newspapers probably lived in Sawyer Village also, and had connections to those who controlled the economic and social life of the county. She ultimately decided to wait it out to see what the next few days would bring.

37

The same day State Attorney General Gordon Clark received the mid-sized, brown envelope, he called Matthew Crenshaw, soliciting his help on a very confidential matter in Thompson County. "How's life treating you these days?" Clark asked. "It's been a long time," he continued with an easy familiarity and without giving Crenshaw a chance to answer the first question.

"Yeah, it has been a long time; but I'm doing great," Crenshaw replied with a slight lift in his voice. A reflective smile seemed to dance across his face and his eyes seemed to focus on a fleeting thought that either was running somewhere in the distance far beyond him, or trying to escape from somewhere in the depths of his mind. Clark informed Crenshaw that the discussion they were about to have could not be discussed with the Thompson County District Attorney. Crenshaw assured him that he would keep their discussion in strict confidence. "You know how that is. Sometimes we have to go after our own kind," Clark declared regretfully.

"Well, if we deserve it, then so be it," Crenshaw said with an uneasiness in his voice. Clark started calling out names to Crenshaw and wanted to know if he had any knowledge of the people he just named or if he had any first-hand knowledge about their involvement in real estate. "Yes, I know all of them or almost all of them," Crenshaw answered, wondering where the conversation was leading.

"What do you know about them?," Clark wanted to know.

"I know virtually nothing about them personally. But, they are attorneys, commissioners, judges, and the general, run-of-the-mill power brokers here in Thompson County," Crenshaw said with sarcasm.

Crenshaw thought for a few minutes and said, "That's not much." Then he added thoughtfully, "No, I have no first-hand knowledge of any of that." Crenshaw was careful to emphasize "first-hand." He had plenty of second-hand knowledge and a lot of idle speculations that found their way to him. "Were you involved with any real estate issues during your time in private practice, that involved any of these people?" Clark wanted to know. "No, that wasn't my forte," he replied. "Most of my work was criminal defense, and a little domestic stuff every now and then." "We've been told that you're a guy we can trust in Thompson County, somebody we can go to and who will point us in the right direction." Clark emphasized the word *right*. Crenshaw knew exactly what he meant.

Crenshaw was wondering how that would involve him. Almost as if he were reading Crenshaw's mind, Clark added, "We just need you to confirm a few things for us; you know, the usual stuff: identify a few people, tell us about the lay of the land; that sorta thing."

"That shouldn't be a problem," Crenshaw said with growing confidence and curiosity. "I'll do whatever I can to assist," he added. Being unable to contain his curiosity any longer, Crenshaw asked, "What's going on?"

"We got a packet of information today giving us what I believe is everything we need to do some serious damage to some "run-of-the-mill power brokers in Thompson County," Clark said mimicking Crenshaw.

"Gotta be some powerful stuff," Crenshaw said with a tone of concern.

"We still don't know where the information is coming from, but this time, I think we got the mother lode. This stuff is laid out so well that a blind person probably couldn't miss it. There've gotta be a lot of people trembling in their boots over there right about now, if they got a copy of this stuff," Clark offered with obvious glee.

"Where does it go from here?" Crenshaw wanted to know.

"We still need to get somebody out there to confirm what we believe we already know," he responded. "If this information is anything like the letter we got, everything we need is right in our laps. We just have to check it. After that, fireworks," Clark predicted. "It's about time," Crenshaw said to himself as he envisioned the looks on some of the faces he had seen many times before. Kind, smiling faces that concealed dirty deeds and evil acts. "What kind of time-line are you talking about?" Crenshaw asked.

"We're not sure yet. We're going to get a special agent over there in a day or two. Are you going to be around?" he asked Crenshaw.

"Yeah, I should be," he replied.

"Expect a call from one of the Bureau's agents who'll need a few minutes with you to get a run down on some of the people. This has to be done away from the job," Clark instructed.

"Sure, no problem," Crenshaw replied. "I'll do whatever I can," he assured Clark.

"Well, we may have to set up a special operations unit down there to uncover what we need to know.

Matthew Crenshaw had not received another call from his old friend Federal Judge Enos Elliston, but he could not tell Clark that he and Judge Elliston had a similar discussion just a few days earlier. That both men would call him concerning what apparently was the same matter was comforting and disturbing at the same time. It unquestionably was a serious matter, but he didn't like the idea that the outcome, to some degree, hinged on him and what he might have to say. He had deduced quite some time ago what he believe was going on, but he wasn't sure he could pass it on as factual information that could withstand a legal challenge. However, the mere thought of it was intriguing. Clark hung up from his discussion with Crenshaw and immediately called Stanton about getting agents from his STF--TC2 detailed to Thompson County to spend some time with Matthew Crenshaw and in the Register of Deeds Office. Clark and Stanton discussed the plan, agreed on it, and congratulated themselves on their mutual cooperation. Stanton informed Clark that the person assigned to the task was Rebecca Burke, the special agent who had confirmed the information outlined in the letter. She was familiar with the area; she had already done research in the

Register of Deeds office; and she would fit right in. Crenshaw quickly became aware of some of the land issues in Thompson County shortly after moving there, but he purposely refrained from getting involved with them when he had his own practice. Land was not his specialty, and he knew that if he had taken on any land cases, he would have been shut out of Thompson County legal and social circles completely.

Crenshaw was the resource Clark had mentioned to Stanton. Before Clark became State Atty. General, he and Crenshaw were opposing attorneys on a minor case involving a child custody battle. Crenshaw won the case because of his greater intellect and better preparedness than Clark. Clark never forgot that loss and he never forgot Matthew Crenshaw, either.

Matthew Crenshaw left his office after talking with Gordon Clark and casually strolled along several streets crossing Main Street. Although he had worked in Humphries and Thompson County for many years and had walked along many of the same streets before, he had never seen them the way he now saw them. There was a new awareness that had engulfed him. It felt that all of his senses loosed themselves from him and behaved as they pleased. His nostrils snagged a variety of aromas as they bounced through the air. The gentle, warm breezes danced about and tugged at his swarthy flesh and at his neat clothing. His eyes saw things they had never seen before and they got him to understand: Antebellum houses perched high on hills overlooking the courthouse below, as if they were saying, "We're above the law." Black, wrought iron fences stately surrounding large plots of land, keeping out the light and holding in the darkness. Streets lined with trees that stretched out their branches to touch each other--what stories could they tell! Crenshaw's lunch hour was over, but his reawakening had just begun. He returned to his office feeling that his challenge that "somebody take on the land issue in Thompson County as a cause," finally, was going to become a reality. He wanted to know how it was; yet, he didn't want to know. During his walk, he had resolved in his own mind the need to be as helpful as he could without making a personal sacrifice. He would tell the Bureau's agents not only what he knew as facts but also what he speculated, as long as he was not identified as the source of the information. He recognized the appearance of cowardice in his position but he justified it in his own mind. He finished out his long workday, hoping to hear from the agent scheduled to come to Thompson County to investigate. He tried to pretend that it was business as usual. But, he had an unexplained feeling that it would never again be business as usual in Humphries, in Sawyer Village or in Thompson County.

🌿 38 🌿

The day after Gordon Clark and Robert Stanton discussed their plan, Special Agent Rebecca Burke was in the Thompson County Register of Deeds Office as soon as it opened. This time, she had been thoroughly briefed on the nature of the issues involving land in Thompson County and was prepared to focus her visit on confirming specific information. She opened a folder that she had secured under her arms and pulled out the listing of information Stanton had given her, information he received anonymously but graciously, information that pointed her in the exact direction she needed to go to confirm all the anonymous informant had alluded to in her letters and packet of information. Using the "BOOK/PAGE#" references on the lists Stanton provided, she located and copied the information. This activity consumed most of the morning. Burke walked into the Thompson County Tax Office during the lunch hour and sat down at the same computer terminal she had used before. She was greeted with the usual hellos and smiles as she typed in a few instructions and accessed the main server for all Thompson County and began her search. Using the alphabetical listing she had been provided, Burke located and printed out a listing of real estate owned by all the individuals identified. She was so delighted with the ease she had obtaining all of the information she needed from both offices that she decided to expand her search to include a list of businesses in Thompson County. She discovered that many of the businesses were owned by some of the same individuals on the alphabetical listing. Their names did not appear on the businesses but they were listed as "Owner of Record" or "Doing Business As." Burke then decided to determine if the system contained a listing of all the individuals who had been issued business or privilege licenses in and around Humphries, Sawyer Village and Thompson County. She found a file containing the listing and printed out a copy of that also. She did not know of any immediate use for the listing, but she felt that it might have some future value. And it did.

Using a fax machine near the copier, Burke immediately faxed to the other special agent on STF--TC2 lists containing the tax information and the names of the individuals who had been issued business licenses. The agent checked the names against individuals listed on incorporation and partnership papers filed with the Secretary of State, and found that some names appeared on all three lists. Of the various connections the agent made among many of the individuals, the one suggested for further investigation was Z & W Real Estate Investment Trust that was formed to purchase the land on which to develop Thompson County Meadows Square Shopping Mall. The land was later sold to the Fox Valley Partnership for actually developing the mall and surrounding office complexes.

Armed with a list of the partners in the Z & W REIT, Rebecca Burke spent the next two days developing intelligence on the activities and movements on several of the individuals, including Dent Madden, J. P. Sellers and Frank Wilcox. The friendly people of Sawyer Village were eager to point out Madden, Seller, Wilcox, or any of the others to Burke. And, they were just as eager to tell her where they probably could be found. In addition to developing patterns of movement on some of the partners, she also located some of the properties the letter referenced and for which she was able to find deeds. The properties included car washes, convenience stores, houses, office buildings, public storage units, strip malls and warehouses, all owned at one time or another by Thompson County's most prominent citizens. It confirmed the information the anonymous packet of materials contained.

Agent Burke then set out to develop additional intelligence on several of the partners. She contacted one possible source that was passed on to her by Gordon Clark. "Mr. Matthew Crenshaw?" the person asked hesitantly.

"Yes, this is Matthew Crenshaw," he replied.

"My name is Rebecca Burke. I think you've been expecting a call from me," the person said.

Crenshaw thought for a few moments, then, after a prolonged silence, asked, "And who are you?"

"I think Mr. Gordon Clark told you to expect a call from me," she said quietly. "Oh, yes." He whispered as he casually looked round about him. "I've been in Thompson County for a few days and have developed some preliminary information that I think you might be able to help me get a clearer picture on," she said.

"I'll do what I can," he responded without giving her any assurance that he could or couldn't.

"Is there any place we could meet this evening to go over a few things?" she asked in a way that suggested she was instructing him

"This evening really wouldn't be good for me," he said apologetically.

"I realize this is short notice, Mr. Crenshaw," she said. "And, I do understand about prior commitments," she said, then quickly added, "Give me a time and a place that would work for you."

Crenshaw thought to himself that she should use a better approach for them to establish a relationship, especially since she was intruding on his time, and suggested that they meet at *Mamma's Dining Room* the following morning as soon as it opened. They would have a chance to talk before the heavy morning traffic. The food is good, he assured her and, besides, they could talk and have a great country breakfast in privacy at the same time.

"Sounds like a winner to me," she said with resignation, and feeling a little less in control than she thought she should be.

"Look for the most handsome guy in the place," Crenshaw said jokingly, then quickly added, "I'll be wearing...Let's see...tomorrow's Wednesday, so I'll be wearing a dark blue suit with a green tie." He laughed out loud and said, "Just kidding, the tie will be red. I'll be wearing horn-rimmed glasses and sitting in the very back of the restaurant, facing the door and reading a paper; and I'll be nursing a cup of coffee, if you get there five minutes after the place opens."

"You'll know me when you see me," Special Agent Burke said in a way that conveyed her displeasure with his attempt at humor, and hung up the phone without describing herself.

Matthew Crenshaw was unperturbed by her curtness, but imagined what she looked like. He also contemplated the kinds of questions Special Agent Burke would ask him and how he would or should answer them. He knew more about the land issues in Thompson County than he wanted to know, but he wasn't sure he wanted the information to come directly from himself. He had often said somebody should take on the land issues as a cause, but he wasn't thinking of himself. He tried to appear as normal as he could, but he was anxious and jittery the remainder of the day. After working late into the evening, he left for home feeling a strange kind of excitement coursing through his body and a kind of mental exhaustion that always seemed to energize him.

During her background work, Special Agent Burke learned that The Belmont Club was a favorite gathering place for many of the individuals whose names appeared on the lists. Therefore, since she couldn't meet with Crenshaw, she decided to pay The Club a visit on the ruse that she was considering taking a job in the area and was checking out all the things the town had to offer. Several people had recommended The Club to her, and she wanted a feel for its amenities and the environment, and to understand its allure to the well connected in Thompson and Sawyer Village. As she drove up the driveway, stopped at the valet stand and stated the purpose of her visit, she got a sample of the attraction. She was escorted from the valet stand to the host's stand where she identified herself as Gabrielle Worthington. She knew that name to be one of respectability, and would grant her instant access to confidential information and gratuitous largess without the bother of having to earn it. The club manager was summoned to personally welcome her and to give her the grand tour. He talked at length about the social advantages and connections membership in The Club would have for her, and told her how to apply for it. He repeated several times that he was more than confident that several members would sponsor her. There would be little doubt about her membership application being accepted, she was assured, because The Club was actively looking for female members. The manager also introduced her to some of the members who were there, including Dent Madden and J. P. Sellers, who were slouched down in huge armchairs in the rear corner of the parlor, their favorite resting area, deep in conversation and nursing their cocktails. Burke knew who Madden and J. P. were because they had been pointed out to her earlier during the day. Madden acknowledged her presence and smiled at her skeptically. J. P. smiled at her and winked, thinking to himself that he was having a much better time at The Belmont Club than the last time he was there, and having his feelings confirmed by the presence of someone so obviously cultured and graceful as Gabrielle Worthington. As the manager continued introducing Burke to other club members, Madden closely followed her movement around the large sitting room. He was sure he had met her somewhere before, but he wasn't sure where. There was something about her that he didn't like, but he wasn't sure what it was. For some unexplained reason, he just didn't trust her. J. P., on the other hand, was captivated by her beauty and her charm, and looked at her longingly as she moved easily about, smiling, nodding and sensually cocking her head and throwing her hair. His preoccupation with his looming concerns quickly vanished as she looked at him coyly and moved with poise and grace throughout The Club. Special Agent Rebecca Burke also charmed the manager and members as she sashayed throughout The Belmont Club, discreetly observing those who gawked at her. Although she added beauty and vibrancy to the otherwise drab and sterile environment, the attitudes and behaviors she had adopted for such occasions were completely uncharacteristic of her. However, she always had fun playing the role, and she had become adept at playing it easily and convincingly. In the midst of her performance, Special Agent Rebecca Burke was gathering information and developing her plan to get to the root of the land issues in Thompson County.

Matthew Crenshaw intentionally arrived at *Mamma's Dining Room* several minutes before it opened for business. He carefully backed his car to the back edge of the parking lot, although the lot was essentially empty, so that he could see who came and went from that position. He looked at his watch as a nondescript car soon afterwards came slowly up the narrow driveway and stopped momentarily before proceeding into the wide expanse of the parking lot. He determined it was Special Agent Rebecca Burke and watched her as she came slowly toward him, then turned sharply to park near the entrance. Shortly afterwards, the exterior lights on the sides of the backdoor to the restaurant came on. The door was opened momentarily; then it was closed, indicating to the early arrivers that Mamma Sylvia was ready to serve them. Crenshaw slowly got out of his car and quickly walked across the parking lot, stealthily passed Burke as she sat in her car applying make-up to her face. He entered, hoping that nobody, including Agent Burke, had seen him. He went to his usual table in the back, sat and nervously waited. Moments later, a well-dressed woman with brunette hair and unblemished skin walked in with a briefcase and went directly to the table where Crenshaw sat with a look of anxiety, as well as anticipation. Mamma Sylvia watched her from the moment she entered and said to herself, "An irregular," and went about her chores as she continued to watch with an unobtrusive interest as Special Agent Burke moved purposefully toward Crenshaw.

Agent Burke introduced herself with a curt, "I'm Agent Burke," without extending her hand, and sat down while pulling her briefcase onto the table. "I'll make this as brief as I can," she said, as she, in one continuous motion, opened the briefcase and pulled out a folder. Crenshaw deduced from this, along with her appearance and reactions from the day before, that she was strictly about business.

She opened the folder, scanned down a list and asked Crenshaw, "What can you tell me about Bennett Zorn?" "Can't tell you anything specific about him, but I believe his old man Anders Zorn was pretty big in real estate before he died. It was well-known throughout the county that you could always get a loan from him even when the bank wouldn't let you have one," Crenshaw told her, and was taken aback by her intensity and no-nonsense approach, and apparent disdain for idle chatter and small-talk..

"I bet you could," Burke replied.

Crenshaw was not surprised by the comment because he was aware of rumors about how Anders Zorn had operated. Crenshaw was confident that Burke also knew what Zorn had done and wanted him to help her to confirm it. He then thought about the legal representation a woman was asking for on a land issue involving Anders Zorn and his son Bennett.

Mamma Sylvia yelled to Crenshaw and asked if he wanted the usual, and what did his friend want.

"Yeah, the usual Ms. Sylvia," he said, and asked Burke, "What are you having?" "Nothing for me," she assured him as she watched him carefully and panned her eyes about the restaurant at the same time. She quickly added, "I only have a few minutes and I have another stop to make before things get too busy. Thanks anyway," she said with a forced smile.

"I understand," Crenshaw said, looking past her toward the door. He was relieved that she didn't have much time to spend with him, because he preferred not being seen with her.

"Have you ever had any dealings with Dent Madden?" was her next question without hesitation.

"No direct dealings," Crenshaw said truthfully.

"What about indirect dealings?" Burke asked with a looked that said Crenshaw was withholding information.

"I remember being in court one day waiting for a case to be tried and heard some of the facts in a case involving Madden and some partnership he headed up."

"Do you remember what the case was about?" Special Agent Burke asked.

"It involved a dispute about some land. Something about an estate and some fellow named Fuller, I think," he said noncommittally.

"What was your assessment of the facts?"

"From what I heard, the plaintiff should have gotten a favorable ruling."

"You mean he didn't?" she asked.

"No, in my judgment, he didn't."

"Who was the judge that heard the case?"

Crenshaw hesitated a few moments and finally said, "Judge Frank

Wilcox."

"Do you recall who represented Madden?" she asked while looking directly at him without blinking.

"I think it was a fellow named Mac Mc Lauren," Crenshaw told her hesitantly.

"You mean Heywood Mc Lauren, who is now Head of the State Board of Ethics?" she asked.

"Yeah, that's the same Mac Mc Lauren," Crenshaw said emphatically.

"What can you tell me about Frank Wilcox?" Burke asked because she thought Crenshaw knew a lot more than he was saying. He picked up on the open-ended nature of her question, thought about it for a few seconds and quickly asked, "What specifically do you want to know?" "Oh, I didn't know if you had any information that might be useful for Atty. General Gordon Clark," she name-dropped, hoping to get Crenshaw to share more.

"What can I say? He's the judge. I don't always agree with him. And, if I don't, I can always appeal his decisions," he said, sensing that he had to give her something for the subtle pressure she was trying to put on him "Do you know a guy named James Sellers?" Burke asked.

"You mean J. P.," Crenshaw said with a chuckle. "Yeah, I know who he is."

Special Agent Burke gave him a look of disbelief. "Really!" he said. He's a small-time real estate broker who suddenly made it big in Thompson County. He, Madden, Wilcox and some of the others I understand run in the same circles."

"Yeah, I've determined that already," Burke volunteered.

"They're all out of my league, that's for sure," he said sarcastically.

Special Agent Rebecca Burke wanted to know whatever information Crenshaw could provide her about some of the county commissioners and developers and their involvement with some of the land issues in Thompson County. He stated emphatically that he could provide none because he had not practiced law as a private attorney for many years and had no first-hand information. His job now as an assistant district attorney limited him to certain kinds of cases. "Mostly criminal cases," he said with pride, that suddenly faded from his expression, as he thought about what the land issues entailed.

He then added that there are always rumors about unfair and fraudulent land deals being made, but he had no knowledge of any of them. Agent Burke was sure that Crenshaw had more to tell, but that he was astute enough to tell her as little as he could and protect himself while also trying to be cooperative with her and the State in the investigation. When his breakfast was served, she thanked him for his help, gathered up all materials and left just as quickly as she came. Burke had everything she needed from Thompson County and was on her way back to provide detailed information to Robert Stanton and Gordon Clark.

Crenshaw finished eating his breakfast and sat quietly at his table, characteristically holding a cup to his mouth with both hands. He thought about what he had told her and how much more he could have told. He felt sure, though, that the land issues in Thompson County would finally be resolved. As Crenshaw got up from his table, Kaye Webster walked in. She nodded in his direction as she walked confidently toward the table where she usually sat. Crenshaw was surer than ever before that she was the person behind the letters and the other information that were mailed anonymously. He was delighted with her for her bravery and risk-taking, and he was disappointed with himself for his caution.

Kaye wanted to thank Crenshaw for recommending Atty. Norman Winfield to her because he was able to resolve the land issue to her satisfaction. Before she could get his attention, he was on his way out the door. She always got the feeling that he was afraid of her. Kaye was rather certain that details of the land issues in Thompson County would explode soon; she just didn't know when or how. She took some comfort in knowing that she was a catalyst for getting some action; but she took more comfort in knowing that few, if any, people would know the role she had played. She sat quietly, ate her breakfast and tried to play out various scenarios in her head.

39

"Mac, I tell'ya, something's going on down here," J. P. declared.

"How do'ya know that, J. P.?" Mc Lauren asked.

"Madden and Wilcox were with this fellow in the mall the other night, but Wilcox swears that he wasn't there."

"Are you sure?" Mc Lauren asked.

"Hell, yeah, I'm sure. I was there and I saw'em with my own eyes," J. P. responded with anger.

"Maybe he forgot about it."

"Not after a couple of days, he didn't," J. P. said with indignation. "Besides, we had only one cocktail; so he can't blame his loss of memory on that."

J. P. Sellers called Mac Mc Lauren to express his concern that Madden and Wilcox were shutting him out of something involving the mall. J. P. also wanted to know if Madden or Wilcox had called Mc Lauren with any information. He believed he and Mc Lauren had a right to know everything involving the mall because they all were partners in the Fox Valley Partnership, which was organized to purchase the land from Z & W Real Estate Investment Trust and to develop the 150 acres of land from the Fuller estate. It was unusual for Madden or Wilcox to visit the mall, J. P. knew, unless it involved some business pertaining to the mall. J. P. approached Madden in The Belmont Club to inquire about his visit to the mall two days earlier. Madden denied being anywhere near the mall on the day in question. J. P. became more suspicious of Madden and Wilcox. J. P. wanted Mc Lauren to explain to him what this could mean. Mc Lauren didn't know what it could mean, and he didn't know anything that he could share with J. P. Mc Lauren told J. P. he knew nothing about the third man he said was with Madden and Wilcox, and asked J. P. to stop worrying about it. J. P. could not stop worrying about it. Something was amiss because he could feel it. Mc Lauren didn't say it but J. P. could hear it in his voice.

In fact there was a lot that Mac Mc Lauren knew but that he could not tell J. P. Sellers. He and J. P. had been good friends for many years, but they were in very different social classes. Mc Lauren always knew it and J. P. always felt it. J. P. knew he was tolerated by Madden, Mc Lauren, Wilcox and many of the other "Big Mucks" in Sawyer Village and Thompson County. They used J. P. and J. P. used them, forming a relationship of mutual convenience and uneasy trust. It was a relationship they all understood and lived with as long as it was mutually beneficial. J. P. was getting the feeling that he was no longer tolerated and was, in fact, being cut out of the exchange of information among those in the inner circle. Madden had determined that he could contain any damage that might come their way from the Register of Deeds Office, and that he could justify any decisions he made as the county land attorney. Wilcox also felt that any decisions he made involving land issues could be justified based on the facts of the cases. All of the information that appeared in the mid-sized, brown envelope could be explained as sheer coincidence. There was nothing illegal about the transactions and any missing paper work was due to sloppy record keeping procedures that happened before the introduction of computers and more sophisticated procedures. Mc Lauren was still skeptical about his ability to get the "State Boys" to see things his way. Everything that happened was ethical and legal, he assured Madden and Wilcox, and that the information they received anonymously had no factual basis. Madden and the Register of Deeds Office could attest to that.

Madden, Mc Lauren and Wilcox discussed how J. P. was beginning to act rather strangely, not making a lot of sense in his discussions, displaying paranoid behaviors, etc. Madden and Wilcox rationalized that his strange behavior was justification for having him removed from the picture. The technical details of the problem could be taken care of, but the issue of people problems was a different matter. Madden and Wilcox were skeptical of Mc Lauren and they definitely did not trust J. P. They had determined that J. P. was the weak brick in their wall of invincibility. They believed that J. P. knew too much and would probably break under any kind of questioning, no matter how mild. He had too much to lose and would do anything he could to protect any financial gains he had made. Therefore, he was the most expendable. It was better to sacrifice him than to have him sacrifice all of them. The third man at the mall was the same man who arranged to take care of the old man who was making noise about being swindled out of his land by J. P. and the investors in the Fox Valley Partnership. Madden and Wilcox rationalized that the old man made a deal fair and square and later was trying to back out of it. Whatever happened to him he caused by his own behavior, they told themselves. Madden and Wilcox always suspected that's what had happened, but they didn't ask and they didn't want to know. Madden and Wilcox had initiated a plan to get J. P. out of the picture. The deal was made the night J. P. saw them at the mall. They could not share their plan with Mc Lauren because of his relationship with J. P. It was one of sympathy rather than one of genuine care and concern. Mc Lauren never stated it, but they both could sense it. J. P. wasn't well educated, but he wasn't stupid either. So, he became extremely cautious, paying close attention to everybody and everything around him. J. P. had a feeling that somebody was always watching him, and he was right, but he didn't know it. He was being tailed from early morning until he went home at night. He became suspicious of everybody, and began to vary his patterns of going and coming.

J.P. drove his sports utility vehicle into his usual parking space, carefully surveying the landscape to detect anything that was suspect or caused him reason to be concerned. Satisfied that there was nothing to cause him alarm, he grabbed his briefcase, jumped out and pressed the remote keyless entry system device. J. P. crossed the parking lot hurriedly and rushed into his office while surveying around him and feeling certain that nobody had followed him. He breathed a sigh of relief after painstakingly unlocking his office door, gingerly opening it, gradually panning his questioning eyes around the room, and carefully closing the door behind him after he was had assured himself that all was safe. J. P. then cautiously approached the window and peeped through the vertical blinds before opening them. At the far end of the parking lot, with the front pointed away from the building, was a nondescript car with slightly tinted windows. A man sitting behind the wheel, but looking in his side view and rear mirrors, observed his every move and held a small electronic device over his right shoulder, pointing it toward J. P.'s. suv. The instant J. P. pressed the remote entry device to lock his suv, numbers registered on the frequency meter the man was holding. It had recorded the frequency of the remote keyless entry system, and if he had desired, could have activated or deactivated the remote keyless alarm and entry system at will. He had another purpose in mind, one that was meant to make a great impact.

The man who had been waiting for J. P. waited awhile longer until more cars began to fill the vacant spaces in the parking lot. He then punched a few buttons on a crude device in the passenger seat, picked it up carefully and walked swiftly toward J. P.'s suv. As he approached it, he reduced his pace and walked nonchalantly to the back of the suv, stooped down suddenly and attached the device under it. He then stood up slowly, walked casually back to his car and quickly, but cautiously, drove away. He was quite certain he had placed his packet on the intended target unnoticed. He had accomplished many such assignments before, and was quite good at his craft. He was so sure that he was good at his work that there was no need to wait to see the results. Besides, there were too many unnecessary risks in confirming results that had always been one hundred percent successful. The device was a bomb set to explode 25 seconds after the car alarm was deactivated, and for him to stay around that kind of result was not worth the kind of money he could have commanded. Except for feeling a little jittery about all of the events that had occurred during the past few months, J. P. was having a normal workday. He sorted through the previous day's mail and the mail he had picked up from the post office on his way to his office. There was nothing there that needed his immediate attention. He made several phone calls, carefully measuring his words and monitoring himself. J. P. then picked up the paper and started to peruse it, starting with the real estate section, but began to feel sickly after looking at the first entry. He could not bring himself to continue. He realized that he was not having a very productive day, and decided to leave at noon for the rest of the day to vary his pattern. He packed his briefcase, which had been a constant companion since he first got wind of the letter, and left the office. As he began to cross the parking lot, J. P. pushed the deactivation button on the remote keyless security system to his suv.

"J. P.," a gravely voice called out from behind him immediately after he pushed the button. J. P. was startled and turned around to discover that it was Bennett Zorn. "Got a minute?" he asked. Realizing that he had frightened J. P., he smiled broadly and immediately extended his hand to him. "Sure, I have a few minutes," J. P. said as he moved in Zorn's direction extending his hand also, with a sigh of relief and some apprehension.

The two men shook hands and exchanged greetings, and Zorn proceeded to update J. P. on the land dispute he was having. "We decided to walk away from this one," Zorn said. "There was too much to lose; and we weren't sure what and who we were dealing with."

"What do you think will happen next?" J. P. asked with genuine concern because he was trying to determine why Zorn was sharing his decision with him, but was steadying himself for the answer.

Before Zorn could answer, there was a loud explosion. J. P. turned around in time to see his suv being engulfed by flames and blown to smithereens. Immediately after the explosion, there was chaos, with people running and screaming, dodging and falling. J. P. wanted to run toward the vehicle, but was frozen by fear. He screamed, "Holy Crappoly!," but just stood feeling helpless. Other cars near J. P.'s burst into flames and exploded. All of the cars were empty except one, a Lincoln Town Car that had just parked next to J. P. when the explosion occurred. As soon as the driver, an older woman, opened her door, the force of the blast violently threw her back into the car, and her car burst into flames, along with several other cars that were parked nearby.

Fire and other emergency vehicles rushed on the scene and contained the disaster to the parking lot area. A preliminary investigation revealed that the initial explosion was J. P.'s suv, and that the Lincoln Town Car was registered to Dent Madden. The older woman, the only casualty of the disaster, was Estelle Madden, Dent Madden's wife. J. P. knew that the bomb was meant for him, but he wasn't exactly sure who wanted him out of the way, but he had an idea. The first thing that came to mind was the meeting with Madden, Wilcox and the man he could not identify. J. P. knew his life had been spared this time and that, if he were the target of the bombing, he still was not safe. The State Bureau of Investigations was brought in to investigate the bombing, which was a State as well as a Federal offense. Robert Stanton was particularly interested in the case because his office had plans to exert some subtle pressure on Estelle Madden to corporate with his office in understanding some of the land transactions that occurred while she was Register of Deeds. It was going to be tricky to get the information they wanted without getting her to finger her husband as the mastermind of the scheme. But, he felt certain Special Agent Rebecca Burke could gain Estelle Madden's confidence and get the information they needed. Now, that possible source was gone. Stanton was also interested in the case because J. P. Sellers, the apparent target of the bomb, was implicated in many of the land issues in Thompson County. Stanton and Gordon Clark had determined that given the right set of circumstances, J. P. would help them to get first-hand information on some of the dealings. They thought maybe the bombing would help J. P. to talk.

And talk, J. P. Sellers eventually did.

40

J. P. Sellers called Mac Mc Lauren at his home the same evening of the bombing. As soon as Mc Lauren answered the phone, J. P. screamed, "Dammit, Mac, somebody tried to kill me. Holy Crappoly! You should have seen it," he said with excitement and disbelief.

"I heard about it, J. P.," Mac responded serenely. "I heard it on the radio right after it happened. And, I saw pictures of it on the evening news." Trying to remain calm, Mc Lauren asked, "How do you know it was meant for you?" Mc Lauren felt certain that it was meant for J. P. and he thought he knew who may have planned it. However, he had to ask the question.

"Hell, the SBI determined it was attached to my truck," J. P. snorted. "Who else could it have been for?" J. P. asked angrily, but Mc Lauren did not answer.

"It's too bad about Madden's old lady, isn't it?" Mc Lauren asked, trying to divert J. P. s attention away from himself.

"Yeah, it's bad, but I'm not concerned about his old lady right now. I'm concerned about me," J. P. snapped back. "It seems like somebody out there wants me out of the picture."

"How do you know that?" Mc Lauren asked as calmly as he could.

"That bombing was not a coincidence, Mac. A lotta shit's been happening ever since that letter started making the rounds," J. P. said with fear and anger dripping from his voice. Recounting some of the events, J. P. said, "Then that list connecting a lotta folks arrived out of nowhere. Bennett Zorn settled the land issue he was involved with by walking away from it. The Zorns have never walked away from a land deal unless there were some serious problems with it," he asserted with confidence. "I believe Madden and Wilcox were planning something when I saw them in the mall and Wilcox denied they were there. All of this shit can't be coincidence." J. P. said with rage and conviction. Mac Mc Lauren was listening attentively as J. P. made his case. Mc Lauren, in fact, had come to a similar conclusion as soon as he heard about the bombing. "Yeah, it all seems to fit," he finally said. "It's a little too convenient for me, too" he added in a way to say he had J. P's interest at heart.

"I tell you what, Mac, I'm only concerned about me right now," J. P. said.

Mc Lauren wanted to say, "That's what Madden and Wilcox are afraid of, too," but he couldn't tell J. P. that because he knew it would spook him even more. J. P. continued. "This whole thing is falling apart and it seems like everybody is running for cover. I believe somebody's trying to knock me off because they think I know too much. That's attempted murder," he said with undeniable confidence.

"I wouldn't go that far," Mc Lauren offered apologetically in an attempt again to calm his fears.

"Hell, I would," J. P. said with assurance. "They probably think I'll say something about the deal with Jake Fuller, and some other stuff that's not quite right. I'm not that crazy," he said in a way that appeared to be reassuring himself, rather than to Mac Mc Lauren.

"I don't know anything about old man Fuller," Mc Lauren said.

"I know about him but I don't know what happened to him," J. P. said. "But, if anybody tries to get me again, I'll go directly to the Federal Prosecutor or the SBI and tell what we've heard happened to him."

Mc Lauren obviously became uncomfortable with the direction of their conversation and was ready to end it. He quickly said, "I don't know what you're talking about J. P. Listen, I have to go now. Lots of stuff going on tomorrow."

Before Mc Lauren could hang up J. P. said, "Okay. But, you know what the word is about where Ole Jake Fuller's buried?" he stated in the form of a question.

Mc Lauren immediately slammed the phone on the cradle as though he were angry with it. He could not believe what J. P. had just said. Mc Lauren had heard the story also and believed it to be true, but he knew better than to repeat it, especially over the telephone.

The tap on Mc Lauren's home phone had recorded the entire conversation between him and J. P. Sellers. The Attorney General Gordon Clark authorized the wire tap after the preliminary determination that Mac Mc Lauren was implicated in the land issues in Thompson County. The tap was proving to be quite useful. J. P. Sellers' comments would give Rebecca Burke and her partner another piece of information to pursue in conjunction with the Fox Valley Partnership. If Jake Fuller's body were entombed where they thought it was, it no doubt would be a case of murder they were looking at.

To the public, Dent Madden took his wife's death very hard, sending him into deep mourning; in the privacy of his own mind, however, he was more anguished and conflicted about what he was certain would follow in just a matter of time than he was concerned about the reality of her death. She had played a key role in helping him to accomplish all that he had with his current and past real estate holdings. Although Madden had initiated the plan to eliminate J. P. Sellers, he felt no responsibility for his wife being at the wrong place at the wrong time. He could not figure why she was in the vicinity of J. P. Sellers' office anyway, unless she was going there to determine how much he knew and what he intended to do with the information. The bomb was meant for J. P. Sellers. "If she got in the way, she got in the way," was his private and emotionless attitude, however. Estelle Madden's death was a great disappointment to Rebecca Burke, and how she died troubled her. She had determined that Estelle Madden had intimate details of how Dent Madden's scheme had yielded him titles to land through his office and official position as the Thompson County Land Attorney. Burke had talked with some of Dent Madden's relatives to inquire about how they had acquired several tracts of land that eventually were transferred to Dent Madden after he was no longer in the employ of Thompson County. While they did not know exactly how the land was titled to them, they were sure they did not pay for it, and they paid no property taxes on it. Dent Madden took care of all of the paper work and he paid the taxes. The property was later transferred to Dent Madden and his wife Estelle, and they paid the relatives a small amount of money at the time of the transfer. Burke told Madden's relatives that they were not to inform him about her visit with them. She wanted to believe they were innocently drawn into an illegal scheme to steal people's land and to make it appear to be legal. If they apprised Dent Madden of her visit, she would have to conclude they were willing participants in the scheme and, therefore, could face criminal prosecution. That was a way of ensuring their cooperation and their silence.

Kaye Webster had figured out the scheme and had put some of the details of it in the first letter she sent out. Burke followed up on the information the anonymous source had provided and found all of it to be substantially true. Although Estelle Madden now could not provide any information about her role, Burke knew she already had enough to bring conspiracy and fraud charges against Dent Madden. Enos Elliston had continued to take a hands-off position in the land issue in Thompson County, feeling certain that the State would investigate the matter. When he heard about the bombing, he called his friend Matthew Crenshaw to get his assessment of what was going on. Crenshaw was certain there was a connection between the land issues and the bombing of J. P. Sellers' suv, but he wasn't sure exactly what it was. Crenshaw told Elliston that he knew who Estelle Madden was and that he was really sorry about her death. He also shared with him that Dent Madden was considered "Mr. Land" of Thompson County when he was the county land attorney, and that Estelle was one of his key people because she was the Register of Deeds. Elliston's response was, "Seems like it was a real cozy and highly improper relationship to me."

"I always thought so myself, but it was none of my business," Crenshaw replied.

"So, what else is going on?" Elliston asked.

"I'm not exactly sure, but rumor has it that the State is bringing some pressure on a few folks around here," Crenshaw offered without revealing to Elliston that he was one of the persons who had talked with the Special Agent on the case.

"Well, at least they're doing something," he said. "Maybe now they'll get to the bottom of this thing and press some charges soon," he added.

"I get the feeling they have everything they need. They're just trying to tie the whole thing together," he said. "At least that's the rumor," Crenshaw quickly added. Crenshaw, in fact, had heard no rumors about what the State was doing. After his meeting with Agent Rebecca Burke, he became more observant of the goings and comings in the County Office Building and Court House. He also speculated that the anonymous letters and lists were creating quite a stir in the county and causing a lot of anxiety. Crenshaw knew a lot and saw a lot, but he had learned how to say very little. "Keep me on board," Judge Elliston instructed Crenshaw, feeling more certain now the issue would be resolved.

"I'll do that," he promised as he hung up, then leaned back in his chair and laughed. He continued to work long hours and wait for the Thompson County land issues to become front-page news.

🎐 41 🎐

Three days after the bombing, small advertisements that appeared in the *Evans County Gazette*, the *Humphries News Leader*, and the *Perkins City Evening Star Telegraph* attracted lots of attention. The ads were identical and read:

If you or any of your relatives have lost land under questionable circumstances within the past 50 years, there may be help for you. Possible class-action lawsuit being considered to get land returned. No charge to you unless successful. Call Atty. Norman Winfield at (986) 555-5287.

Winfield's office began receiving telephone calls almost immediately. When the first call was received, Monica, the paralegal, was baffled by it. She asked the caller to read the ad to her. Monica acknowledged that the number called was that of Atty. Winfield, but they had not placed an ad. After the second call was received and Monica relayed the story to Atty. Winfield, he became curious. He asked her to find a copy of the papers and let him speak to any caller who called in reference to the ads. Winfield was fascinated by the stories he was hearing, but he wasn't surprised. He was sure his office had not placed the ad and he wasn't exactly sure who had. However, he had a good idea who had. Monica called the newspapers to determine who had placed the ads. The newspapers' records showed that the ads had been paid for with cash, but the signature approving the ads was illegible. One paper was sure that the person who placed the ad was a young man, but they did not know his name. The other papers were not sure who had placed the ads. There was no problem, Monica assured them. Atty. Winfield just wanted to be sure the ad had been paid for. A week after the ads appeared, Winfield knew he had enough information to initiate several class-action lawsuits against several people in Thompson County. This was something he was itching for because Bennett Zorn and Chad Pollard had denied him that challenge. They settled out of court without much of a fight. Many of the stories were similar to John Wilkinson's. Others involved agreements to farm cotton and tobacco allotments that resulted in individuals losing all or most of their land because they did not understand what they were signing or what they were agreeing to. Others involved the sale of land for back taxes, but the individuals never received any notice about the property taxes being in arrears or any information about the pending sale of the property to pay the taxes. Once the land was sold, there was no right of redemption. Winfield and his small staff of lawyers had gathered enough information to keep them busy for a long time. Totally unaware of the activities underway by the State, they began to take formal statements, to secure agreements, to conduct research and to plot their strategy.

Special Agent Rebecca Burke began to zero in on J. P. Sellers. One morning shortly after the bombing incident, she watched J. P. as he got out of the taxi and rushed into his office. He refused the rental car his insurance offered him after his suv was bombed. He felt safer taking taxis. Burke casually walked into his office immediately behind him and called out, "Mr. James Sellers." She detected instantly that J. P.'s body went into a fight or flight mode. She extended her hand immediately, smiled and said, "I'm Rebecca Burke. I think we met at The Belmont Club sometime ago." J. P. was about to panic. His heart began to race and a sinking feeling crept into his knees. But, he composed himself after remembering that he had met her and found her quite beautiful and charming. She continued to smile and hold on to his clammy hand.

"Oh, yes, I remember. I'm James Sellers," he said. "Most people call me J. P.," he added with a big grin. "Have a seat," he continued while gesturing toward a chair in front of his desk and settling in for a friendly chat. He vaguely remembered the face, but her name could not register with his memory, and attributed it to the stress pervading his body and mind. If I met her at The Belmont, it must be okay, he reasoned with himself.

Burke cordially thanked him and gracefully sat. She then calmly pulled a cassette player from her briefcase, handed it to J. P. and asked him to push the "play" button. He took the player reluctantly and nervously followed her instructions. As the tape began to whiz, he appeared anxious. It was a tape of the conversation he had with Mac Mc Lauren in which he talked about the bombing and Jake Fuller. J. P. knew instantly that this was not a laughing matter. "Is that your voice on the tape, Mr. Sellers?" the agent asked as the taped continued to play.

"Yes, one of them is," J. P. responded and looked perplexed.

"And the other voice is that of a Mr. Heywood Mac Mc Lauren?" she asked.

"Yes, it is," J. P. said reluctantly. She knows too much, he thought to himself.

He pushed the "stop" button because he had heard enough. J. P. Sellers was speechless. He knew what was on the remainder of the tape. "Now that we've established that, let's talk about a few things," she said authoritatively. "I'm a Special Agent with the State Bureau of Investigations and we are looking into some issues involving land here in Thompson County. You're not under arrest, but if you would like to have an attorney here with you, please feel free to call one. I just have a few questions to ask you."

J. P. sat stunned and his face suddenly became pallid. He collected his thoughts and started to talk. Special Agent Burke interrupted him and said, "By the way Mr. Sellers, when I met you at The Belmont Club, I was introduced to you as Gabrielle Worthington, just in case you're wondering."

J. P. knew he was in serious trouble and the gravity of the problem was quickly registering in his consciousness; and her tactics were beginning to enrage him. He wanted to scream his favorite expression but it would not come up and it would not come out. J. P. tried hard to manage his appearance and to contain his emotions. He began to sweat profusely. He reached into his back pocket, produced a dirty and rumpled handkerchief and swiped nervously at his clammy forehead. He wanted to run, but he felt paralyzed. "Oh, no. I don't need an attorney;" he said, "I have nothing to hide."

Special Agent Burke sat quietly for a few minutes and purposely let J. P. think about the information she probably had about him and the evidence she probably had on him and others involved with the land issues in Thompson County. J. P. knew he had no way out. He wondered what was happening to Madden, Mc Lauren, Wilcox, Zorn and the others? Were they being visited by the SBI? What would they say? He was a small player in this whole thing; why was he being harassed by the SBI? How many other conversations did the SBI have of him and the others? These and other questions rattled about in J. P.'s round, squatty head.

"Mr. Sellers, we are in the process of issuing indictments against several people here in Thompson County on a variety of charges, including murder and attempted murder," Burke said matter-of-factly. "I'm sure you are aware of the fact that you were the target of the bombing that killed Mrs. Estelle Madden." J. P. dropped his head, but could say nothing.

"The land fraud issues are small in comparison to murder and attempted murder," she added. "And, of course, Mr. Seller, there is the issue of the whereabouts of Mr. Jake Fuller. The SBI always suspected there was foul play when he was initially listed as missing. I think you've provided us the break we've been looking for after all these years."

J. P. was still speechless. He started gasping for air.

"Are you alright, Mr. Sellers?" Agent Burke asked as she got up and moved in his direction.

"Yeah, I'm okay," J. P. struggled to push the words out of his mouth.

"Mr. Sellers, we know who the partners are in the Fox Valley Partnership, and their connection with Thompson County Meadows Square Shopping Mall. What we need to know is the specific connection between the partnership and the disappearance of Mr. Fuller."

J. P. thought for a few minutes and said, "I honestly don't know the specific connection."

"What do you know?" Burke looked him directly in the eyes and asked.

J. P. looked at the cassette player, then looked at Special Agent Burke. He knew she knew what the rumors were. Therefore, J. P. knew that he at least had to repeat what he had said on the tape. He struggled to remember what it was. Not being exactly, he finally said, "There are rumors that Jake Fuller is buried somewhere on some of the property owned by the partnership." "Where did you hear the rumors?" she asked forthrightly.

"I honestly don't know," J. P. said nervously.

"Do you think there are any truths to the rumors?" she asked probingly to see just how much he knew, and if he was willing to share it with her. "Think seriously before you give me an answer," she admonished J. P.

J. P. wanted to cry. He believed the rumors to be true. He had heard them whispered too many times for there not be a shred of truth to them. "Yes, I do," he said with obvious anguish on his face and tortuous pain in his voice.

Burke believed them too and had already arranged to get a court order to begin a search for the body. She would tell J. P. that later, but she wanted him to suffer some in order to extract as much information from him as she could while she had him directly under her influence.

"What role do you think Mr. Dent Madden, Mr. Mc Lauren or Judge Frank Wilcox may have played in the disappearance of Mr. Fuller?" she asked softly as she looked him squarely in the face.

J. P. tried to think of what else he said on the tape that might have implicated Madden and Wilcox. And he thought of other conversations he may have had with Mac Mc Lauren that mentioned Madden and Wilcox. He didn't trust Madden and Wilcox and had grown more suspicious of them lately, but he didn't want her to know that. He was less suspicious of Mac Mc Lauren, and he wanted to believe Mac trusted him. But now, he wasn't exactly sure. His mind went back to the evening he saw Madden, Wilcox and a stranger in the mall. He thought initially that there was something suspicious about them meeting there. Now, his instincts told him that he was right. They were there making plans to eliminate him, he thought to himself.

Special Agent Burke interrupted his train of thought and interjected, "Mr. Sellers, we already have the security tape of Mr. Madden, Judge Wilcox and the third man you were wondering about."

J. P. looked at her with disbelief. He wanted to ask who was the stranger, but he couldn't bring himself to ask the question.

Recognizing his curiosity, Burke volunteered, "Mr. Sellers, he is a known go-between for rub outs. That means murders for hire, Mr. Sellers, just in case you don't know what that means. A guy's known as "The Moose". His real name is Homer Glidden. We've concluded that he probably was hired to kill Mr. Fuller and to kill you. Maybe it was Madden and Wilcox who hired "The Moose" for both jobs." She shared that information with J. P. matter-of-factly and watched him carefully to gage his reactions.

J. P. sank a little deeper in his seat and began to wring his hands. He twisted and squirmed, and grew angry at what he was hearing and angry at himself for feeling that way.

Burke watched J. P intently, waiting for the appropriate moment to add to his discomfort.

"It looks like you might have some information somebody doesn't trust you with, Mr. Sellers," Burke said nonchalantly. "Or, they think you might not be able to keep secrets," she added, after she had weakened his resolve to protect his friends and feeling that she could get him to share more of what he knew.

J. P. thought how ironic it was that she was right on both counts. He knew exactly what happened with the Fuller land deal, and he was willing to tell it because he knew it would help to save himself. Since Madden and Wilcox had tried to have him killed, he would share any secrets they had among themselves. He told Special Agent Burke exactly what happened in the Fuller land dispute and the role he played in it. J. P. was emphatic about one point and he repeated it several times:

"I had nothing to do with the murder of Jake Fuller."

"We've never suspected that you did, Mr. Sellers," she assured him. She added, "Mr. Sellers, you might be interested in knowing that we have a taped conversation between Mr. Mc Lauren and Mr. Madden, suggesting that Mr. Madden discuss the issues with Judge Wilcox. It was the same day that Mr. Madden and Judge Wilcox met with "The Moose". We believe, however, that we can convict Mr. Mc Lauren for accessory to murder and accessory to attempted murder." Burke was very deliberate about the facts because she wanted them to have a profound impact on J. P. And, they did.

J. P. felt shattered. He could not believe it. His life-long friend may be involved with murder and attempted murder. His life-long friend also may have been involved with trying to have him killed. "Mr. Sellers, is there anything else you want to share with me?" Agent Burke asked.

J. P. shook his head back and forth, meaning no, and began to sob. He sat quietly, looking down at the floor as tears filled his red eyes and slowly dripped off his pudgy cheeks. The humiliation he was feeling then did not outweigh anger he had for himself for his stupidity.

"Mr. Sellers, just for your information, we also have a warrant for the arrest of "The Moose". I don't think you'll have to worry about him again If he tells us where Mr. Fuller's body is, we can save everybody a lot of time and money." In a strange sort of way, J. P. felt relieved. He no longer had to live with a secret that was always bubbling just below his consciousness. He no longer had to keep looking over his shoulder to see who was watching him. His confused state of mind was attempting to lead him to the conclusion that the image he was maintaining was no longer important to him if it came at the expense of his life. J. P. had done well, not so much by his own efforts, but by helping take advantage of others; or, by reaping some of the benefits manipulated or stolen by people such as the Zorns, Madden, Mc Lauren and Wilcox. J. P. knew that; he had always known it. He thought it was easier for him to live the delusion that whatever he could acquire at others' expense justified his behavior. He now had to face up to the reality that his greed and the greed of others caused pain and suffering, and that their unearned wealth caused undeserved poverty for others.

J. P. continued to sob and wipe his fat, ruddy face, struggling with an image of himself that he knew his wife would detest and that he found pitiful. Special Agent Burke learned little new information by talking with J. P. but thanked him for his cooperation. "You've been enormously helpful," she told him.

J. P. felt proud of himself because of his ability to shed some light on the case for the State. He was also interested in receiving any favorable treatment he could get from the State for his cooperation. Attempting to find a way to end this painful experience, he asked Burke politely, "What's next?"

"We'll just have to wait and see," she said noncommittally. "We expect to get everything in place today so we can make some arrests early tomorrow morning." "Who will be arrested?" J. P. asked.

"I can't say for sure right now, Mr. Sellers. I think you'll know most of the individuals. I don't think you have anything to worry about for the time being, but you are implicated in some of the cases."

J. P. sighed and attempted to chuckle, still not sure what he was really feeling. "Mr. Sellers, if I were you, I would not try to make contact with Mr. Madden, Mr. Mc Lauren or Judge Wilcox," Burke advised him, emphasizing *not*.

"Oh, I had no intentions of doing that," J. P. assured her.

Burke took the cassette player from J. P.'s desk, put it back in her briefcase and stood up to leave. J. P. bolted from his seat and thanked her for coming by to talk with him. He actually sounded as though he really meant it. Before she opened the door, she turned around and asked with genuine concern, "Are you sure you're going to be alright, Mr. Sellers?"

J. P. was silent for a moment, and had a faraway look on his face that belied his response. "Oh, I'll be just fine," he assured her. He sat at his desk and smiled as Special Agent Burke casually walked out the door.

Special Agent Burke had an uneasy feeling about J. P. as she closed the door and began to walk away; but she tried not to let her personal feeling override the job she had to do. Before she reached her car in the parking lot, there was a sound of a gunshot that came from the direction of J. P.'s office. "Oh, my God!" Special Agent Burke screamed as she turned around and ran back in the direction of J. P.'s office. She reached it, she quickly opened the door and saw a blaze on top of J. P.'s desk. J. P. was leaning back in his chair with blood oozing from the side of his head, out of his mouth and down the front of his clothes. It appeared that J. P. had doused the papers in his briefcase with a flammable substance and set them afire, then put a small caliber pistol to the side of his mouth and pulled the trigger. Special Agent Burked tried frantically to put out the fire and to revive J. P., moving as quickly as she could from one to the other, and screaming for help at the same time. J. P. Sellers could not be revived, and all of the papers that he guarded so closely were destroyed. For a few moments, there was sheer bedlam and mayhem, people scurrying about and screaming, frantically trying either to escape the scene or being drawn deeper into it. Whatever additional secrets he had went with him or burned in the flames, unless there were others who knew the same secrets and were willing to talk. Burke called Gordon Clark and Robert Stanton immediately and informed them of the tragedy with J. P. Sellers. They made the decision to arrest Mac Mc Lauren in his office right way because he was convenient and for his protection, but not to make it public knowledge. The Governor had already been briefed on the developments in Thompson County and the role that Heywood Bradford Mc Lauren played in the land fraud when he was an attorney in the county, and before he was appointed Chairman of the State Board of Ethics. The evidence against others was so compelling that Clark and Stanton gave Special Agent Burke the authority to act as she saw necessary. Word of J. P.'s suicide spread very quickly throughout Sawyer Village and Thompson County. From the moment the 911 Call was made and the emergency vehicles started rolling, the ever-present police scanners broadcast what had happened. By the time the news hit Thompson County Office Building and the Courthouse, the District Attorney had already been instructed by Gordon Clark and Robert Stanton to prepare and issue warrants for the arrest of Dent Madden, Judge Frank Wilcox, two of the five county commissioners, several attorneys, and two real estate developers the next morning, and to keep the matter concealed until 8:00 am the following morning. Only the arresting officers should be apprised of the matter, and only one-half hour before they were to take suspects into custody.

Gordon Clark contacted Federal Judge Enos Elliston and informed him of the plans he and Stanton were devising. Elliston was delighted with what the State was doing, but he did not express his feelings. He simply said, "Thanks for bringing me in the loop. If I can do anything, Gordon, let me know." Judge Elliston hung up the phone and immediately called Matthew Crenshaw. Because of some good detective work and a little luck, Special Agent Burke and the other STF--TC2 agent learned that the last known address of "The Moose" was three counties away, and had arranged to have a stakeout at that address the past two days. Based upon his patterns of movement, they were certain he would show up soon and would be able to give them the information they needed about Mr. Jake Fuller. They were also sure that a little pressure on Madden, Mc Lauren or Wilcox, once they were arrested, would give them a lot more information to clarify and to validate what they had already found out.

⟡ 42 ⟡

Most of the radio and television stations in the State had live, same-day coverage of the tragedy of Mr. James Preston Sellers' untimely death in Thompson County. There was a lot of speculation about what had happened, but there were very few facts. It was known that J. P. Sellers had committed suicide, but it was not known how his death was connected to the land fraud issues. However, those who knew him praised his standing in the Thompson County/ Humphries/Sawyer Village Communities. No Thompson County officials claimed any knowledge of why J. P. may have committed suicide. Splashed across the front page of most evening newspapers was a blaring headline about the suicide and in Sawyer Village and Thompson County, all speculating about why he may have done it; none mentioned the real reason for it. Many of the Thompson County residents, however, talked among themselves about the horrible land ownership problems they had heard J. P. was connected with, but few could give any specifics. People in the surrounding counties also were interested in what had happened because many of them had recently provided information to Attorney Norman Winfield about land they or their relative had lost because of suspected fraudulent activities they knew J. P. was connected with.

Somewhere in the distance long before the break of dawn the next morning was the sounds of hammering, pounding and grinding that ricocheted off objectives as far as the ear could hear. The strangely familiar but curiously misplaced sounds were coming from the direction of Spring Meadows Shopping Mall and piercing the eerie silence that normally blanketed Thompson County most mornings. This added drama to the previous day's events and betrayed all sense of tranquility everybody was accustomed to As the morning wore on, the monotonous drone of life began to rise again, and word of the hammering and grinding noises started making the rounds in and around the county. Many of the residents who should have known what was going on, to their dismay, discovered that they did not; and those who weren't supposed to know started feeling a bit smug because those who were supposed to know, like themselves, didn't know either. There was much discussion and guessing; and after it was determined that no satisfactory explanation was forthcoming for the commotion coming from the direction of the Mall, the only way to know for sure was for the curiosity seekers to go on a fact-finding mission. Most of the roads leading there soon became crowded with cars, pickups and suvs, causing congestions and evoking memories of a typical Saturday night when Thompson County's upper-crust teenagers who, apparently with nothing better to do, took to the same roads on thrill-seeking missions; and those who wanted to look like they too were well-heeled joined in the ride to nowhere in particular.

The main entrance to the Mall, elaborately decorated with a waterfall and a wishing well, was cordoned off; Thompson County Sheriffs directed traffic away from it; several large dump trucks stood idly by; some ominous and heavy equipment moved in and out of the entrance; and the hammering and grinding noise emanated from the entrance loud and clear. These were sure-fire indicators that something significant was going on there. Those who were determined that they would not to be denied the satisfaction of a close-up and personal examination of their intended mission quickly made their way to the nearest accessible entrance and headed in the direction of the waterfall and wishing well. They learned in a matter of minutes after entering the Mall that the route toward the waterfall and pool was blocked also. State Troopers and State Bureau of Investigation agents stood guard, preventing anyone from entering the wing leading in the direction from which the noise was coming. The curiosity-seekers yelled a barrage of questions at the agents, including, "What's going on down there?" "Why can't we go down there?" "What are y'all looking for?" All questions received the same unemotional response: "I'm sorry madam/sir, there is an official State matter underway here; that's all I can tell you." The buzz of cell phones and the muted sounds of private conversations interrupted the solemnity surrounding them.

Those who were tall enough, or could stretch their necks high enough, saw a woman and two men busily marking on the concrete floor, then directing a heavy-equipment operator to pound the floor with a steel blade attached to the front-end of the machinery. After the equipment revved up, then bounced and rocked for a few seconds as it gouged into the floor, moving chunks of concrete and digging up piles of sand, the operator maneuvered it out of the way to allow the woman and men to inspect the results and decide what they wanted to happen next. When it was apparent that they had not found what they were looking for, they directed a front-end loader operator into action. The loader ambled up and gingerly scooped up the concrete pieces and sand and carted it out to the trucks waiting in the Mall parking lot. This activity was done with a practiced orchestration and precision, and was something they apparently had done many times before. The ritual, continuing for quite some time, grew on the patience of the workers and wore on the patience of many of the onlookers, who soon tired of it; retreated for a while; then returned to gaze in amazement and wonderment again. The suicide was the only one anybody could ever remember occurring in Thompson County. The news of it, along with all the activity at the Spring Meadows Shopping Mall, consumed interest and speculation of all who were aware of it. The idea of it was appalling and tragic at the same time; and most of the whispered conversations in *Mamma's Dining Room* were about where it probably would lead.

Matthew Crenshaw sat at his favorite table and scanned through several newspapers. He too was trying to decipher what the sketchy information was not revealing and to anticipate apparently what was yet to come. He was not holding a cup to his mouth as he usually did; nor was he seated in his usual trance-like position. He was unusually animated and was actually smiling while he was reading and talking to a young man sitting at the table with him. All of the reports and newspaper stories he read amused him. He was particularly amused by the comments from the Attorney General and Head of the State Bureau of Investigations about their cooperation and joint effort to pursue and apprehend criminals wherever they may be, and no matter who they are. There was no comment about the help they received from an anonymous source. They also did not mention that there was no land issue in Thompson County as far as they were concerned until that anonymous source brought it to their attention. Somebody else had put the case in their laps and solved it for them, but they were willing to take all of the credit for it.

Kaye Webster nearly glided across the floor after she entered the door, carrying three newspapers snuggly under her arm and swinging her ever-present shoulder bag. She saw Matthew Crenshaw sitting at the table in the back where he usually sat. But, this time there was a young man sitting with him. It was a young man she had seen before. His eyes followed Kaye as she walked briskly toward her usual table. As she approached it, she pulled the newspapers from under her arm, waved them at him and yelled, "It looks like you finally got your wish." "Yeah, it's about time," he yelled back. "But I had nothing to do with it," he said, then wished that he had not assumed they were talking about the same thing. Kaye laughed freely because Crenshaw confirmed for her that they were. She yelled her usual morning greetings to Mamma Sylvia as she carefully dropped her shoulder bag into one of the chairs, gracefully removed her coat and prepared to seat herself at the table. Crenshaw continued to look at Kaye and to admire her beauty and her charm, and was captivated by the way she carried herself. He just realized he had really seen her for the first time, this time. While Kaye was perusing her newspapers, Mamma Sylvia served her breakfast. She commented to Kaye that Crenshaw was not worshipping his coffee cup like he usually does and laughed. "I think he's really admiring you this time," she added.

Kaye chuckled and said, "Oh, get serious girl. He appears to be smart but he's probably like the rest of them. You know, a dude, a dog, a deadbeat or a low-life," Kaye said with sincerity. Mamma Sylvia laughed hysterically and repeated the expression, "Dude, dog, deadbeat, or low-life." I have to remember that one," she said. "No, I don't think he's either one. I told you he's a little strange, but he's really a nice guy."

Kaye appeared to be interested in hearing more about Crenshaw. "What do you know about him?" she asked with a tone of serious interest.

"He's an okay kind of a guy. Says the kid with him is his son Tony; but nobody believes that. Believe his name is Antonio, and he seems like a real nice kid." Then, Mamma Sylvia slyly looked toward Crenshaw and the young man, waggled her hand limply and said in an effected, high-pitched voice, "My name is Antonio;" then chuckled and said, "You know what I mean?" "Oh, stop it! To each his own," she said chidingly as she discretely looked round the room, then in the direction of Crenshaw.

Kaye wasn't sure what to say or do. So, she turned to look in their direction again and then immediately remembered where she had seen the young man. He was the receptionist at Attorney Jarvis Freeman's office. It seemed that her visit there had been so long ago. Mamma Sylvia thought for a few moments and said, "What else can I tell you?" she asked herself then said, "Not a lot. He stays to himself from what I see. Comes in here religiously. He's been one of my most faithful customers since I opened, I guess, about twenty years ago. If he says six words the whole time he's in here alone, he's said a lot. But, when Antonio is with him, which is rare, he acts like a normal guy. Laughing, talking. Really comes to life. Almost like a different person."

"Oh, I see," Kaye said with an apparent growing interest as she looked in their direction again.

The stakeout for "The Moose" was also successful. He denied that he was "The Moose" initially, but eventually admitted that he and Homer Glidden were the same person after he was shown the security tape from the Mall where he was talking with Madden and Wilcox. As the work was continuing at the Spring Meadows Shopping Mall, Wilcox was arrested in his chambers and Madden was arrested at his house. Neither protested. It appeared that each expected to be arrested and was relieved that the time had come. The attorneys, county commissioners and real estate agents were also taken in custody without incident. By noon, the workers at the Mall had found what they had been looking for. Entombed under the waterfall and wishing well they found the body of Mr. Jake Fuller, just as "The Moose" told them they would. Special Agent Burke had learned through her research that Mr. Fuller had gone missing about the same time the concrete was poured for the floor in the Mall. She was quite certain that, even if "The Moose" had not provided them the exact location, they would find it there. Her intuition told her that was probably the most logical place where the murderer or murderers would bury it and believe it unlikely that it would ever be discovered. She was right. Johnny "Big Boy" Dawson had been kept completely out of the loop on the events that were unfolding in Thompson County, but, out of necessity, he was in the midst of the excavation and was attempting to make sense of all that was happening to his county. As he witnessed the unraveling of some events for which he had some personal knowledge during his eleven-year tenure as sheriff, he looked on with stunned silence and contemplated how his connections to and assignments for Judge Frank Wilcox might determine his eventual fate.

The *Land Fraud Trials* were going to be the biggest events ever in Thompson County, everybody predicted. They were filled with intrigue and murder, and they were fueled by greed. It seemed that word of them had spread throughout the State and to distance states that had experienced similar problems. There were rumors circulating that the US Justice Department was interested in the case, because of numerous complaints it had received, from many citizens in many states over the years, and had too many similarities for them to be coincidences. There were clear patterns and practices that made the most ardent skeptic nervous about what they would probably uncover.

Kaye Webster was delighted with what her efforts had wrought for her cousin John and for other people in Thompson County. She would listen to the various reports and reflect on the letter that initiated the series of events that led to the uncovering of what had been a history of deceit and thievery. The history was shameful, and it enraged and saddened her because it was orchestrated and sustained by the very people who were paid to ensure that such things did not happen. In her mind, that was the ultimate insult to her sense of equity and justice and exposed just one of the unforgivable stains on the innocence of humanity. While Kaye felt a lot of empathy for J. P. Sellers and Estelle Madden, she also felt a lot of remorse because their lives ended so tragically. However, she felt a sense of relief that Judge J. Francis Wilcox, Bennett Zorn, Dent Madden, and Heywood Bradford "Mac" Mc Lauren, and what they had done, finally, would be exposed, and that they would have to face some semblance of justice. She knew Chad Pollard was involved in many of the schemes, but she wasn't sure of the details of his roles. She made herself a mental note, and let her mind explore how she would probably feel while sitting in the courtroom carefully listening to the evidence and testimonies, closely examining the behaviors and expressions of all witnesses, and attempting to get an innocuous, but relevant, comment to any reporter willing to ask her a question. She also was wondering how to get introduced during the trials some of the information Atty. Norman Winfield undoubtedly was collecting, once the trails began. Her mind continued to race and strategize, along with the swift passage of time, calculating what needed to be done and how best to make sure it was done.

With great anticipation and a little apprehension, Kaye Webster, along with the general citizenry of Thompson County, waited for *The Land Fraud Trials*, as they were popularly known, to get underway. When any mention of them was made in her presence, she acted as interested and as surprised as anyone who had no knowledge of what had led up to them, and no understanding of the intricacies of the legal maneuvering involved with them. She wanted to keep it that way. She had made up her mind to attend every day of the trial, or trials, no matter how long it took. If it took more than a year, from start to finish, she was determined to be there, soaking up every bit of information presented by the prosecution and the defense, and surreptitiously providing them more if she felt they needed it. Kaye felt that if they were going off in the wrong direction, she would have to be the person to get them focused back on what had happened and why it had happened, in addition to what must be done about it. She wasn't sure how she was going to do it, but she would find a way. It was not her nature to allow one minor inconvenience to keep her from accomplishing anything that was important to her. Kaye had grown to consider the land issue in Thompson County one of the most important she had ever encountered. It was not in her heart to leave the spirit of her fight to the technicalities of the law and the machinations of politics, and was defiantly unapologetic for her position.

During times of solitude and moments of silence, she would repeat in her mind, almost verbatim, the contents of the first letter she wrote to get the attention of those she believed could assess the problem objectively and quickly take corrective actions as they found necessary. That did not happen as she anticipated because some of those who should have been helpful were also part of the problem, and had no intentions of exposing themselves and others they were expected to protect. Nevertheless, the way she crafted the letter caused her to marvel at herself and her powers of persuasion, and the passion she ultimately found to be her true calling. Occasionally, she would think of the path that got her to that point, and mockingly would recite portions of the letter out loud and laugh at herself for the way she allowed the issue to invade and consume her life, and for the boldness she had learned from her disappointments and her persistence. The letter read as follows:

18 June 2000

To Whom It May Concern:

There is an unconscionable land fraud being perpetrated on the good and decent citizens of Thompson County. The real tragedy of this situation is that the very people who are employed by the County to help the citizens are the very ones who are carrying out this atrocity. This is disgraceful and shameful! While I don't know all of the details of how the fraud is occurring, I have been privy to conversation that lets me know it is widespread and is participated in by members of the legal, political and real estate communities. I do know however that it is a problem that will not be resolved by local leaders. Too many of them are personally involved with the problems and are financially benefiting from it, or they have friends and family members who are. There is no other way to categorize this but conspiracy.

I also know from first-hand knowledge that some county employees have used their offices to hatch schemes to swindle citizens out of their land, and personally have falsified, or induced other county employees to falsify, official County documents to make them appear that illegal land transactions were, in fact, legal. Subsequent paper trails are so convoluted that they are almost impossible to follow. Or, they have been sanitized to the point that they are almost perfect.

Basically illiterate and unsuspecting people have been advised to sign documents they did not understand, but were told served their best interest. They discovered later that they had agreed to relinquish all the rights to their property. There is something grossly wrong with this mode of operating a local government, one which is complicit with private interests to take advantage of the citizens. I urge you to talk to each other about this matter immediately, and take the necessary actions to rectify past injustices. As a start, you may want to look at the real estate holdings of Dent Madden, a retired Thompson County employee. Also, by examining Anders Zorn's estate, you will discover that much of the holding inherited by his son Bennett Zorn was taken in exchange for a minor indebtedness. Indebtedness that was impossible to repay because of the way Anders Zorn and his attorney structured the repayment arrangements. You have everything you need to get started. You must act now! I am in a position to know if you have or have not done anything about this problem. I know most of the player and know what they are capable of doing. I want to give you an opportunity to do something before I make it public matter.

Sincerely

A Person with a Conscious
and High Ethnical Standards

Copy to:
State Attorney General
Head, State Board of Ethics
State Bureau of Investigations
Bennett Zorn

Her second letter contained much of the same information that was in the first. However, a copy of the first letter, along with the informational grids and spreadsheets with the names and connections, was included and sent to Federal Judge Enos Elliston, the Governor, Judge Frank Wilcox and Dent Madden.

Only a few weeks before the trials were scheduled to begin, Katherine Webster resigned her position as an Insurance Adjuster, and told her associates and friends that she wanted to take off a year and enjoy life. She could not force herself to tell them that she had no intentions of ever returning to that kind of life and profession again. She didn't bother to give the customary two-week notice; so that should have told them something. She would leave it to them to eventually figure it out on their own.

Kaye Webster came home, filled her bathtub nearly to the top with delightfully warm water and an abundance of fragrances, then eased in and metamorphosed herself to another world.

❧ SOME THINGS TO CONSIDER ❧

- According to the U.S. Agricultural Census, blacks have lost 80 percent of 5.5 million acres of farmland they owned in the South 32 years ago.

- Up to 83 percent of black landowners do not leave wills, resulting in their heirs owning their estate in common.

- 1862—U. S. Congress creates the U.S. Department of Agriculture.

- 1862—U. S. Congress passes the Morrill Act (or Land Grant Act) to create land grant colleges for agriculture and mechanical arts for whites.

- 1865—After meeting with freed slaves in Savannah, Georgia - in what became known as the Savannah Colloquy - General William T. Sherman responded to their pleas for land. In January he issued his famous Field Order 15 setting aside a huge swath of abandoned land along the Georgia and South Carolina coast for black families on forty acres plots. He also said that army mules no longer in use would be offered to Black farmers, creating the "Forty Acres and a Mule" idea. Sherman never stated whether this was to be a permanent or temporary land acquisition.

- 1865—U. S. Congress establishes the Bureau of Refugees, Freedmen and Abandoned Lands (Freedmen's Bureau) providing for the allocation of "unoccupied land" to freedmen (not to exceed 40 acres) - rather than 40 acres as requested, Congress allowed the Freedmen's Bureau to sell only 5 to 10 acre tracts of land to freed slaves.

- 1865—President Johnson announces his Reconstruction Plan. The plan calls for the Southern States to abolish slavery but does not offer a role for Blacks in Reconstruction. The southern states are to determine the role of Blacks themselves.

- 1865—Some 40,000 freed slaves were settled on what was

referred to as "Sherman's Land" on some 400,000 acres of land in Georgia and South Carolina. Much of this land was for rice cultivation. The Freedmen created their own government, denied white access to the area and cultivated their land.

- 1865—President Johnson reverses Sherman's Field Order 15 by ordering that virtually all plantation lands given to freed slaves be returned to the original plantation owners.

- 1865—A reluctant General O. Howard, Chair of the Freedmen's Bureau, assigned the task to tell freed slaves in Georgia and South Carolina that they must return the land they had settled on to the original owners. Some 2,000 Blacks came to the local church on Edisto Island to hear his comments. Howard said the freed slaves need to "lay aside their bitter feelings and to become reconciled to their old masters." They responded "No, never!" "Can't do it!" "Why, General Howard, do you take away our lands?" Petitions by Blacks were drafted to protest betrayal. The first stated: "General, we want Homesteads, we were promised Homesteads by the government. If it does not carry out the promises its agents made to us...we are left in a more unpleasant condition than our former....You will see this is not the condition of really free men." (Eric Foner & Joshua Brown Forever Free: The Story of Emancipation and Reconstruction)

- April 9, 1866—THE CIVIL RIGHTS ACT OF 1866—Guaranteed blacks the right to personal liberty and the ownership and use of property. The U. S. Congress overrode Andrew Johnson's veto to pass the legislation. Johnson opposed federal protection of the rights of Blacks.

- July 9, 1866—FOURTEENTH AMENDMENT TO THE CONSTITUTION- Intended to make former slaves citizens of the United States, and states in which they live.

- 1866—The U.S. homegrown terrorist organization known as the Ku Klux Klan is created in Tennessee by Nathan B. Forrest to disrupt the progress of changing the framework of the south away from a "slaveocracy," and to engrain white supremacy into southern life. It spreads into "nearly every southern state, launching a 'reign of terror' against Republican leaders both black and white." (Foner & Brown)

- 1867—Congress passes a series of Reconstruction Acts abolishing Southern State governments under Johnson's plan. Election boards in each state required to register all adult Black males and all qualified adult white males. Johnson vetoes these acts and Congress easily overrides the veto.

- 1877—The Compromise of 1877 ending reconstruction: The 1876 presidential election between the Democratic candidate Samual Tildon and the Republican candidate Rutherford B. Hayes is in dispute. The tallies in Florida, Louisiana and South Carolina are questioned. Congress appoints an election commission composed of 5 representatives, 5 senators and 5 Supreme Court justices. Hayes wins but a compromise is agreed upon behind the scenes. The Hayes will be recognized by the South if the federal government agrees to no longer intervene in southern affairs and consequently remove the Federal troops from the South. The Compromise of 1877 was the death knell of reconstruction and laid open the tragic decline into the devastating Jim Crow period in U.S. history.

- 1877—Reconstruction ends with Democratic control of the South and laws are passed throughout the south denying Blacks the right to vote.

- May 10, 188—YICK WO V. HOPKINS--The U. S. Supreme Court ruled that it was unlawful for the City of San Francisco, CA, to prohibit a person to establish, maintain, or carry on a laundry business within the corporate limits without the consent of the board of supervisors unless the business was located in a building constructed of brick or stone. (The ordinance was aimed at putting out of business people of Chinese ancestry.)

- February 8, 1887—DAWES SEVERALTY ACT (INDIAN GENERAL ALLOTMENT ACT)--The U. S. Congress Established guidelines for individual allotments of land to Indians on reservations.

- August 9, 1888 --DAWES ACT (MARRIAGE WITH INDIAN WOMEN)--Enacted by the U. S. Congress, the Act prohibited white men who married Indian women from acquiring any right to any tribal property, privilege, interest whatever to which any member of such tribe is entitled. 1890—Congress passes the second Morrill Act to create land grant colleges for Blacks.

- 1890's The "Colored Farmers National Club and Cooperative Union of the United States" is created in Arkansas.

- 1896—U.S. Supreme Court passes Plessy v. Ferguson legalizing separate but equal facilities for whites and Blacks which supports the "Jim Crow" laws passed in the South denying Blacks their rights.

- 1910—Peak of land ownership for blacks. Collectively, blacks own 15 million acres of land of which 218,000 black farmers are full or part owners. A steady decline of landownership begins after 1910.

- June 2, 1924—CITIZENSHIP TO AMERICAN INDIANS--By way of Public Act Number 175, the U. S. Congress authorized the Secretary of the Interior to issue certificates of citizenship to Indians born in the United States, provided tribal rights would not be effected.

- June 8, 1934—INDIAN RE-ORGANIZATION ACT--The U. S. Congress granted greater authority to tribes on reservation regarding their land.

- December 18, 1944—KOREMATSU V. UNITED STATES--The U. S. Supreme Court ruled that during the time of war, individuals could be removed from their homes and forcibly imprisoned until their loyalty is established, on the "basis of military necessity."

- 1946—Congress creates the Farmers Home Administration (FmHA) to offer credit designed to improve the income of the small farm owner often known as the "lender of last resort."

- 1964—The Civil Right Bill is passed to enforce the constitutional right to vote, to confer jurisdiction upon the district courts of the United States to provide injunctive relief against discrimination in public accommodations... (U. S. Gov't source)

- 1965—The Voting Rights Act is passed - By 1965 concerted efforts to break the grip of state disfranchisement had been under way for sometime, but had achieved only modest success overall and in some areas had proved almost entirely ineffectual. The murder of voting-rights activists in Philadelphia, Mississippi, gained national attention, along with numerous other acts of violence and terrorism. Finally, the unprovoked attack on March 7, 1965, by state troopers on peaceful marchers crossing the Edmund Pettus Bridge in Selma, Alabama, en route to the state capitol in Montgomery, persuaded the President and Congress to overcome Southern legislators' resistance to effective voting rights legislation. President Johnson issued a call for a strong voting rights law and hearings began soon thereafter on the bill that would become the Voting Rights Act. (U. S. Gov't source)

- 1967—Federation of Southern Cooperatives founded to assist in the economic development of black farmers and the rural poor.

- 1969—James Forman releases "black manifesto' in Detroit calling for $200 million for a southern land bank.

- 1973—"Only Six Million Acres" is published by Black Economic Research Center under leadership of Bob Browne. Browne and others were concerned at the pace of land being lost by the Black community.

- 1973—Emergency Land Fund (ELF) formally organized to address the issue of black land loss. Bob Browne was the founder.

- 1981—With a grant from the United States Department of Agriculture, the Emergency Land Fund conducts its seminal research on heir property in the Black community in the rural south. The study is known as "The Impact of Heir Property on Black Rural Land Tenure in the Southeastern Region of the United States." It was found that one of the primary reasons Blacks loose land is because of heir property - land being owned by the family - which can more easily be absconded by developers or the government.

- 1982—U.S. Commission on Civil Rights reports one of the primary reasons blacks loss land is because of discrimination from the USDA and that the FmHA's policy of being the "lending institution of last resort" did not apply to Black farmers.

- 1985— ELF merges with the Federation to become the Federation Of Southern Cooperatives /Land Assistance Fund (LAF).

- 1990—Federation/LAF successfully leads efforts to pass the first "Minority Farmers Rights Bill" (section 2501) to provide technical assistance to black farmers.

- 1990—The first law suit filed against the federal government on behalf of all black farmers by the Farmers Legal Action Group with the assistance of the Federation/LAF.

- 1992—The US Census of Agriculture reports there are 18,000 black farmers left owning 2.3 million acres.

- 1992—The Federation/LAF leads the first black farmer "Caravan to Washington" to address the plight of black and other minority farmers.

- 1997—The USDA holds listening forums to hear from minority farmers.

- 1997—The USDA's Civil Rights Action Team develops 92 recommendations to end discrimination within USDA.

- 1997—A second law suit on behalf of black farmers is filed against the federal government.

- 1998—The Coordinating Council of Black Farm Groups created.

- 1998—U.S. District Court Judge Paul Friedman designates Pigford V. Glickman as a "class."

- 1999—A Consent Decree arranged between attorneys for farmers and USDA attorneys - attorneys agree to settlement in class action suit filed by farmers. Attorney J. L. Chestnut in Alabama was the only black attorney serving as class counsel.

- 1999—U.S. District Court Judge Paul Friedman holds fairness hearing on Consent Decree in the U.S. District Court.

- 2008—The U. S. Congress passes the Farm Bill which includes provisions for "late" filers in the Pigford lawsuit to proceed with the claims process - it is known as "Pigford II."

- 2009—President Barack OBama's Secretary of Agriculture Tom Vilsack issues a 14 point statement on civil rights initiatives at

USDA entitled "A New Civil Rights Era for USDA."

- December 8, 2010—President Barack Obama signs bill authorizing $1.25 billion dollars in appropriations for the Pigford II lawsuit after Congress approved the legislation in November 2010.

ABOUT THE AUTHOR

Wilbur L. Brower is an educational and management consultant and trainer, specializing in human and organizational development. He has been published in *Harvard Business Review* and *Cultural Diversity at Work*; and has had a presentation printed in *Vital Speeches of the Day*.

www.ingramcontent.com/pod-product-compliance
Lightning Source LLC
Chambersburg PA
CBHW070058260626
47160CB00004B/1243